In the Empire of Dreams

ALSO BY THE AUTHOR

■

A Much Younger Man

In the Empire of Dreams

DIANNE HIGHBRIDGE

SOHO

Published by

Soho Press, Inc.
853 Broadway
New York, N.Y. 10003

Design by Pauline Neuwirth, Neuwirth & Associates, Inc.

Library of Congress Cataloging-in-Publication Data

Highbridge, Dianne,
In the empire of dreams / by Dianne Highbridge.
p. cm.
ISBN 1-56947-190-8 (alk. paper)
I. Title.
PR9619.3.H5332I6 1999 98-43842
823--dc21 CIP

10 9 8 7 6 5 4 3 2 1

ACKNOWLEDGMENTS

■

This work was assisted by a writer's grant from the Australia Council, the Australian Federal Government's arts funding and advisory body.

■

For M.T.

Ai o komete

■

Yet at home in my random corner
on truth, with no choice but to play
the world sung in a transposed key,
mine was another mourner's voice:
And again I say rejoice.

—Mary Jo Salter
Henry Purcell in Japan

1

Apparitions

AT THE END OF SUMMER, when the woman who came out of nowhere was haunting the dreams of the young, Liz arrived in Tokyo.

Liz can see her now, as clearly as if she had once looked straight into that beautiful, terrible face. And the story's still in her head as she first heard it, in Elaine's voice.

This woman had been appearing all over the place. For instance, in the warm autumn evening a child would be walking down the street minding his own business, gently swinging the little green plastic cage that held his precious insects—his bell crickets, perhaps, clinging to a slice of cucumber. He would lift up the cage from time to time to talk to the insects, encouraging them to chirp, and, thus innocently occupied, would not notice until too late the woman who stepped out of the shadows before him. He would look up, wondering. The woman would stand for a moment, slender shoulders slightly turned away, with a graceful gesture lifting the lacy stole she wore over her kimono, so that it obscured the lower part of her face. The child would think, nevertheless, because of something about her perceived in that instant, what a pretty lady! Then she'd turn full-face, and let the stole drop, or the handkerchief, or whatever, and she'd take a step towards him—

"Well, I'm not sure if she could take a step exactly, maybe she'd have to just glide," said Elaine.

"What do you mean, glide?"

"Japanese ghosts don't have feet," said Cathy. "But Elaine, this isn't one of those, it's not an obake. It's got to be a—what?—a yokai, an apparition. They have feet. She can walk. So this unhappy child—"

"Okay. Let's say she can. So there he stands, poor little guy, rooted to the spot with terror, because she's *moving* towards him, and she's smiling, she seems to be smiling, and then he can see—she has no mouth, but where her mouth should be there's this horrible, horrible slit. . . ."

Cathy and Elaine got such a kick out of it. They didn't make it up. It was all over town, it was even in the newspapers, about how all the children believed in the kuchisake onna, the woman with a slit for a mouth, and saw her everywhere.

For a while Liz found herself actually looking over her shoulder for the woman when she walked home at night from the library. That was silly. After all, the worst thing she ever really saw was the occasional drunk throwing up a bowl of noodles in the lane.

So she walked undisturbed, moved from light to light, hearing through wooden walls the clatter of dishes, the NHK news, the splash of bathwater. After a day of struggle, learning how to use the catalogue and the microfilm reader, she allowed herself to be soothed by the homely rituals, the knowledge that rice was being cooked, that backs were being scrubbed. She started to look forward to the walk, to love certain houses, to watch for the yellow light behind a favourite panel of pierced wood carving above a door, maybe a silhouette in the shape of bamboo leaves, always to look up at a child's room with his name spelled out in tape on the windowpane. A lot of those old places are gone now.

This was all soon after the awful journey. Over the Pole. At the airline office, they'd made it sound like a voyage of exploration: we'll route you over the Pole. But once on the plane, the Pole was neither here nor there.

She'd been dozing, half-watching the movie, a comedy, the kind where people are standing out on fire escapes in New York, yelling "I love you!" and passers-by are smiling along with the lovers, when, towards the end, before her drowsy eyes, the sides of the picture began to blacken and curl, and then leaping orange flames were projected on the screen, and everyone stood up and started screaming. Liz stood, too, but she didn't scream. She simply expected to die, to fall burning into the icy sea. Stewardesses were pushing down the aisles begging people to sit down in different languages, in Japanese, English, and German, and then, after no one knew how long, the screen turned to a smoky blur and finally to white again. The chief purser rushed up and stood in front of it and bowed and apologized. It was the first time Liz heard in real life the most formal and also the most humble of the apologies she'd learned. Green tea and damp towels were handed round, and she sat looking down at the still sea, and thought, "Who would have missed me?"

On the ground at Narita, she was disoriented still. She came out of Customs and found herself not exactly in Japan, but instead completely surrounded by American men in dark suits and white shirts, wearing tags saying "Elder This" and "Elder That." She did nothing in particular about it, but was found among them, helplessly clutching her winter coat and her bags, by the man from the Organization for Taking Care of Foreign Students or whatever it was called. He crossed her off his list. She looked uncomprehendingly into his harried, sweaty face, said "Hai" to everything, gave him the paper with Cathy's address on it and let him pack her into a taxi and wave it away.

The first thing she saw clearly, as dark fields and forests were left behind and the light in the cab became brighter with the reflected glare of the approaching city, was an advertisement stuck to the back of the driver's seat. It seemed to show. . . . yes, Jesus and the Disciples at the Last Supper, eating steaks that were part of a set menu for three thousand yen. All you can eat, all you can drink, she read laboriously. She leaned closer, but that was what it said.

Neon flashed all around and now, on the city skyline, she could read, written in light, words that seemed to belong to the known world. They leaped out at her, triumphant versions of the flashcards from which she had learned their characters, testing herself over and over again till she could see them, like this, in brilliant colours, in her sleep. Toshiba! Hitachi! Asahi Shimbun!

Then the taxi left the freeway and dived into dark streets that got narrower and narrower. With every turn her brief surge of confidence ebbed away. The taxi stopped. The driver, smiling a broad gold smile, pressed a button, and her door flew open. She struggled out, knowing she'd lost all power of speech. A sentence from a translation exercise in the ancient textbook of her first-ever Japanese class came into her head: I'll have the one the tip of which is shiny. No, no use! But nothing else came.

It was Cathy who saved her, running down the path with her sneakers half on and half off, thanking the driver, making sure he'd been paid ("You must have looked really pathetic, clever Liz! A taxi!") carrying Liz's heaviest bags into the tiny entranceway of her apartment.

As Liz bent down to take off her shoes, she heard a wailing sound. Clutching a shoe, she turned and saw, through the gate, an old man in baggy pants and straw hat, pulling a cart. It had a pitched roof and a lighted paper lantern swinging behind. She saw that the man held a flute in one hand—a kind of flute, though it didn't sound like anything she had ever heard before. Its notes floated in the darkness, died, returned, moved away.

"Ramen," said Cathy, and Liz remembers gazing out into the strange night, hearing the flute faintly mingled with the sounds of the traffic on the main road, listening intently until it was gone.

In bed, lying sandwiched between the musty quilts of Cathy's spare futon, she thought, I have no idea where I am. What if there's an earthquake now? I don't know where I am! In 1923 this city heaved and burnt. Why not now? Too exhausted to sleep, she lay for a long time waiting, with all the conviction that was left to her, for the disaster.

This was how it had always been. Waiting for the door to open, the light to pour down on her, the voices. I'm taking her now! You're not! You're not! To be rolled roughly in a rug, and put on the backseat of a car, prickly wool and slippery vinyl. To be driven all night, staring out at the tops of dark trees passing endlessly by, at the long straight road, nothing there but an occasional carcass picked out by the headlights, a stretched-out kangaroo, a smear of dog. To feel herself shaken if she started to nod off and be told to sit up love and talk and sing songs so that whoever was driving wouldn't go to sleep, though once it happened and she woke to see the side of the road sliding away at an angle in the half-darkness, and screamed a loud scream just in time. And to be pulled stiffly out in the frosty morning, the rug still around her, to drink lukewarm black coffee from a thermos in a park in a sleeping country town. There was always a silent bandstand, and a begonia house with dusty glass so you couldn't see inside, and a public toilet with spiderwebs on the back of the door, and little things scuttling away from under dry leaves in the corners. She had never known where she was going, or when she might return. The memory made her sigh heavily or murmur in the sleep that must have finally come, so afterwards she remembered Cathy's voice asking fuzzily, "Are you all right?"

She woke to the voices of children from the nursery school next door, and to music from the radio, a Japanese pop song. Cathy was softly singing along. Liz understood a few words: Yesterday, I cut off my hair. (Why would that be, though?) From today I will forget everything. Sun came in the window, and on the sill was a small brown pottery vase with a spray of pink chrysanthemum buds in it.

Cathy pushed aside the door and brought in a lacquer tray

with coffee and toast. "Proper toast," she said. "No nasty surprises here. No biting into a roll and finding red bean paste. Did you sleep okay?"

"I started to worry about earthquakes," said Liz. She hoped that Cathy would say, Oh, earthquakes, they're not so bad.

"Oh, earthquakes," said Cathy. She put the tray down on the tatami beside Liz, went to the closet and dragged out a backpack.

"This is my kit," she said. "Water, see. A can of these crackers, they're supposed to last forever. Flashlight, matches, radio, tissues, underwear, a space blanket—you know, it folds up tiny like this, but it keeps you warm at night, even on the moon or somewhere—toothbrush, Swiss army knife—you can get most of this stuff in the disaster corner in a big store—I'll take you sometime."

"Do they happen? I mean often?" Maybe Cathy would say, hardly ever really. But—*disaster corner?*

"Oh, every so often. You'll see. You won't like it when it goes too long without one—it makes you nervous. They say the little ones let off the pressure. Last month we had a four. It was all right. The epicentre was up north."

"A four? What was it in 1923?"

"I think it was about a seven or eight on the Richter scale. That's different from the Japanese scale. With the Japanese scale, they tell what it is by whether the tombstones rock, or whatever. I think the tombstones rocking makes it a five."

"You mean someone runs out to look?"

"I suppose so. Or they used to."

"Well, anyway—if four—a four, I mean—wasn't so bad . . ."

Cathy sat back on her heels and made a humming sound. "I hate to be the one to have to tell you this," she said at last. "It increases exponentially. It's not just one, two, three. That means a seven is many times worse than a four. A lot worse. Many, many times . . . w ell. Let's not go into it. What you do is, you get this kit together, and then you don't think about it anymore. That's what you do." She shoved the pack into the closet and slid the door closed with a bang.

For her first visit anywhere, Cathy took her to a shrine dedicated to the patron god of learning. "The best way to start," she said, "before you have to have anything to do with those old farts of professors. Tenjin-sama is the real thing."

Hung on frames around the courtyard of the shrine were thousands upon thousands of little wooden boards, about the size of envelopes, on the back of which students had written prayers. Please let me pass. Please let me get in. Cathy wrote something on one, though Liz didn't like to ask what. She'd shared a seminar in Canberra with Cathy, not a friendship. It was out of the neutral comradeship of the seminar that Cathy had invited her to stay. They, alone of that old group, would both be studying here. That was the idea. Later, she would find that Cathy didn't study at all, at least not what she was supposed to be studying. Her scholarship had run out and she taught English. Also, she studied ink painting. She took workshops in traditional papermaking. She went on long trips to places where people did a special sort of weaving, or pottery, or made baskets out of bamboo, cherry bark or the vine of the wild mountain grape, or sometimes all three together. She spent all her spare money on this kind of lovely thing, and didn't seem to feel the least bit guilty about her thesis.

Liz held her pen over her sliver of wood, hesitating. What should she write? She had never prayed for anything before.

Study itself had always been her protection, her salvation. The one thing that had always come easily to her, the one thing that had not ended badly, the one thing always rewarded. Report cards, scholarships, prizes, these had been her comfort. Her first real grant money, for the northern summer just over, profitably spent in a German library. And this, the big one, given only to a few: a year in Japan, renewable. And yet—last night she had forgotten in a moment of panic all the Japanese she had ever learned, except that ridiculous sentence. Perhaps it would be better to write something, just to make sure. She wrote her name carefully in katakana. The god of learning, in his picture, did look rather beautiful and benign in Heian-period dress, black kimono and tall black hat, his eyes narrow and thoughtful. So then she wrote: Let me understand. Cathy, who had no scruples about reading other people's prayers, even those of people she didn't know very well and to whom she had not shown her own, laughed over her shoulder.

That evening, Cathy and her American friend Elaine took Liz to a local restaurant, a noisy cement-floored place where the chefs bawled out orders and cries of welcome and farewell, as the mood took them, making her jump and turn her head towards the hubbub. Cathy and Elaine ordered for the three of them. The first thing that came, on a thick blue-and-white dish smacked down brusquely on the table, was a whole fish, its flesh sliced into sashimi. Its eyes were very bright.

Cathy and Elaine talked over the fish, fast and loud. They seemed to assume that no one around spoke enough English to make out what they were saying, but Liz wasn't so sure. They told her lots of useful things, however. They told her that

Japanese spermicidal jelly was effective for ten minutes only. They seemed to think this was pretty funny. They told her that the Japanese for "come" is "go." They told her that the Koreans in her Japanese-for-foreign-students class were notoriously gorgeous, with lips like the ones you see on sculptures of the Buddha. They told her the sexiest sumo wrestler was Chiyonofuji, because he raised his leg so high before he stamped it on the dohyo, and because of his tremendous glare, and the sweetness of his expression when he wasn't glaring, and his great shoulders, and that she had to see him in action as soon as possible.

"I think the fish is moving," said Liz.

"Good heavens, so it is," said Cathy mildly.

The fish was twitching so vigorously that its plate was being propelled across the table.

"Do something!" cried Liz. "It's alive!"

"It's dead," said Elaine. "Very recently, but it is dead. It's just reflexes."

"I can't watch!"

"Let's put the menu in front of it," said Cathy. She moved the plate to one side and stood the menu up like a folding screen. "There. It'll stop soon."

A waitress, rushing by, briskly picked up the menu and folded it back in its proper place, giving them a brief, puzzled look. Cathy and Elaine burst into laughter. "Look, it's stopped," they assured Liz.

"*Really* fresh," said Elaine. She picked up her chopsticks and took a slice of the raw fish. "Oh, good."

"You'll have to get used to this," said Cathy, leaning over to pour a drop of soy sauce on a miniscule plate for Liz, and expertly mixing green wasabi paste into it, "if you're going to marry a Japanese."

"She's not here to do that," said Elaine, "Are you, Liz? She's here to work. Not like you, goofing off from day one."

Their eyes were challenging and amused.

Liz picked up her chopsticks and broke them apart. Nervously, she lifted up a piece of fish, dipped it, praying now that it wouldn't fall off and splatter sauce all over everything, and quickly ate it. It was sweet. It melted. She took another piece, and ate that.

They talked about the woman with a slit for a mouth. They agreed that women made the most wonderful demonic spirits. Look at the classics! The Snow Woman, whose chill breath could freeze a man to death. The faceless servant girl of Akasaka. The old woman in the kabuki who was a cat demon in disguise, but you didn't know until the scene when she made sure she was alone, and then she knelt down, all dreadful eagerness, to lap fish oil from the lamp, and the lamp cast her shadow on the shoji, and it was—the shadow of a giant cat!

Across the table from Liz, two faces. Pretty Cathy, swinging back her fair hair, smiles her sideways smile at a young chef who's sent over, unasked, an offering of silvery slivers on a scallop shell. ("It's the scallop muscle. Waste not want not, these guys.") Elaine, animated, undistracted, lifts up her thin hands to make a point. And this image of them remains fresh in her mind, overlaid though it is now by others, more or less transparent, that have fallen gently down upon it, layer by layer, as leaves do with the seasons.

Liz drank too much hot sake, and felt lightheaded, so they took her home. She remembers telling Elaine, out in the street,

"You're the first American I've ever really known," and Cathy repeating mockingly, "*Really* known?" (truly, not something she'd say now, after all these years) and Elaine laughing and admonishing, in a tough-guy kind of voice, "We're all gaijin here, kid," and then—her voice changing, "*Abunai!*"—pulling Liz sharply out of the way of a motor scooter loaded behind with a rack of lidded bowls. "You want noodles in your hair?"

After they'd said goodnight to Elaine in front of the Fuji Bank, with its neon-lit row of posters of Mount Fuji decked both in snow and blossom, and Elaine had turned down the lane that led to her place, Liz asked Cathy, "How long has she been here?"

Cathy said, "Oh, forever."

"Is her place like yours?"

"It's like nobody's."

When she saw Elaine's apartment, it was hardly an apartment at all, just two rooms divided by a plain screen and containing nothing like Cathy's things, nothing lovingly chosen, but only heaps of books and an old typewriter on a rickety desk and fewer clothes even than Liz had brought in her suitcase. It was not yet really forever that Elaine had been here, it only counted as forever then.

Elaine lived in different places after that, but always she lived like that. She'd take a place, get a boy with a van to help her move her books—the boy was always willing, though she promised nothing—stack them around the walls, dismiss the boy. And there she was. In the centre of it all, concentrating.

The strangest thing: That second night there was an earthquake. Liz had gone right to sleep, because of the sake. She woke to find herself being bumped up and down in her futon, and the walls rattling and groaning, and Cathy dashing to open the door, crying, "Oh, damn, oh, bugger!" as she fell over the table. Half a minute and it was finished. They sat on their futons, hugging their trembling knees. "Breathe deeply," said Cathy, but her voice shook, which Liz was pleased to hear. "I hate the up and down ones," she said. "Side to side's a lot better. I don't mind side to side."

"Your vase is broken." It lay in a shaft of moonlight on the bookshelf beneath the window, split in two clean pieces.

Cathy gave a moan. "I loved that vase. It was from Mashiko. The first thing I ever bought here." She fetched a towel from the kitchen and began to mop up, in the dark. Liz picked up the spray of chrysanthemums and sat holding them. They glowed pale grey in her hand.

Suddenly, she jumped up. "Sirens! They're coming!" And in a moment, the room was filled with a wild shrieking. "They're coming here!"

"It's started a fire!" Red lights flashed in the windows. They dashed to the door, and then dashed frantically back again to drag on jeans and T-shirts, hopping and fumbling.

Outside, fire engines, ambulances and police cars flashed and honked and backed up in the narrow lane. People came running out in cotton kimono, and pajamas with coats flung over them, and trodden-down sneakers and beaded sandals. Policemen urged them back. Firemen leapt from the sides of moving firetrucks and ran towards the door of the nursery school.

The firemen! They looked like young samurai, samurai out of a vision, all in silver, in silver helmets wide at the shoulders like samurai helmets, and high silver boots, running through the beams of flashing light.

Liz, standing at the gate, laughed out loud for the delight of watching them, for the beauty of them.

There was no fire. Probably the earthquake had set off an alarm in the nursery school. The firemen shouted at each other, smartly reversed all that they'd done, jumped onto their trucks and were gone. The ambulances and police cars sped down the lane, and people folded their arms and walked contemplatively away.

It was dawn. Liz and Cathy drank a pot of tea, ate a whole box of sponge cakes given to Cathy by a grateful student, and went to bed.

Liz had put the chrysanthemums in a glass of water and set it by her pillow. She lay awake looking at them, considering. She had always thought of herself as an unlucky person, beset by dangers. Now she began to see that, on the contrary, her history was one of miraculous escape and survival. And here, in a city where she was totally lost, where there was a strangeness to everything she encountered, in a city that could crumple and burst into flames at any moment, she felt as if she had successfully completed a perilous voyage and arrived somehow at a place of relative safety.

Years later, when they were talking on the telephone one night, she asked Elaine, "Whatever became of the kuchisake onna? When the hot weather was over?"

"Who knows?" said Elaine. "Maybe she went to Saipan for the winter and never came back. She liked it on the beach and decided to stay. Or she stayed without deciding. Just like you stayed here, you know. That's the way it goes."

2

On the Line

CLAUDINE TRAVELS ON THE Yamanote line almost every day. There are twenty-nine stations on the circle that defines the centre of the city, and the green trains go round all day and most of the night, only a couple of minutes apart, the outer line clockwise and the inner line counterclockwise.

She and Michael live near the prettiest station, where in summer there are bell crickets in cages near the ticket office, and the station staff grow rice in large boxes right on the platform. Local schoolchildren make scarecrows, marvelously detailed, to protect the rice as it ripens from nonexistent birds, and when it's harvest time in the country it's harvest time at the station, too, and the rice is cut and hung on poles to dry. It would make a couple of good-size bowls, Claudine supposes, but as to who eats it, she'll never know.

On this station there are signs by the flowerbeds that say, LET'S LOVE FLOWERS. Claudine takes her notebook whenever she goes out, and she copies down the characters she sees on signs, and deciphers the hard ones from her character dictionary when she gets home. LET'S LOVE FLOWERS is an easy one. The line curves through areas where at night the neon signs of love hotels flash brightly block after block, so from the train she often sees the character for "love," made up of the one for "heart" plus some other squiggles. There's Castle of Love, Dreams of Love, and a lot of others. The characters for "mahjongg", above a thousand seedy doorways, were harder when she first saw them. Also the ones for loan sharks, emblazoned on billboards at every station. There's a lot to learn. Even when she sees a sign in English, like LET'S SWEAT TOGETHER, it takes her a while to figure out the place is a dance hall.

On the train she's also acquired smarts she never had before. She's learned from her bruises, from lost necklaces and stripped heels. She knows not to wear a long scarf outside her coat in winter, so as not to be strangled in the crush. Once this almost happened, and she knew that if she died no one would realise it till the doors opened at the next station, because her body would remain upright. It was this knowledge, somehow, that gave her the strength to bring up her trapped hand, inch by inch, till it reached her throat, and pull the scarf away from her windpipe, just enough so she could breathe again. And she also knows how not to get caught with the horizontal railing by the door at her back, in case the crowd should be thrown on top of her and push her too hard against it, maybe breaking her spine. That could happen. And she knows how to let herself be popped out of the train when the doors open, like a pea from a squeezed pod, unresisting. Hesitate and be trampled to death. These are things that Michael, who drives himself to the office, or, when there's an important meeting, is picked up by a car with a driver, has no way of knowing.

Sometimes she can't face the rush hour. These mornings she goes very early, and catches the old ladies in from the countryside, in their baggy indigo pants and kerchiefs, with enormous baskets of vegetables on their backs. Old ladies! Some of them aren't so old. It's just that their faces are weatherbeaten, their teeth made of some silvery metal. When they're really old they won't be able to straighten up now as they do, gratefully, without the betrayal of sound or gesture, when they put down their loads. It's impossible for Claudine to envisage the world they come from, far outside the circle they ride with her. At this time of morning she sees day laborers, too, in one particular park by the line where they stand in the cold around a brazier, blowing on their hands, shabby men waiting for someone—Michael said, when she told him, gangsters—to give them jobs on construction sites. An hour later these people are gone. Office workers, immaculate in English raincoats with belts tied just so, fill the trains. Children with alert young mothers play in the park. It is a transformation.

On nights when she has late classes or socializes with her students, the train's crowded again, full to bursting with red-faced men, and girls pretending to be drunker than they are, Claudine thinks, so they can put their heads on boys' shoulders. When she gets on the train this late, she feels as if she's swimming against a tide of whisky fumes. Occasionally, some man will say something to her. Once a man—an ordinary middle-aged man with a perspiring nose—rubbed himself against her, trapping her against the door. He got off at her station—

it really was his station, too—and, beside her in the crowd pushing towards the stairs, muttered urgently in her ear, "I rub you!" Claudine broke away and stood at the bottom of the stairs and laughed till he was out of sight.

She didn't tell Michael. She knew he wouldn't think it funny. Nor does she mention the mornings when sometimes, nobody's fault, she is crushed against someone much more attractive, smelling faintly of aftershave, whose face, near her own (because he's usually not very tall) maintains a polite neutrality to the last, but who is clearly finding the whole thing as interesting as she does. She likes Japanese men on the whole, their thick hair and neat bodies, their cool. So perhaps she shouldn't blame Michael for Miss Ueda or Miss Watanabe, but she does. She does blame him.

When they first came to Japan she and Michael took a trip to Kyoto, where they stayed in a phony-traditional inn that had notices in English: PUT OFF SHOES and HOW TO USE JAPANESE BATH. When they went out walking, she looked longingly behind fences of woven bamboo, and down water-splashed stone paths to hidden doorways. She said to Michael, "Don't you wish we could see inside these real places?"

Michael said, "No place is more real than any other. For God's sake, Claudine, you sound like a tourist. A cliché tourist."

They passed a small temple, and in the driveway of the temple she saw a man with a bucket, sweeping. He looked up, and his mouth opened as if he had something to say to her, so she stepped forward, through the gate. Perhaps, she thought, he wanted to say something about the temple, its history or something like that, or invite them in. But when he saw her moving towards him, the man let out a gurgling scream and turned tail and ran, knocking over his bucket and hurling his broom away. Claudine, in an instant, turned too, and fled back the way she'd come. She looked over her shoulder once, only to see the man, still panting up the slope to the temple, looking back at her with a terror that mirrored her own. Michael, at the gate, guffawed. "The village idiot! The poor old guy!" And then, "Are you satisfied? Is that real enough? Who's the idiot now?"

Maybe she is an idiot, although Michael hasn't always called her one, hasn't always spoken to her this way.

Their trips together since then haven't been much more successful, and it's been her fault mostly. For one thing, she's developed a fear of earthquakes. Once she insisted on leaving a movie theatre in Shinjuku when it began to roar and shake, and then felt a real fool when she found it was built under a bowling alley, and it always sounded like that when the balls went down. Michael says she's neurotic. But that isn't really why they don't go anywhere much together anymore.

She should be scared of earthquakes when she's on the train, but for some reason it's all right then. Well, except for the morning after the big tremor that had sent her flying around at home, heart pounding, to turn off the gas and open the windows. She'd done all the right things, but she'd ended up under a table and didn't have the strength to come out till long after it was over. That morning, tension vibrated down the train, and the sobbing, half-hysterical giggle of a girl with a boy somewhere in the crowd panicked her. Everyone else was silent, with only one thought, perfectly clear: "What if it happens again now?" Somehow that oneness had sustained her, until the girl broke the silence, and then Claudine, sweating and trembling, fought her way off at the next station and let a dozen trains go by before she found the courage to get on again.

But it helps that the line is aboveground, and generally she's amazed and emboldened by the calm of the people crushed together this way in a country where anything might happen, the earth might fall in just like that. There they stand, with their noses, some of them, squashed against the glass of the doors, so that if you see them from outside you have to laugh, and yet they are for the most part very collected, and she likes being part of them, knowing something of what they know.

She and Michael live in an apartment big enough so that they don't have to be close if they don't want to. If they had to live the way most Japanese people live, in a tiny place with two children and a grandmother, how would they survive?

Not that Michael knows anyone who lives that way. He meets the sleeker kind of Japanese in his work. He doesn't speak the language (it's not what he's paid for, he says, and it's true). He's not particularly interested in anything Japanese, though he likes to think he knows all the inside stories. He believes he knows all about political corruption, and who owes whom in the sumo world, for example. This is foreign businessmen's bar gossip. He sometimes refers to people as Japs, though maybe he does this just to annoy.

The office ladies are not Japs. "Wonderful girl," says Michael of Miss Ueda or Miss Watanabe, "Worth her weight in sushi." They smooth his way.

Claudine is sympathetic to Japanese working women. She understands how hard it is for them to get ahead in the big companies, and how in a foreign company like Michael's they might have some sort of chance, but still are used, the way she supposes Michael uses them. She deplores the way they're called "office ladies," no matter if they have degrees in economics, like Miss Ueda, or linguistics, like Miss Watanabe. She admires Japanese women in general, their resilience, the fierce old characters they become. The grandmothers who push her onto the train then zip in front of her for seats, she admires their guts.

Still, all this having been said, she doesn't know whom she hates more, Miss Ueda or Miss Watanabe. She doesn't know which one she ought to hate, so she hates them both.

Miss Ueda, all in black, designer black from head to toe, her hair cut alarmingly straight, her lovely impersonal smile, her considering stare. Miss Watanabe, soft round chin, soft eyes, soft pale skin like a rice cake, as the Japanese say, though Claudine likens it more to a steamed dumpling from a station stall. When they went to a company wedding Miss Watanabe wore a brilliant kimono and smiled behind her hand. Her smile is toothy, and she has the prominent eyeteeth the Japanese think are cute, and can be. But on her, thinks Claudine, they give at certain moments a foxy look that's at odds with the softness. Michael raved for days about that kimono, so perhaps it is Miss Watanabe. On the other hand, Miss Ueda is perfectly elegant, and will be even more elegant the older she gets, and Michael appreciates elegance, so perhaps it is Miss Ueda. It has to be one of them, and it has been one of them almost from the beginning.

In the beginning, Claudine was lost. She didn't know what to do with herself, without a job for the first time. It's not as if there isn't enough for gaijin wives to do, but she just couldn't seem to hit on the right thing. She isn't charitable, or theatrical, so the Benevolent Society and the Players were out. She's not good at getting bargains, somehow the dealers see her coming, so there was no point in working on one of the city's great collections of Edo period lacquerware or samurai sword chests. She tried ikebana, but on bad advice joined a modernist school, where every arrangement seemed to have barbed wire in it, so she quit. At an embassy party someone invited her to join a course in calligraphy, and she thought it would help her to learn characters, so she tried that, but she sensed the condescension of the teacher, and feeling humiliated to be doing an inferior course, a gaijin ladies' course, she soon gave that up, too. She even tried tea ceremony, but her first time in the tea room her feet went to sleep from kneeling, and somehow the paralysis worked its way up to her fingers, so she couldn't do anything right, the way it absolutely has to be for the whole thing, the tranquillity, to work.

But she wanted to learn, so finally she got a teaching job, ten hours a week, teaching English, though she'd never taught anything to anybody before. At first she thought it was really quite wrong to inflict herself on these students, from whom she hoped to learn so much, without experience. She soon found out, in this disreputable little school whose ad she'd picked from a magazine, that the other teachers were no more teachers than she was. They were fly-by-nights, young gaijin go-getters looking for cash, some still living in gaijin hostels, just back from getting their visas in Korea. They'd been living, before that, in San Diego or Maui, on welfare or on the beach, or they'd come up from Bangkok, or Manila, or Bali, where they'd heard there was money to be had pretty much for the asking in Tokyo. And the students were an innocent, biddable lot, lacking the brains or the confidence to take themselves to a better school, and in desperate need of English conversation, for reasons Claudine could not always comprehend. Overhearing the other teachers' classes, since most of them had loud, assured voices, she heard harangues on the shortcomings of Japanese society, and incipient seductions, almost anything but real teaching, so she felt a bit better about her own efforts with textbook and tape recorder.

She was older and better-dressed than the other teachers, and she wasn't sure what they made of her. One or two of them got round to asking, "Why do you have this crummy job anyway?" She knew better than to admit that she was looking for some way into the culture, that she did it for the snippets the students told her about their home lives, and about what they did on the weekend, in the course of practicing speech patterns from the book. That sounded foolish. But however she tried to get round it, these gaijin just looked at her and said, "Oh, right."

One afternoon she invited some of them home. She was embarrassed at how impressed they were with her apartment. Most of them had college educations, and they must have been brought up in middle-class homes, and yet they acted like children of the Third World, wandering around touching things and going, "Wow! Two bathrooms!" or "Wow! A dishwasher!" They watched sumo on TV, and drank beer, and talked.

The conversation turned to love hotels, who'd been to one, and what theme it had, beds shaped like racing cars, or space capsules, or whatever. Claudine was arch. She and Michael had never been to any such place, but she didn't want to admit that, of course not. The talk got pretty noisy. She was relieved when the sumo finished and they drifted off to their evening jobs in time for her to clean up before Michael came home. He was happy, so maybe he'd had drinks with Miss Ueda or Miss Watanabe.

It must have been two or three days after that when one of the Americans who'd been at her place, a tall, hairy fellow, came into the room where she was teaching, before her class arrived, and started to kiss her. This was Gary. Afterwards she was ashamed to face her students, who couldn't be that innocent, with a red, swollen mouth, and she could hardly concentrate even on her rudimentary lesson plan for the terrible impatience she felt. She wanted to leap across the table and shake poor little Miss Hino, who kept saying, "I have ever been to Disneyland."

After their classes were over, she and Gary went to a love hotel. It was called The Empire of Dreams. They went every day for two weeks, and every day for two weeks he came into her classroom and put his hand down the front of her blouse, or pushed her over a desk with a long blue-jeaned leg between hers. It got worse and worse, but they always stopped enough seconds before the first students arrived for her to make herself somewhat decent again. Gary would pick up his textbooks in a businesslike way and make jokes with the students as he went out the door. She was sure they must know, and the thought made her hand clumsy as she changed the cassette to the next lesson, but she let it continue.

The Empire of Dreams was just around the corner from the school, and every afternoon she and Gary hurried through the vine-screened door and into the tiny lobby, where they got a room key from an invisible person behind a shaded glass window. The funny thing was, if they stayed longer than the specified time, someone, maybe the same person, telephoned the room and then came up and knocked at the door and had to be paid again, not furtively this time but with the bows and polite language of any other transaction. It was Gary who went to the door, more often than not with Claudine's money—but then, they both knew she had more.

The hotel was just what she wanted. It had everything. There was a swing draped with plastic flowers, and a round revolving bed with mirrors above it, and a vinyl mattress in the bathroom, and all sorts of extras, like a spare pair of cheap panties, which would fit Miss Ueda or Miss Watanabe, but did not fit Claudine, who always put them in her bag anyway. There was a big video screen and a selection of videos, which she was curious to see, but there was never time. Gary did not like to go into the next hour if they could help it. He preferred this economy, perhaps on her behalf, or perhaps because he had other places to go, other people to see.

He told her all about his Japanese girlfriend, and his girlfriend in Detroit. She didn't care. He told her a lot of other things, too. He liked to instruct her, though most of the information she would never need. For instance, he told her how to finance a trip to Korea to renew a tourist visa by buying a certain type of Japanese camera, and making sure never to touch the inside of it, especially the shutter, so it would look absolutely new, no fingerprints, but of course you would carry it as if it were your own, and sell it to a certain guy in a certain street in Seoul, for enough money to pay for the whole trip, provided you found a cheap enough hostel. Since he also told her about a time in one of these hostels when an Australian martial arts maniac in the next bunk spent the whole night screaming and making chopping motions with his hands, Claudine was sure she wouldn't want to stay there. The place where he was staying in Tokyo didn't sound much better. The guy in the top bunk sometimes threw up over the side in the middle of the night, Gary told her, miming his disgust but enjoying hers.

He warned her that he didn't want to get involved. Claudine replied drily, "It sounds as if you've got more than enough involvements already," but what she really thought was, Why would I want to get involved with you? She understands why he might have been nervous about it, though, because she liked to hang on to his arm as they left The Empire of Dreams. She regrets this impulse herself, now she comes to think of it.

God knows how long it might have gone on. As long as it did, Claudine stopped thinking. At home, she hardly noticed if Michael was there or not. She focussed only on those few hours of each weekday. Gary came into her classroom. He left. She heard the students go through their exercises, smiling, correcting, watching herself do it right, more or less, somehow keeping herself in that room, even lingering for a moment to answer a question that could have waited, making herself wait. Then The Empire of Dreams. Later, when she left Gary at the station, he waved a casual hand and loped off, heaven knows where, and she went home. Once Michael said to her, "I'm really glad you've settled down," and actually stroked the back of her neck. He liked her this far out of it.

One day it ended, in a matter of minutes. She was sitting on the floor behind a filing cabinet in the little room the teachers used, looking at textbooks from the bookshelf, when Gary and two of the other teachers came in with some of their students, guys from a small import company nearby. There Claudine was, in the classic situation, invisible, and all these guys began to talk. That is, the gaijin talked. They were talking about—motorbikes. Claudine was only half listening. She had to find an exercise in the use of the future tense, fast, otherwise there was nothing she could pretend to do with her class. It wasn't about motorbikes, not exactly. It was about some prostitute in Kawasaki that Conrad had heard of, who would do it on a motorbike. It was clear the students were uneasy, and they murmured something to each other in Japanese, but Conrad pressed on. He needed advice. He'd taken his little brown envelope last payday and tried to make contact with this woman on his way home, but the yakuza around the place had stopped him. Kind of forcefully. Was it because he was a gaijin, he wanted to know? Was this some kind of discrimination? He reproduced his conversation with the yakuza, grunts and all. The students declined to assist with interpretation. Claudine could imagine the way they were smiling. There was a silence.

Conrad seemed to have given up, and said something plaintive to Gary. Gary laughed, and then he asked in his rather pleasant deep voice, "Does your wife know that you—you know?" Conrad's wife and baby were in Japan with him, living in a two-room apartment on the Toyoko line.

"I don't know," said Conrad, "Well, maybe she does, like she must have some kind of an idea."

There was a pause. "But she loves you, right?" said Gary. At first Claudine thought he must be joking, but a moment later it came to her that he sounded horribly sincere.

"Right," agreed Conrad eagerly. "Right—she just wants for me to be happy, that's all."

"Sure she does. That's really great, man," said Gary, in a warm, serious kind of way. Claudine felt queasy.

Conrad's voice thickened. "You know," he began sentimentally, "When she found out she was pregnant, this was in Seattle, we had just about fifty dollars between the two of us, I tell you, man . . ."

The students were backing out of the room. Claudine didn't listen to Conrad's story either, though she heard phrases like, "do anything for me," and "wonderful girl," and "lucky guy," and "goddamn yakuza."

She waited with a book in her hand until Gary and Conrad left, too. She found the exercise she was looking for.

She couldn't have put a name to what it was she felt, not that it mattered. She went to her classroom too late for Gary to meet her there. When the class was over, she quit the job and she quit Gary. It was easy.

She's seen him only once since then, on the morning train. He was wearing a suit and carrying a leather file under his arm, and he'd had a haircut. "Hey," he yelled to her over the heads of the crowd. "Know what I'm doing now? Writing English instruction manuals for cameras! They wanted a native speaker! Know how much I'm getting?" But she never heard. They waved as the crowds swept them apart.

Claudine is glad she did all that, anyway. Maybe she'll never go to a love hotel again. But she's sure Michael has never been to one like The Empire of Dreams. It must surely be a more elegant class of place that he goes to with Miss Ueda or Miss Watanabe.

Now she has a better job, working with real teachers. Most

of them have degrees in teaching English as a second language, and know all about audiovisual aids, and are members of the Japan Association of Language Teachers. She listens to them with admiration when they talk about their experiences teaching in other countries. Some of them have worked in the Sudan, in Nigeria, in Indonesia. They speak airily of locust plagues and spiders as big as your fist. They live in well-organised little apartments and invest their salaries in the money market and nothing bothers them at all. Claudine will never be one of them, but she's learning.

The rest of the time, she has to have something to do, so what she does is travel on the Yamanote line.

She's found a book, a guidebook to the line. It has a chapter for each station, and tells you what to see there, where you can find some special shrine, or buy some special cake, or watch some umpteenth-generation craftsman at work, making combs or sashimi knives or whatever. Claudine depends on this book, and she's doing all the stations, one by one, even the ones where she's been already, because there's always something she didn't know. Even at her own station, with the help of this book, she's found a temple with a peony garden, and a monument to the reconstruction of Tokyo after the earthquake of 1923, though she'd rather not think about that. She ticks off each station on the contents page as she does it: God's Rice Field, Nightingale Valley.

Michael is not pleased that she has this project. It annoys him. When she told some people in his office about it, just trying to make conversation, he said, "That's Claudine—always going round in circles." It passed for a joke, but she could discover no affection in his voice.

On the line, she looks and looks. She continues her study of the posters inside the train. You can get a special ticket to a hot springs resort and sit up to your neck in a wooden tub on top of a mountain. Claudine thinks she'd like that. You can get married in a pink fake church, with a dry ice machine making swirls of mist around your feet as you walk up the aisle. You can do all sorts of things.

She pays attention to the grammar of loudspeaker announcements. Watch your feet, don't forget your umbrella, stand away from the doors. There are people looking out for her safety. Sometimes the security of it makes her daring. She says. "Move, dummy," under her breath when people get in her way. The chances are good that even someone who understands English isn't going to stop long enough to take revenge.

On the other hand, she's more self-conscious than before, because she's always being watched. In the past, when, for example, she dropped a bag of grapes on the platform, and it burst, she stamped her foot and swore out loud, and everyone stared at this display of self-indulgence. She wouldn't do that kind of thing now. But she does make a point of reading her newspaper on the train, because she's noticed that Japanese women rarely do. Maybe they don't want to take up the space, maybe they don't like inky fingers. She crackles hers under men's noses.

She is watched, and she watches. Men and women primping before the mirror on the station. Tiny children, in hats too big for them, travelling across town to school. Workmen in split-toed boots. Teenage boys sitting with their legs wide apart as if they think they're in some samurai movie. Wild-eyed vagrants with long, matted black hair like mountain hermits. A man still in a salaryman suit, frayed cuffs rolled up, carrying a bundle and a bottle of pep-drink from a vending machine, starting out as a homeless person in the subway—but from which point of departure?

She watches a shoe repairer in the street outside a station. She's fascinated by the way he works, putting his whole body behind the knife as he cuts and shapes the leather, polishing with one economical finger. He has a face like a court noble in a classic scroll.

In the evenings the fortunetellers come out, to catch the office workers going home. They wear strange hats and sit at card tables lit by lanterns, and young women queue to speak to them. Sometimes Claudine sees girls come away crying. She's glad she wouldn't understand her fortune, or she might be tempted to try it.

One day an old woman, bent and almost bald, at a shop where she's bought some little thing, presses a piece of candy into her hand. The gesture, not felt since she was a child, brings tears to Claudine's eyes.

She hasn't been so open since she was a child. Everything is fresh, her eyes are fresh. Her senses are all alert. She smells the mothballs from the wedding guest's kimono, the sweet heavy scent of the sumo wrestler's hair oil before he looms up beside her.

There's a plastic statue of a sumo wrestler pursuing a salmon-pink Marilyn Monroe around a revolving platform just outside a station Claudine passes often. They're both naked and larger than life-size, crouched in sumo poses, and, whatever they're advertising, they chase each other unceasingly round and round.

Claudine, too: no-one's following her, but round and round she goes.

❖ ❖ ❖

There's to be a twenty-fifth-anniversary reception at Michael's company. A representative of the Minister will be present, or maybe even the Minister himself. Claudine wasn't listening very hard when Michael told her.

Anyway, she promised to be on time, and she is, only slightly breathless. She promised not to wear trousers (one of Michael's peeves) and she isn't.

Some of the gaijin women in the room are dressed up in a different kind of way, in dark droopy things by Japanese designers, or belts and jackets made from faded kimono fabric. They make Claudine think of the farmers' wives with their packs of vegetables, or of the old gardener-women she's seen picking up leaves, one by one, in temple gardens. But her hand tightens around the too-pink patent leather strap of her own designer shoulder bag.

No Michael.

There are people here that she knows, but they're all, at this moment, very far away.

"Hello, Claudine." A familiar face, met a couple of times in—yes, in the ladies' room of that first school, between classes. It overlooked a lumberyard, and the scents of pine and cypress drifted in with the traffic noise over the transoms of dingy windows. Chipped mirror, cracked basin, a sprig of flowers in a glass. Cathy talking of some shampoo made from a special camellia oil, on a remote island. A bright girl, wasting her time. Not the only one.

"Cathy! Why are you here?" But doesn't that sound rude?

"Not sure," says Cathy, apparently taking no offence. "I teach here once a week, but tonight the class is off because of this, so they invited me." A bit of window-dressing, thinks Claudine. She knows that, she's not unsure at all. Young, pretty, smart—something of the student about her still. "Why are you?"

"My husband works here."

"Really? Which one's he?"

Claudine flushes. "I haven't found him yet. I just got here."

Cathy looks the room over. "Interesting, you see a whole different class of gaijin at these affairs," she observes.

"Different? From what?" Let her explain. Not that I care.

"From my kind. A different world. Super-gaijin salaries, huge apartments, antique kimono hanging over the master bed."

"What's wrong with that? The kimono?"

"Oh," says Cathy. "Now tell me you've got one."

"I haven't."

"What a relief."

She doesn't look as if it's that much of a relief. She doesn't care what I have, or what I don't have, thinks Claudine. I'm a company wife, a gaijin okusan, a nothing to her.

They stand awkwardly, until a good-looking man comes by and says something to Cathy in Japanese. She says something back—very fluently, thinks Claudine enviously—gives Claudine a nod, and he takes her, smiling now, away.

Claudine hovers at the edge of a group in which she recognises one or two people, resolved to join the conversation, but it's the wrong group, the wrong conversation. "Corazon's married my sailing sensei. No, really, she's got a perfect right to be in love, only now she's got a spouse visa of her very own, and I haven't got anybody," she hears.

"Sailing sensei?" she says to the woman next to her, Stephanie Wagner, in a voice that may be too loud.

"There's a sensei for everything," replies Stephanie with a shrug. "Speaking of which, I gather you quit the shodo class?"

"Yes," says Claudine. "I quit a lot of things."

"I gave up, too. I just couldn't stand the way the sensei kept grabbing my hand with the brush in it. I wanted to write it all myself. Rampant individualism, I guess. I'm not proud of it."

"Yes, that's their way," says Claudine. "But I don't think he was much of a sensei, or he wouldn't have wanted students like us."

Stephanie laughs. "Talentless bums! I was never going to have a scroll fit to hang."

She calls her husband from a nearby cluster of men. Arms folded, they're echoing each other's body language. He's just finishing a story about an incompetent taxi driver, which ends, "And the guy tells me, 'There is no American Club!' No American Club! And I said, 'The hell there isn't, fella, and we're there!'"

"Hon," says Stephanie. "Let's ask Claudine and Michael to come with us to see the show? Tomorrow afternoon, Saturday? Kind of a tap-dance revival thing, Claudine, original cast. Someone gave Phil tickets—a bribe, I guess," she adds roguishly.

"Hey, it's not like that," protests Phil, unfolding his arms and spreading his hands wide, deprecating, entering into the joke. "It's in the culture. I did the guy a favor, that's all."

Claudine is pleased. The idea of going out to see a show with another couple, doing the sort of things people do, is appealing out of all proportion. She catches sight of Michael over on the other side of the room. She gestures, but he doesn't see her. "Thank you," she says. "We'd love to."

She sets out across the room to Michael, but it soon turns

into a major expedition. "Excuse me," she says. "Sumimasen, excuse me." It's like the rush hour.

There's Hiromi Nakayama—or could it be Yamanaka? The one Michael thinks is so clever, and also a pain in the neck. Hiromi saved Michael from a bad mistake and has never been forgiven. He'd let his attention wander, and she'd had hers fixed on the cruzeiro. Well, so she should have had. Took her next New Year's vacation in São Paulo, worked on her Portuguese, made herself the expert. A bit much, he says. Won't do her nearly as much good as she thinks. Claudine makes a diagonal gesture meant to be a bow to Hiromi in the crush, but Hiromi, tall for a Japanese woman, is looking over her head. Trying, as it happens, to catch the eye of the President, who is bowing to a couple of—might be Brazilians. Good luck to her.

A waiter holds a tray in front of Claudine, and she takes a glass. A sip, a step. Then an unknown Englishman bars her way. He introduces himself with a determination that clearly indicates he no longer wishes to be alone in the crowd, that he needs right this minute to be with someone, and Claudine will serve his purpose.

"What are you doing here—I mean, here in Tokyo—what are you doing here, actually?"

Claudine knows that if she stops to reply he will never leave her. Besides, what is she doing here?

"I'm sorry," she says, "Excuse me."

The heat and smoke are beginning to make her feel dizzy and slightly nauseated. She looks around for somewhere to put her glass, and finding nowhere, feels it falling sideways out of her hand, and she's powerless to stop it. It's all happening in slow motion, and she can only wait for the stream of wine to show up as a dark stain on the slender black silk dress of the woman in front of her. Then, in an instant, the woman turns, takes the glass from her with one hand, grasps her arm with the other, and begins to steer her through the crowd towards an open door.

The woman is Miss Ueda.

They are in a little kitchen, where there's a narrow window and a chair. Miss Ueda opens the window, places Claudine on the chair, gets a glass and pours some iced water from a jug in the refrigerator. Claudine sips it. Miss Ueda produces a cool, damp towel and presses it to Claudine's forehead. Claudine, feeling flushed and stupid, is about to burst into tears, but Miss Ueda dabs her temples delicately with the towel and says, "Daijobu. It's all right. The room is too hot, ne?" so calmly that she thinks better of it.

They stay in the kitchen for a while. It's peaceful, and the sound of the party in the next room is now like white noise.

Claudine has a conversation with Miss Ueda. Miss Ueda tells her that she's leaving the company soon. Michael hasn't mentioned this. Miss Ueda is going to graduate school in America. She's going to do a master's degree in Development Studies.

"I intend to specialize in Women in Development," says Miss Ueda. "So-called WID. You know?" Claudine does not. "But I have to level up my English before I can write a dissertation, don't you think so?"

"Have you always wanted to do this?" asks Claudine, perplexed.

"Certainly, by all means! I have been saving money these several years. It is my dream."

"What will you do—after that?"

"I shall join the United Nations. I want to work for all the human beings," says Miss Ueda grandly.

"You do?"

"I am not, like, typical," says Miss Ueda. "I do not agree to any plan, such as to marry. I am young—" Now Claudine sees that this is true. This monster of sophistication is very young. "I want to go anywhere, even it's an underdeveloping country, I don't mind, even I have to speak African English, I will learn!" Her little foot in its black-strapped shoe is tapping, ready to go.

Claudine smiles at her. She stands up and pushes the door open. There are Stephanie and Phil, and Phil is shaking his finger at someone. There is Hiromi, with the Brazilians now. There is Cathy, laughing with three guys. There is Miss Watanabe, standing somewhat to the side of the crowd, holding a glass in both hands the way she would a green tea bowl, and a cocktail napkin neatly under it. She is absolutely still, but it is a stillness without tension. A tranquil stillness. And there is Michael, making his way across the room towards Miss Watanabe, careful not to look too obvious, but so very purposefully. Claudine turns to Miss Ueda. "I don't feel really well," she says. "I think I'll go home. Please tell my husband."

It seems this is a perfectly correct way to remove herself from the scene. Miss Ueda insists on coming with her, takes her down in the elevator, calls a taxi, rides home with her, and makes her a cup of tea when they get there, all the while explaining enthusiastically the politics of Overseas

Development Aid, so-called ODA. She advises Claudine strongly against taking a hot bath tonight, shakes her hand with a pretty smile, declines thanks, and returns to the reception.

The next day Michael refuses to go to the show with Stephanie and Phil. "I have other plans," he says. "I mean, you didn't consult me, did you?"

"What will I tell them?"

"I don't care what you tell them. Tell them what you like."

"They'll know something's wrong."

"What's wrong? Nothing's wrong."

She tries to call, but Stephanie and Phil have left already.

At the station, there's an exhibition of children's art, paintings of trains. On her way down the covered bridge towards the stairs she stops to look at them. There aren't any old-fashioned trains with puffs of steam. These are mostly the green trains of the Yamanote line, and some of them have faces and are grinning.

She's nearly to the bottom of the stairs when she notices that there's a green train stopped, oddly, half in and half out of the station, and that although there are people on the platform they're not making a sound. They are all standing silently, looking to the right. Something has happened, and it has happened no more than a moment before. Then she hears a voice, the voice of an American woman down in the crowd, high and clear above the silence, echo of her own confused thought: "Oh, God, it's a suicide!"

A telephone rings behind her in the station office, and already, incredibly, there's the sound of a siren in the distance. Claudine takes a step down the stairs. She will walk past the crowd, and she will not look. This is something you shouldn't look at. But it's early and the crowd is small, and for all her dread she cannot stop herself from looking where everyone else is looking, down at the track.

A man is lying there. Claudine has never seen a dead person before. She has reached her thirties without seeing anyone dead. Now she is looking at a dead man.

There is nothing special about his face. It is a very ordinary face, with no particular expression of shock or pain. His eyes are closed. He is wearing an ordinary navy-blue suit and white shirt, and his tie is loosened. Perhaps he loosened it standing on the platform, waiting for the train to come. His left leg is bent sideways, and—this is the only thing about him, really—the trouser leg has been ripped away below the knee, and his foot is bare too, and from the knee to the foot his leg is streaked red, stripped of skin.

The sirens get closer. Some way down the track a man in railway uniform picks up a shoe and starts back with it dangling from his hand. Someone brings a plastic sheet. Claudine turns away. Her train comes in quietly on the other line, and she gets on, and stands all the way to Harajuku.

She isn't even late. Stephanie and Phil are there in the lobby. She tells them that Michael has hay fever. It's almost spring.

"It's the dust from Mongolia," says Phil. "They have a dry winter there, it blows over here, all this yellow dust."

Claudine knows she shouldn't say anything about what she has seen, and she's made a good start, but she can't help herself.

"I saw an accident at the station," she says. "No, not an accident. I didn't see it. Somebody said, it's a suicide." She seems to have lost control of her voice. It comes out thin and trembling.

"Not so common now," says Phil. "Used to be the preferred method. Then it all but stopped. Reason was, the authorities started making the suicide's family pay up."

"What? Pay what?"

"Lost revenue," says Phil. "Stopping the trains, cleaning up, the whole darn thing. Can you imagine what that would cost? Not many people want to do that to their families. A Japanese family would accept the responsibility. That was the thinking behind it, and it seems to work, mostly."

"Then I suppose a person who would do it mightn't have any family," says Claudine bleakly.

"Not a very helpful piece of information, Phil," says Stephanie, putting her arm around Claudine. "Now listen, honey, try not to think about it anymore, okay? Happens in the big city."

"That's right," says Phil, reddening at the reproach. "Why don't we just go in? Enjoy ourselves, forget it? Life goes on."

They're both looking at her, waiting for her to reply, to move. As the moment lengthens, she can see they're getting anxious, but she can't seem to speak.

Finally, she manages to smile and nod, and they smile encouragingly back, and Phil takes her elbow and they go in.

She sits through the performance wrapped in silence. She makes an effort to concentrate, but the music slides through her brain, so she doesn't really hear a thing. Now and then she becomes conscious of the dancers tapping and twirling on the stage. It seems as bright and far away as the moon. She always joins in the applause, and exchanges glances of appreciation with Stephanie and Phil, who sit on either side of her, leaving Michael's seat empty at the end of the row.

Afterwards, she won't join them for dinner, though Phil knows a place near here that serves great ribs, and where the chairs are big enough for his rear end, he says. She has to hurry home and take care of Michael. She sounds so sincere about this that she almost believes it herself, that Michael is at home waiting for her, watching sports on TV and sneezing, that he'll greet her with a hug.

She walks to the station along with a lot of other people who've been to the theatre. They're all carrying programs like hers and looking very happy with each other, as far as she can tell.

3

Teaching the Nightingale

IT'S ALWAYS SHOCKING to come back to the city after being in the mountains. When the doors of the train open and they step out of the air-conditioned car that has brought with it the illusion of mountain coolness, they're blasted by the heat from the machinery that has created it, rising up from the gap between car and platform straight into their faces. The city air is thickened and yellowed by the afternoon sun. It is particle-laden, almost tangible. The noise of loudspeakers, right above their heads, makes speech pointless. Not that they have anything in particular to say.

They find a place by the wall where they can stand for a moment. They nod in sketchy bows and raise their right hands slightly in tentative waves, and then Seiji is gone, lost at once, even to her eyes, in the stream of black heads moving towards the green signs of the Yamanote line.

Teruko thinks, I can't go home, not yet. Standing alone, she becomes invisible. People press closer and closer to her. She's jostled and bumped. A man half falls over the bag at her feet and glares back at her as the crowd carries him on.

She digs around for her change purse, finds some coins, joins the stream and lets it push her jerkily towards a phone.

Larry is there. "Glad you called, Terry," he says. "I was just sitting here missing Yoshi. He left today."

Teruko doesn't say, "Yoshi?" Larry has so many boyfriends, always arriving from Sapporo or Naha, going back to wherever. It's hard to remember which is which. How can he miss them all? And yet it seems he does.

There's no place that isn't crowded. She struggles onto the Yamanote a few trains behind Seiji's, which must be halfway around town by now, and off again at Shibuya. The plaza in front of the station is a mass of teenagers, boys and girls with ears pierced several times over, black hair bleached to the colour of clay, all in their best, ready to shop, or dance, or whatever it is they do on Sundays. Teruko carries her bag, made heavier by the cookies bought for her mother in the hotel lobby, up the hill and into a building where the shops are full of the same kids, trying on shoes, testing makeup, shrieking in a foreign language she no longer knows, kids' language.

In the elevator she's jammed into a corner. Her own face, frightened and ghostly, is beside her, reflected in the bronze-mirrored wall her shoulder is pressed painfully against. When she reaches the coffee shop on the top floor there's a long queue of kids waiting to get in—has there been a kids' weekend coup?—but she sees Larry, already inside, waiting for her.

"Don't you love Shibuya on a Sunday afternoon?" he says, waving a hand through the cigarette haze as if to dispel it. "I've seen the future, and it scares me half to death."

Their table is tiny, and Larry has to stretch his legs out into the aisle, and draw them in every time a waitress passes. They're by a window that reaches to the floor, and the effect is of perching on the edge of a precipice.

"I know just what you're thinking," says Larry, following her eyes down. "Me, too. All we need now is an earthquake, right? I guess we'd be pitched out, coffee and all. I'd try to snatch another one of these almond things on the way down. Sorry, I went ahead and ordered, couldn't wait. My, are these good. So where've you been?"

Teruko has been away. In the mountains with Seiji, Professor Maekawa. She tells Larry this, though until this minute she never thought she would, or could. Who else can she tell?

Two or three times a year, when Professor Maekawa's wife goes to Kobe to see her parents, Teruko and the Professor go away for the weekend. Since Teruko returned to Japan, it's become a sort of habit (that's how she describes it to herself, not to Larry), a difficult one to break. There's been no reason to break it. Nor has Mrs. Maekawa seen any reason to break her habit. Although she must have some idea what's going on, she calmly takes their daughter to Kobe just the same. Seiji seems to be a fair-to-middling kind of husband, and there will never be any question of divorce. Unless, that is, after their daughter has finished college and married one of her father's more promising graduate students, Mrs. Maekawa should decide she's had enough of being a professor's wife, of living in a tiny house of which every corner is surely littered with piles of old academic journals tied up with string (journals her husband may or may not ever get round to reading), so that her cleaning has to be done around them, of cooking huge platters of fried chicken wings for his seminar students while they sprawl laughing and gossiping on the floor at his feet and drink themselves silly, and opt for a quiet little apartment by herself somewhere. Teruko would sympathise with her if she did, but thinks it unlikely.

Teruko has always considered it fortunate that she herself never had any thought of marrying Seiji. She's known him since they were students together, and members of the climbing club. He was senior to her, but he was kind, and she used to think of him as being far out of her reach.

On these weekends, they do some of the same things they used to do then. They hike, and look at flowers, and watch birds in an amateurish way. Teruko takes photos, but, for obvious reasons, he doesn't. Sometimes, like this weekend, they stay in a Western-style hotel at a mountain resort, and in the atmosphere of such a place they have sometimes acted like true lovers, rather than the old friends they've always been.

Teruko has noticed couples somewhat like themselves on the trains they've taken to these romantic places, and around the inns and hotels where they've stayed. The middle-aged man with his almost middle-aged mistress, a little giggly for the occasion—she spots them in a flash. She thinks, though, that while Seiji definitely looks like somebody's husband, she—perhaps because she was abroad so long, perhaps because she looks as if she might have a real job, and pay her own way, which she does—has not settled into the mould. She still looks as if she has possibilities. Just.

When, on Friday afternoon, she opened the doors to the balcony of their room, the mountains, still covered almost down to the valley floor with snow, rose and encircled her. She had to put her head back to see the highest ridges and the sky. She focussed her binoculars. Along the ridges, against a background of clouds, were countless tiny, black, moving spots.

"Come and look at all the climbers!" she called. "Isn't that amazing! Nose to tail!"

"You used to like it."

"It wasn't so crowded then, was it? Yes, I did. The air, the way it stung the inside of my nose, I loved that!"

"My idea of a good time's changed," he said. "I don't want to sleep huddled up in a hut on top of a mountain anymore."

He put his arms around her. It gave her an odd feeling. They're always shy at first. It isn't as if they have much contact between times. One might consult the other on some point of English when preparing an article for a foreign journal, maybe, or they might see each other across a library reading room. Occasionally this might lead to an hour or two in some love hotel in a corner of the city, but not often. They are both busy. They have their own lives.

"Me either. Anyway, I'd be nervous up there, now."

He kissed her neck. Voices floated over the balcony of the next room. A bird sang.

"Listen to that," he said. "An uguisu singing its love song."

"Oh, uguisu!" she exclaimed, in mock disgust.

"You surprise me. I mean, it's such a poetic bird! The foremost literary bird."

"That's just the problem. There's one in every other poem and they drive me nuts! How do you translate uguisu? It's always been 'nightingale,' but that seems wrong to me. On the other hand, 'bush warbler' is rather prosaic, don't you think?"

"You're talking about your article? 'Aspects of Nature in Japanese and English Poetry,' etcetera?"

"That's what I'm talking about."

"Forget it," he said. "Put a footnote. Explain that they're really bush warblers and they sing in the day."

"Is that your answer to everything? A footnote?"

"Certainly. It's only a little bird."

"Thank you, Professor."

She leaned against him. He was wearing his favourite hiking shirt, one of the plaid flannel shirts he gets from the catalogue of some famous mountain equipment shop in the States. Admittedly, they're always too neatly ironed, and it could be funny—slight, bespectacled Seiji as weekend backwoodsman—but it isn't. His arms are sinewy, though as far she knows he hasn't done any serious exercise for years, and they feel good.

"Do you remember the haiku by Issa, Professor?" she asked. "The one about the uguisu that wipes its muddy feet on the blossoms of the plum . . . ?"

"Mm, yes," he said, frowning, but by the way he moved on too quickly she was pretty sure he didn't. "Do you remember Sei Shonagon complains the uguisu never sings in the palace, but she often hears it warbling its heart out in the scraggly plum tree beside some peasant's hut?"

"Oh, come on! Everyone knows that!"

"Okay. Can we finish this later?"

She knows Seiji too well. She's known him longer than his wife has. She knows how much he hates to be outdone, even in the smallest thing, how he revels in the adoration of his students, how he loves being on NHK TV, how much he always wanted to be just the person he is today, the perfect sensei, not rich, not too famous, but entirely admirable. She knows what he's doing when he name-drops older, more famous, American scholars that he knew, however slightly, when he was there, and she's sure he sends them Japanesey Christmas cards still, though they probably don't remember him too well by now. She knows that one of the reasons he likes to be with her is that she recognises the names.

Larry often says to her, "You know what it's like out there in gaikoku, Terry!" He thinks it's so funny, the way some Japanese say "gaikoku" like that, innocently, like "foreign parts." Sometimes they even say, "What do they have for breakfast in gaikoku?" As if all countries not Japan were the same. Well, she and Seiji have both lived in countries not Japan. And Seiji's wife hasn't, because he left her behind for the three years of their engagement while he went to Michigan to get his doctorate, and, incidentally, have a lot of fun. "Pig," Teruko's gaijin friends would probably say, though Mrs. Maekawa might not. Teruko thinks Seiji is rather a selfish person, but then again, it isn't her problem, and, lying warm beneath him with the uguisu singing outside, she was certainly prepared to overlook it.

It rained all night, and in the morning, as they set out, huge drops were still sliding from the leaves of the trees, dripping down their necks. They climbed down into the riverbed and crunched over the wide expanse of smooth grey stones. The river was running fast and clear with melted snow, and when Teruko knelt down to dip her hand in it, she felt a thrill of cold, almost of pain, up to her elbow. The banks were lined with new-furred pussywillows, and shoots of wild rhubarb—"the foremost literary vegetable," she said, teasing—had already pushed through the earth, but there was no sun. She and Seiji, on this spring morning, were bundled in layers of down, and glad of it.

Trailing mist obscured the dark walls of the mountains, but the little black spots could already be seen moving slowly along the clearer ridges. It was very quiet—and then, out of nowhere, there came a helicopter buzzing overhead. It hovered, moved on, hovered again. The sound reverberated from peak to peak.

Teruko, standing in the riverbed with a perfectly oval stone in her gloved hand, felt momentarily claustrophobic. It wasn't the first time. She remembered that once a gaijin friend had asked her, "What happens to claustrophobic people in Japan?" and Teruko had laughed and replied, "There aren't any. I've never met any. They couldn't survive." Now she felt, in this beautiful gorge, as if the mountains were leaning towards her.

Before, she's felt this way in more likely places. In elevators, and theatres, and buses, she's felt a desperate need for air, for space. This is since her return. She knows what it is, what she really wants, and she knows what she wants is impossible. She wants to feel young, the way she did right up to the moment she got on the plane home. It's the impossibility of this that constricts her lungs.

She sometimes wakes up in the morning thinking of her life as it was, not of anything special but of everyday things like jumping in her car and driving to the supermarket for milk. Then she feels trapped and breathless, even in her own bed.

She must have made a sound, because Seiji took her arm and asked. "What's that sigh? In this beautiful place?"

She smiled at him, and they clambered up to the path again and started to walk, more seriously. The path was wet and in places streams had burst over it, so they had to climb around on wet rocks, or cross miniature bridges of fallen branches. People on their way up to the peaks passed them, striding heavily in climbing boots, and hung about with ice axes and bright nylon ropes.

What would her parents say, if they knew she was there? Not on a girls' outing, as they like to think of it, with her old high-school friend Hiromi, whose rise in the bank they've followed with interest and a certain anxiety, for Hiromi, successfully unmarried, is perhaps not the best influence—but with Professor Maekawa? She's told them lies, like a teenager, but how else can it be done? How else can it ever be done?

They've been so worried about her being an "old miss." What an expression! (And that earlier generation, borrowing it from some passing Victorian, couldn't even get it right!) They were so worried that they were driven to lie to her, to bring her back. They lied. Her father isn't really sick, never was. He was well enough to meet her at the airport, large as life, and how could she express anything but joy at seeing him there? Could she have said, "You lied!" then, or ever?

Larry was incredulous when she said that it made her realise, in spite of everything, how much they cared about her. "Terry," he said, "I would've been on the next plane out again!" There are some things it's impossible to explain, even to Larry. He says, "If you keep refusing omiai, if you won't meet anyone they find for you, what's the point? You came back, you stayed, but now you won't do anything they want. Isn't that a bit contrary?" Yes, it is contrary. They all thought—her sister, playing her allotted part, had actually voiced this thought—she was selfish to stay away as long as she did. Now they think she's obdurate, as well.

Maybe she was born out of sync. She loves to read about the young feminists of the Taisho period, say, how they ran away from home and cropped their hair and read Ibsen and drank rainbow-coloured cocktails in wild bohemian bars and had affairs and wrote outrageous poetry and demanded the vote. That was running away! Now she sees everywhere on the street girls who look just like them, with their hair cut short all round and wearing long dresses, the latest thing, and heavy black flat shoes. They look like they stepped out of a magazine photo of 1920, except for the multiplicity of earrings, and they look like they do just as they please. And here she is, Teruko, with her two master's degrees, not just one, right back where she started.

Only not quite. She smells of butter, as they used to say in the old days. Her sister says she even walks differently, and flings her elbows around, to demonstrate. Maybe this is why her mother makes a point of telling everybody, "Yes, of course we were anxious about her, going abroad alone. We were so afraid she'd overdo it. The study, you know. She had to write a whole thesis in English!"

It made Teruko cringe when, not long after she came back, she saw a young girl on the train wearing a T-shirt that said, I GOT LAID IN HAWAII. Sometimes the craziest things are written on T-shirts, nonsense things in broken English, just for decoration—she and Larry make fun of them, and he says he wants to be a T-shirt writer, only he's not sure he's got the talent. But here was a real American T-shirt. She couldn't know whether this plump little girl with the dumb face would have made much sense of the message emblazoned across her chest, or if it's true, but still she hated to see it, because it was her own truth. She herself, good-daughter Teruko, had done just that, and not only in Hawaii.

Also, she once quite seriously thought of marrying a gaijin.

Something stopped her. Maybe it was only that he enjoyed her Japanese manners too much, the way she poured his beer for him, or that he thought it was too charming that she still couldn't say words like "lyric" properly. Anyway, something struck a wrong note, made her back off. Or could it be that she just lacked the courage to take the risk? It might have been the right thing. She might be one-half of a real Western two-career couple now. She might have a toddler in nursery school, while she finished her Ph.D. and taught. She might have a large sunny house with her own study, and a station wagon, and he might have been a decent husband after all, and not wanted her really to fulfill some geisha fantasy. And her parents would have come round, and they would have loved their grandchild and forgotten to worry at all about its being a haafu, and she wouldn't have this problem she's got now.

In her sister's apartment one day, the claustrophobic feeling came upon her so strongly that she had to go outside, down six flights of stairs and into the apartment-house playground, on the pretext of taking the children out to play. She was just overcome.

She leapt up, and her sister and her aunt, mid-gossip, stared at her in surprise. (Aunt! How easy it had been to cast off the discipline of respect for family bores, in all those years without Aunt!) She talked nonsense to the children as she hastily put on their jackets. Auntie, my zip won't go! Yes, she is an aunt too, and maybe she'll end up with nothing to talk about but other people's marriages, if she doesn't end up crazy. "Oh, your auntie's so stupid," she cried, fumbling to get it right, because she had to get out of there, and she hustled them into their shoes and down the stairs, not wanting to wait for the tiny, dim elevator, and she kept them down there playing frenetically for an hour, until the elder one started to complain of the cold, and the younger one got overexcited and felt sick.

Now her brother-in-law has come up with another man for her. She has to give them all credit, they put a lot of thought into it. This man is thirty-nine, and divorced, but not of bad character. It was a sad story, everyone agrees about that, and they would have considered it from all angles. She herself has so far declined to hear it. Amazing that they should be able to lay their hands on a man like this. He's worked for his company abroad. He speaks English and German. She's seen his photo—curiosity got the better of her there—and he looks jowly and low-browed, but she understands that they think he's just right, or, rather, the best she can do. She is clearly the best he can do.

Her sister says, "It's not too late to have babies. Don't you want one like this?" When she looks at them, she has to admit the thought appeals. They are lovely. She took dozens of photos of them when they all went to see, on a clear blue winter's day, the last fall of snow clinging to the boughs of plum blossom like a vision of all she had ever been homesick for, and the children were laughing in their pink woolly hats and mittens, like blossoms too, that was the only way to think of them.

But wait a minute. Her brother-in-law is handsome. What would her children look like, the ones she'd have with this homely man with the sad story whom she's never met, never wanted?

It was funny in a way, the thought of her jowly, low-browed, thick-lensed babies, but when she told Seiji, he didn't laugh. He turned his face away and muttered, "You have to do what you think best."

"Don't worry." she said, "I won't do it."

"It's your own affair," he said coldly. "Just don't talk about it like that."

She was sorry she'd said anything. It wasn't in the best of taste. It showed a lack of dignity. But perhaps Seiji was really upset at the idea of a change in this very pleasant arrangement they have. If so, it's a pity, because probably there will be no change. Probably they'll go on just like this.

Her whole life will go on just like this. She'll go on working quietly at the college where she carries her books along the hall from class to class, day after day. This part would be better if she were doing great original work, but she isn't. And though her students are clever girls, most of them are going to end up well married and they don't need her for that. Sometimes the President herself arranges important marriages for her graduates, the best ones. The girls would envy Teruko if they knew she'd been in the mountains with Seiji, who is on TV. It would be a wonderful scandal, though it certainly wouldn't do her career any good, but they'll never know. All this could go on for a very long time.

The other day, the President gave a lunch for a group of visiting African women educationists. The head of a girls' school in Mali spoke of the low life expectancy in the country, and the role of women's education in improving the situation, and so on, and the President said—this is what woke Teruko out of a reverie, since, as a relatively new member of staff, she was placed at the end of the table and rarely addressed: "Pity us poor Japanese women. We have to live forever." It made Teruko jump. It's true. Japanese women have a longer life expectancy than anyone, longer than any human beings in history. Teruko's own grandmother is ninety-five and still going strong. Teruko herself, well nourished and with those genes, can expect to live—well, practically forever.

That's what she was thinking about when, in the distance, the helicopter reappeared, skimming very close to the mountainside beneath the ridges.

They stopped and looked up, shielding their eyes from the glare reflected by clouds. "It must be the rescue helicopter," said Seiji.

A short distance along the river was a rough bridge, where they planned to cross. As they approached it, she kept looking back to see what the helicopter was doing, but by the time they reached the other bank it was gone.

"It's all over, whatever it was," she said.

On this side of the river the path followed close to the foot of a thickly wooded mountain. Ahead of them was the gate of a shrine, its two single tree trunks and curved crosspiece a faded vermilion, glowing in the grey light of late afternoon. The mountain rose straight up behind it, but its peak was hidden by curling mist.

Teruko said, "It's really possible to feel there's a god here."

"The restaurant's here somewhere, too," said Seiji, pulling his guidebook from his pocket.

She laughed. "I'm talking about the god, and you're talking about food."

"This is a famous restaurant," he said defensively.

The famous restaurant was a wooden shack before the shrine gate, and they could smell woodsmoke and grilled fish before they saw it. But when they reached it, they walked past the hut and into the shrine, and said a prayer.

Teruko's prayer was longer than she'd meant, and she found when she'd finished that Seiji was still beside her, his palms joined beneath his bowed head.

There was no-one else in the restaurant. A girl with a mountain woman's bright red cheeks skewered two fish and placed them upright in the ashes of the open hearth.

Teruko, curious, walked around the interior of the hut. She saw an old sepia photo on the wall, and stopped to look closer. It showed gaijin in Victorian walking dress, a man in knickerbockers and a woman in a plain ankle-length skirt and buttoned boots. Beside them was a Japanese man who looked like a woodcutter.

"Who are these people?"

"Missionaries," said Seiji. "The other man was a famous mountain guide, an ancestor of the owners here. It's in the guidebook."

"Everything's famous in that book."

"The purpose of the book is to point you in the direction of the best things," he says.

"They look like they think they're in some colony, India or somewhere."

"It's all the same to a missionary."

"What a nerve they had, to think they could evict the gods!" Teruko was surprised at the outrage she heard in her own voice.

"Well, they didn't have much of an effect on the gods, did

they? They had more success spreading the word on recreational hiking, wouldn't you say?"

Teruko didn't smile. She burst out, "Sometimes I don't know where I am! Sometimes I feel like a foreigner!"

Seiji, turning the book sideways to study a map, only answered calmly, "That's natural. You'll get over it."

The fish were crisp and salty on the outside, and the flesh was very sweet. When only the bones were left on their plates, they smiled at each other. It was really something, after all, to be together, to have eaten fish from the cold river at the feet of the mountain god.

The path they took from the shrine, back in the direction from which they'd come, was quiet. There seemed to be no other people walking on this side of the river. It ran through shadowy woods, and they could no longer see the peaks.

The snow line came right down to the path, but there was a deep hole in the snow around the base of each tree trunk, melted by the miraculous warmth of the living tree in its spring growth.

One tree not far from the path was surrounded by shreds of bark. Sharp claws? Teeth?

"Deer," said Seiji confidently.

"Aren't there bears?"

Their eyes met. Seiji was wearing his plaid shirt under his down jacket, but right then he didn't look like much of a woodsman.

"They'd have cubs," she said.

"Let's sing," he offered. "They hate human noise."

So they sang. They sang old pop songs, Beatles songs, and

student songs, from the days when they were always in a big group of friends in the mountains, and never gave a thought, so it seems now, to anything that might happen. In the woods, or teetering along the ridges, they never felt anything but safe.

Whether or not this strategy worked, there were no bears.

Instead, unbelievable good fortune! Among the trees, standing there completely unafraid of their singing, they saw a mountain antelope. It had long, pale hair. It was deerlike, and goatlike. It gazed at them, its expression mild and interested. They stopped dead. Finally, after it had looked its fill, the creature turned and delicately, unhurriedly, picked its way up the mountainside, through the patchy snow and into the underbrush, and was gone.

Then they moved towards each other, they laughed and hugged and kissed and stayed there kissing till they became aware once more of the silence that was around them. It seemed even quieter than before, and from now on they walked faster, their boots crunching loudly on the path, crushing the delicate icicles that lay just under the surface of frozen mud.

After a while the path turned downhill, and gradually it ran out of the woods and into the middle of the valley. Again they were following the river, as it split into several narrow streams, swollen with melted snow, and rushed around the roots of trees and over rocks, and then as it widened out into pools that reflected the darkening mountains and the shifting mists.

An uguisu called above their heads.

Teruko paused to look for it, but, as if sensing her searching gaze, it immediately fell silent.

"I can't see it," she said regretfully.

"Come on," said Seiji. "It's leaf-coloured, and I'm cold."

"No, wait."

He sighed and leaned against a post, on which was a sign advising persons intending to climb above this point to leave their names and details of proposed route in the attached box. He began to rub his hands together briskly and blow in them. In his know-it-all voice he said, "You know, that song doesn't come naturally."

"No? What do you mean? Of course it does!" she said, still methodically trying to follow each branch in turn.

"Ah, you don't know!" he said with satisfaction. "They have to learn how. In the old days—it's not allowed now—but then people used to keep uguisu in cages. If you had one that had been raised out of the nest, it wouldn't know how to sing."

"It wouldn't?"

"No. So what they did was, there'd be a man who had some singing birds, and he'd come round with his birds, and they'd teach the other one to sing."

"How long did it take?"

"I don't know."

It was impossible to distinguish the shape of the bird in the failing light. Teruko gave up. "So you don't know everything," she said.

It had started to rain, though gently enough. With their hoods pulled up, arm in arm, they left the river and climbed a slope wooded with spindly birch trees. Through the trees they saw the lights of the hotel glimmering.

At dinner, Seiji was thoughtful over the wine list. He considers himself something of a gourmet, and for relaxation he reads a lot of books about food. He brought one with him this weekend.

The gastronomic philosophy of a famous writer, preferably a Naoki Prize winner, that's the kind of cookbook he likes. Teruko doubts that Seiji himself really cooks, though once he was featured in a magazine article about men who do, and there were arty black-and-white photos of him doing it. Surely it was a put-up job? Nothing Teruko knows about Seiji or Mrs. Maekawa leads her to believe that Mrs. Maekawa ever lets him in the kitchen. Still, she envies him his way of making something of his fantasies.

The waiter said, "You saw a kamoshika! That was a bit of luck!"

"It's the first time," said Teruko.

"Well, the thing is, the snow line's usually much higher by this time of year, and they follow it up, so you hardly ever see them down in the valley once spring comes."

"It looked right at us!"

"They do," agreed the waiter. "That's why they're so easy to shoot— Oh, not here!" he added hastily, seeing her expression.

"They're protected here. They're a Natural National Treasure! But outside, the farmers . . ."

"Don't think about it," urged Seiji, when the waiter had gone. "Just think, we were lucky."

"Oh, yes," said Teruko. "So much for Nature."

"Handsome kid, the waiter," said Seiji, determinedly changing the subject. "Maybe your friend Larry should come up here."

This kind of remark has always irritated her. He refers to Larry quite often, and usually this way. "Larry wouldn't come to a place like this," she answered shortly.

"Oh, is that so? He only stays in ancient inns or temples, I suppose? He's more authentic than we are? Gaijin like that are a pain in the neck."

"I didn't say that. It's no use talking to you if you're going to be annoying."

"I'm jealous," said Seiji.

"You're joking." She stared at him in honest amazement.

Half cross, half ashamed, he said, "You talk to him more often than you do to me. You talk about him."

"I talk about him because he's my friend. I talk to him because—I can talk to him."

"Better than to me?"

"Don't be silly. I just can't see you so often."

Seiji said nothing but looked down at his plate and pressed his lips together.

After dinner, he said, "Let's go outside. I want a cigarette."

"It's raining."

"You don't have to come."

"I'll come."

Huddled together under an umbrella borrowed from the doorman, they followed a lighted path to a place where there was a small wooden footbridge over the river.

The sound of the fast-flowing stream filled their ears, but when Teruko leaned over the rail, she could see nothing, not even a glint of moonlight on foam.

Seiji said to her, his breath warm on her ear, "We're like the lovers in a woodblock print, aren't we? Sharing an umbrella like this?"

She answered, amused, "But theirs is always a lovely old-fashioned paper one, not an ugly striped golf umbrella with the name of a hotel on it!"

❖ ❖ ❖

Later, as she came out of the bathroom with her hairbrush in her hand—this next part, of course, she doesn't tell Larry, and nor has she told him he was talked about at dinner, nothing of that either—she found Seiji sitting on the bed, legs crossed. Most nights, she imagines, he sleeps not on a bed but on a futon laid out beside his wife's, in her fine old family home, now his home.

With Teruko, he sleeps entwined on double beds, in hotels.

He stood up and put his arms around her from behind, slipping his hands through the slits in the sleeves of her blue-and-white cotton kimono to touch her breasts. "The old-fashioned ways are best," he said. "There's nothing like kimono for ease of access." This is no more than the kind of talk they've always enjoyed on these weekends, but in that moment, in the time it took for her to breathe in, and raise her hands and place them over his, the words died between them.

Why should this time have been so different? How could it be that this time they were lovers, not playing at love because they were together, but real lovers?

He turned her gently around so that she stood in his arms, and held her away from him and said deliberately but in a voice that shook, "I made a terrible mistake in my life! How did it happen? We should have been together—it would have been right, Teruko!"

She remembers crying, "Don't say that! Please don't say that!" She ran to the balcony door, her kimono open, clutching it round her, and the icy air hit her like a slap in the face. Outside everything was dark. The trees, the great wall of mountains almost close enough, this morning, to touch, were obliterated. There was no river sound, only the sound of her own gasping breath.

"Come in! This is crazy! It's cold, you'll die! Please, Teruko, there are people in the next room! Oh, Teruko, I love you!" He grabbed her and pulled her in, and they stumbled on the doorsill into the room, making love there where they lay.

When they woke, they were in bed. It seemed they woke at the same moment, both having heard the same sharp birdcall. They looked straight into each other's eyes, and Teruko, before any conscious thought had entered her brain, was pierced by a single, lucid truth. She recognised it at once. An old fear, in the past half-comprehended, now transformed, clear as a shard of ice. Seiji said, "What is it?" but she didn't try to answer. His body warmed hers, but the knowledge remained, free-floating and irreducible.

She lay there afterwards listening to him in the bathroom. He is always very noisy. He clears his throat uninhibitedly and spits thoroughly. She dwelt on this, as if it could help her undo what had happened, but it was no use. There is nothing he is likely to do, however unappealing, that will make any difference. She loves him, and he knows it. Worse still, he loves her.

It was a brilliant morning. The sky above the peaks was blue, the snow glittered. There were people up there in the brightness narrowing their eyes against the pain of it, breathing the thin sunlight, trying not to look down. The helicopter was already hovering, but with the light glinting on it, it was as pretty as a dragonfly.

"It seems a pity to leave on such a wonderful day," grumbled Seiji. "Why couldn't it have been like this yesterday?"

The truth was, they were both feeling bewildered and heavy-headed. The bags under Seiji's eyes, which made him so interesting on TV, now appeared to her, for the first time, as a true earnest of the way he would look in old age. She could see it. And she should have been with him then, been the grandmother of his grandchildren. Outlived him, no doubt, as his widow, surrounded by piles of dusty journals. It would have been the most natural thing imaginable.

"A pity on any day," she said.

On the train, he put his head back against the seat and closed his eyes. The train ran for a while between the mountains, and then out into a broader valley of fields and orchards, where the apricots were in blossom. She patted his sleeve, and he sat up drowsily and looked out with her at the glowing pink cloud that hovered for a minute or two in the window. Then the blossoms were replaced by fields that were merely green, by farmhouses, by villages that were closer and closer together and then never ended, by the city.

"Terry," says Larry, "all this time you've been holding out on me. And here I am, I tell you everything."

"You don't," she says flatly.

"Well, okay. But you never even mentioned this guy, not once, this very old and dear friend."

"Maybe I was ashamed."

"Don't you mean embarrassed? You weren't ashamed, were you, surely not? One thing I know for a fact you're not, Terry, is a puritan. 'Embarrassed' is a better word for 'hazukashii' in this case. Excuse me for being pedantic at a time like this."

"Embarrassed, then."

"You look awful, Terry, if you don't mind my saying so. What happened? Did he dump you when you got to the end of the line? Not that it's any of my business."

"No. I don't think he'll ever do that."

"So what's the problem? No, you don't have to tell me, I don't mean that. I mean, there might not even be a problem, how should I know?"

"This place is so hot!" She turns her face away from the crowd, but on the other side is the plate-glass chasm.

"It must be beautiful up there."

"It is beautiful."

"Isn't that where the kids were killed?"

"What?"

"Some kids from a college climbing club, they fell."

"I don't know. We saw the helicopters all weekend."

Larry grimaces. "That's how it goes. Anyway. What else?"

"The omiai. The man they want me to meet."

"Another one?"

"The same."

"They don't give up easy, do they?"

"You know I saw his picture."

"Hardly such as to inspire an instant crush, was it?"

"He has a low forehead, Larry!"

Larry laughs. "Oh yes, the low forehead! Well, that settles it. You can't possibly do it. So don't do it. Simple."

"Do you really think so?"

"No. That was dumb."

"What can I do?"

"I don't know what to say, Terry. I guess you're in a bind, but I just don't know. I feel really bad for you."

"I'm sorry. I can't expect you to know."

"I wish I could marry you," he says wryly.

Teruko looks up. "Larry! Why don't we?"

"It was a joke, Terry!"

"But—" She ignores the alarm that tinges his smile. It strikes her now that he's said it before. When they've been laughing together, agreeing about things, having fun, he's said, "We should get married!" Of course, it was just in fun, but now it seems like a wonderful idea. "Larry, we could! Then we could buy an apartment, you could get a loan, even as a foreigner, you'd be respectable to your boss, there are good reasons!"

Then she really looks at Larry's face. He is very upset. She has shocked Larry.

"But Teruko," he says, lowering his voice. "You know as well as anybody. I'm a homosexual."

"You told me they're all married!"

"I told you, they're all married *here.* And I only meant most of the older—no, not most, many—oh, what do I know about it? It's a perception. Based on pretty thorough research, admittedly." He can't resist that self-congratulatory pause, she thinks. "I don't have any figures. Not all. You're so literal, Terry. For God's sake."

"You're here."

"I'm a gaijin!"

"My parents wouldn't know everything about you," she says obstinately. "They'd give in. A gaijin husband would be better than no husband."

"Oh, great!"

"I'd do all the right things! I'd be a good wife, and we're friends. But we'd both be free!"

"You mean you'd be free!"

"We both would be."

"Terry," he says, in a softer tone. "You're not listening to me. I'm free now. I do what I want. I'm not concerned about my position in this society, I don't need this."

After a moment she says, "How fortunate you are. How very far from home."

"Terry, don't be like this. Please. Listen, I'm sorry."

"I'm the one who should be sorry," she says in a low voice. "I was completely wrong. I was very selfish. Now I'm really ashamed."

"Don't be. We're friends, we'll always be friends."

"Although I'm so stupid? Yes, I let myself be called back. I know what you think about that. Now I've made a mess of my life. That's an idiom, Larry. You're right. I am stupid."

He looks at her, for once helpless. "How can I tell you, Terry? I love you. You're not stupid. I know you love your family, you love this guy—"

"I don't want to talk about love," she says, pronouncing the L and the V very clearly.

A dreadful thought comes to her.

This is Larry, open, funny Larry. She's not his only friend, he has countless friends. And he can never resist a story. How can he not tell this to everyone? She has given Larry a story! He'll tell all his gaijin women friends, and they'll feel sorry for her, but they'll think her a fool, too. They must know all about her already, about how her parents called her home, and she came. About the omiai. They know too much. But it's her own fault. She shouldn't be here with Larry at all, telling him all her private things this way.

She picks up the check. "Thank you, Larry," she says. "I'm sorry. I have to go."

"Will you be okay?"

"I feel better now, thank you."

"Don't let anyone make you do anything you don't want to, Terry."

"Please don't worry about me."

"You mean a lot to me." He looks as if he might cry.

"You mean a lot to me," she says. "You're my best friend—" and then something makes her add, "among my foreign friends."

Larry, who has half risen, sits down, as if she had struck him. That is how she leaves him.

Her mother is watching TV. Teruko sits down beside her and watches for a while. It's some domestic drama or other. The wife takes the pillow from her futon and moves it onto her husband's futon. This means they're going to make love. Teruko gets up and opens the sliding doors to the garden.

"It's so hot in here," she says. "Where's Daddy?"

"He was playing golf today."

"It's wonderful that he's well enough," says Teruko. Her voice is cold even before it leaves her lips, as if her chest cavity were filled with icicles, sharp as needles.

Her mother takes her eyes briefly from the screen. "Isn't it?" she says.

Later Seiji calls her. He's never done this before, but this is how it will be.

"Are you at home?" she asks. She looks over her shoulder. Her mother is coming through the hall carrying the box of cookies from the hotel. It has bright mountain scenes on the wrapping.

"No," he says. His wife must be back. "I'm out walking the

dog. Teruko—I just wanted to hear your voice. I couldn't end the day without hearing it again."

"I'm fine, thank you."

"Is your mother there?"

"Yes."

"What are you doing with yourself tonight?"

"Working on my paper."

"Well—all right. Teruko, listen, I want to think about next time. When we can be together again. Let's go to a hot springs, some place much deeper in the mountains. Really remote, hidden away. No helicopters. We'll find an extra day, somehow. Escape. Would you like that?"

"Yes, I would."

"I'll get a special guidebook. I'll find somewhere, okay? There are places. Old-fashioned, with lamplight. Mountain vegetables, all different kinds of mushrooms. A stream right under our window. The uguisu singing there, too, it'll still be spring. It has to be soon, Teruko."

"Yes."

"Let's talk later. But even if—let's not wait. We'll make a place, a time—before." He means a love hotel, some afternoon between lectures.

"Later. Of course."

"All right, Teruko—goodnight."

"Goodnight."

"Who was that?" asks her mother, right on cue, almost before she puts down the phone.

"Professor Maekawa." To say his name. "He's sending me a book."

They sit at the low table in front of the TV. Now she can

see close-ups of the rescue helicopters, stretchers hanging beneath them as they put down gently near a building, a hospital somewhere.

"Isn't that near where you and Hiromi were?" asks her mother, stripping the cellophane from the scenic cookie box.

"I think so."

"I wish you wouldn't go to such dangerous places."

"We don't climb, Mother. We walk."

"Hiromi is a city person, I know."

"Yes, she is. A very city person."

"But still, even walking—rocks can fall on you."

"Not where we were, Mother."

"What did she wear?"

"What?"

"Hiromi must have some expensive new spring clothes?"

Teruko turns her head from the screen, stares blankly at her mother. "Hiromi always does," she says.

Photos of the victims, side by side. Nineteen, twenty-one. The ages we used to be. And yet, here I am. "So you didn't see anything?"

"No."

Her mother pours two cups of green tea, shaking every last drop from the pot. "About this person," she says. "I talked to your sister today. It's getting late, you know."

"I suppose it is."

"Now," her mother says confidingly, "it's a bit difficult. Your brother-in-law's in an embarrassing position, and he's done his best to help."

"I'm sorry."

"Won't you just meet him, this man? You don't have to, you

only have to say. But wouldn't it be better, just once? Don't you think so, Teruko? He might be very nice. He might be exactly right."

"Possibly," says Teruko in an impatient tone, as the camera moves up to the snowy peaks and down again to where the reporter stands, microphone in hand, by the river. "Why not?"

Seiji walks the dog home and ties it up by its kennel at the back door. He goes straight to his study, where his wife brings him green tea and one of his favourite things, a sweet rice cake wrapped in a salted cherry leaf. He takes down a book and looks for the poem about the uguisu wiping its muddy feet. It's been bothering him all weekend. When he finds it, he writes it in his diary in the space for today, which of course is blank, in his rather good calligraphy.

Larry gets on the phone to his friend Elaine. He tells her what has happened between himself and Teruko. "I'm really mad about what she said to me," he says. "I'm hurt, to be honest. But I understand. She's under a lot of pressure. I guess I'll go to her stupid wedding all the same, when it happens."

"It will, won't it?"

"Sure it will. It's terrible, you know, she really loves the guy. I hate to think of it."

"Well, that's too bad," says Elaine. "But it might be for the best. What do we know?"

"Oh, come on! I just hate it! She's changed so much. I wish you'd known her before, in graduate school. She was a different person. She used to fuck like a mink! Can you believe that? Hey, I wonder if he'll be there, at the wedding? She'll have to invite him, won't she? I mean, he's an old friend, too, a very distinguished guy. He's on TV. They'll probably put him right up front. I'm not looking forward to it, though. I always have a perfectly awful time at these things. Damn. I'll probably have to make a speech."

"You make good speeches," says Elaine. "You always get the honorifics right, and all that."

Teruko and her mother wait up for her father. When he finally comes in, supported by a helpful taxi driver, he's too merry to listen to anything they have to say, news or lies, and it's as much as they can do to get him up to bed.

4

Graces

"BASTARDS," SAYS FRANK, waving his hand as Tommy Yamamoto bows his way out through the revolving door of the lobby. "The way they follow you around all the time. Smile, smile, 'I will attend you.' What's all this about?"

"Hospitality," says Lew.

"In a pig's eye! I know what it is. They just want to make sure we're not alone together long enough to think about how they're screwing us."

Lew's shirt is sticking to his back. "We won't hear anything now till Friday at least. There's nothing more we can do."

"So they think it's safe to give us the night off."

"So let's try and forget it, I was going to say."

"That's a joke," says Frank in the elevator, jabbing the button.

"We're in over our heads. We're too small. We didn't do the homework."

Frank looks disgusted. "Well, you don't have to say it. You're being negative, Lew. You think they talk negative when they're jabbering among themselves? Bet your life they don't. Bushido, remember, that's the name of this game."

In Frank's room, Lew opens the fridge and takes out two beers.

"I didn't know it was tropical," he says. "I always see pictures of Mount Fuji with snow on the top."

He takes off his shoes and lies down on one of the beds, just for a minute. He closes his eyes. When he opens them again, there are empties on the table between the beds, and outside the window it's dark, except for a big neon sign with red-and-yellow characters racing down the length of it. There's a smell of steam and aftershave. Frank is standing in the bathroom door with the light behind him, buttoning up a fresh shirt and watching some TV quiz show with the sound turned down. "Look at this," he says. "When they get an answer right their seats go up in the air, see? And when they get it wrong, down they come."

"Sorry," says Lew. "I must have dozed off."

"Out like a light. That's okay. I'm enjoying this. Boy, do they have some weirdos on these shows. How come you never see anyone that weird on the street?"

Lew sits up and shakes his head, but it won't clear. He's been exhausted every day for months. The doctor said, "There's nothing wrong with you. It's a reaction. With some people, this is just the form it takes." He can't believe how tired he is, all the time. At work, he's tried not to let it show. It was silly to think that on the trip it would be better, that he'd somehow be jolted into action.

"How about dinner and a night on the town?" asks Frank. He tucks in his shirt, his movements jaunty.

Lew tries to focus. "What did you have in mind?"

"Well, you know, there's a lot here. My word," says Frank, reaching for his tie. "Some of those bars sound interesting. Positively educational."

"I hear you can get stung," says Lew. "I don't think our per diem stretches that far."

Frank isn't listening. "No-pants," he crows, "That's what they call them, no-pantsu, isn't it marvellous what they do to the English language?"

"Not in the mood, Frank."

"Listen, all those dear little Madame Butterflies out there waiting! And we give Sonny Boy the slip!"

Lew considers Frank, pink and clean and excited, concentrating on a perfect knot. At work the girls fall silent when he stumps out of his office with a fistful of papers, square-bodied, square-faced, tight-lipped. Frank is a Lutheran, and frequently has a few words to say in the cafeteria on family values and related topics.

"Come on, Lew. It's not so much fun by yourself. I mean, the place's full of bloody foreigners. Joke. Moral support. Okay?"

"You'll manage, Frank. I've got to get an early night. I've had it."

"Oh, come on, mate!"

"Frank," says Lew. "I'm sorry. I haven't been many places at all since Joanne died, and this—If I wanted to go somewhere, it wouldn't—" He can't finish. "Sorry," he says again. "I'm tired."

Frank looks stunned. "Lew, I'm sorry. I'm really sorry. I wasn't thinking."

"It's all right. I'm just tired."

Frank is red to his hairline, though his embarrassment looks the same as his office anger. "Well, you just go and lie down," he says finally. "Best thing, that's right."

The resentment that Lew feels at this is almost a relief. Don't patronize me, you fucking idiot. In the corridor he says to Frank, "Have a good time," and knows how that sounds, how he meant it to sound, from the look on Frank's face as he turns away.

He no longer wants to sleep when he gets to his room. He decides to call Deborah, though he has nothing special to say to her. She takes a long time to answer the phone. He supposes she's in one of the kids' rooms helping with the homework.

Debbie, at thirty, looks already like Joanne at forty, only Joanne took care of herself. Matronly, greying early, Debbie doesn't seem to mind. Joanne was big, but she was never matronly. Under the flowing clothes she wore, her spreading hips only made her seem more lush. Once, not long before she got sick, he happened to drive past the school on the way to a meeting. She was walking in the playground surrounded by children. Two or three were skipping beside her, looking up. She was reaching out to one of them. She was beautiful, slow-moving among them.

Debbie is not a headmistress, or even a teacher, but she has a sternness her mother never had. She's been brisk with him since Joanne died. More than once she's told him, as if she'd invented the expression, and as if it were not an incredible impertinence, not to "feel sorry for himself." She speaks to him of the future, of what she calls his own life. "Dad, you've got to start leading your own life, you've got to try," she says.

Still, he wants to talk to her, even about nothing.

"Are you doing anything exciting?" she asks.

"Eating raw fish," he jokes. "That's about as much excitement as I can take."

"Dad, read your guidebook. Go out and see things. Do things! Not just boring old business."

"It's not a lot of fun with Frank," he says lightly. "We don't share the same tastes."

"Oh, Frank!"

He sends his love to the kids. When he hangs up, he thinks. Go out, do things. Her mother wanted to travel. They would have, too. Now here he is, with Frank. One thing that's funny. If Joanne were alive, Frank would still be badgering him to go out on the town. Since she's dead, he's off the hook. Ironical.

He takes a pill and a glass of Suntory whisky, and, without closing the blinds against the neon glare, goes to sleep on top of the covers, having taken off nothing but his shoes.

In the morning he wakes early and thinks what to do. They're more or less free, until the Japanese make a decision. Passing Frank's room, he sees the DO NOT DISTURB sign on the door, and he relaxes.

He has toast and coffee for breakfast in the hotel coffee shop. The toast is astonishingly thick and light. This—exotic toast—gives him the feeling that he's so far been missing, the feeling of being in a foreign country. With Frank at the meetings it's been just like being back at the office, only worse.

Outside the window people are walking swiftly to work, and the fact that their lives, although they're only walking from the station to the office in the morning, as he himself walks from the station to the office, must be different from his own in a thousand ways, now strikes him as unbearably exciting. He wants to run out among them.

The young waiter pours him another cup of coffee. Lew

opens the Japanese newspaper he found under his door. Perhaps it's a mistake, or perhaps they think everyone can read Japanese these days. Several of the young women in the office are doing it at night school, hoping for promotion. He doesn't think it would have helped them much yesterday. On the front page is a picture of baseball players, looking as grave and correct as the waiter, with neat uniforms and upright posture. Inside there's a sumo wrestler, his hair an oiled black fan on top of his head. He's with a slim girl also in kimono, absolutely dwarfed by him. It looks like an engagement photo, and Lew smiles at it. Then he studies a cartoon. The men are caricature Japanese with big teeth, and the women have huge long-lashed eyes. The joke seems to be a simple one. This fellow's doctor tells him he has a heart problem. He sees a woman in a short skirt, and his heart beats too fast. Then it turns out she's wearing culottes, so that's all right. That's what Lew thinks it is, but it might be something completely different.

Once on the street, he walks fast like everyone else, at first. It's hard not to, when you're in among them. Until now, the area around the hotel has seemed like a business district of any big city. Office blocks, fancy shops, taxis. But there are little lanes everywhere, and he turns into the third or fourth one he passes.

The small shops here are still mostly closed. Last night's garbage in plastic bags is heaped up at intervals. A middle-aged woman in dark-striped kimono and enveloping apron comes out of a rickety-looking wooden house with a bag to add to the nearest heap. A chef all in white, wearing precariously high wooden clogs, sluices water over the cement floor of a jumbled kitchen that opens straight onto the street. A woman beats a quilt at an upstairs window, and the sound of it echoes pleasantly through the sunny morning. An old man is bending over a stand crowded with pots of bonsai. Lew sees that he's using chopsticks to pick bugs off a tiny, gnarled apple tree with miniature green fruit. The old chap peers intently at each leaf, chopsticks poised. Two young women in blue jeans and aprons squat in a patch of sunlight outside another house, watching their toddlers play. In the cramped entranceway behind them Lew notices an array of shoes scattered around the step, and a bicycle propped against an umbrella stand. One of the children, barely walking, has a radio-controlled car that zigzags wildly into a fence, sending a tailless cat leaping across Lew's path.

He thinks of Debbie and her youngest child, by the pool, the little girl in her frilly swimsuit, as blond and brown and solid as Debbie was at that age. Debbie was a serious child, and is a serious mother. She's a member of an association for parents of gifted children. Lew has his doubts. They seem like good, ordinary kids to him, whatever the I.Q. tests say, even-tempered as his son-in-law, reliable in learning to swim and play an instrument each. The youngest already has a tiny violin. Much as he loves them, he finds being left alone with them to talk of teachers and best friends while Debbie is in the kitchen a minor ordeal. He would turn on the TV if Debbie didn't have them rationed. They all learned to read early, but they don't seem to have read the children's books he knows, and he thinks he's heard all they have to say about dinosaurs. He'd better be sure to get them dolls in kimonos and robots that turn into rockets before he leaves here.

Looking discreetly into houses as he passes, he pictures his own. He can see Debbie's wedding photo on the bookshelf, and the one of himself and Joanne in the mountains, where he's standing behind her with his arms around her. In the centre of the floor is the rowing machine he bought last month, at Debbie's urging. She's read somewhere that raising the adrenaline level is good for depression. He supposes there must be something in it. Certainly some nights he's been grateful to have the means of creating a reason for his exhaustion, but now the thought of the rowing machine in the silent room, the vision of himself rowing through his grief, seems pathetic and distasteful to him.

He rounds a corner into another lane, where shopkeepers are wheeling out displays of china, magazines, shoes. At the end of the street he sees the garbage truck pass. Men in pressed grey overalls and grey gloves toss bags into the whining jaws at the back of the truck, with none of the noisy banter he associates with garbage collectors. He stops to watch but moves on when a group of schoolgirls, charms tinkling on their bags, come up behind him, giggling.

He walks and walks. A building with a curved roof, behind a high fence, must be a temple. Above the gate, on a massive lintel, gold-painted characters gleam in the sun. The gate is open, and he can see a garden, and a ladder against a tree whose branches are trained with poles and knotted ropes. He thinks of going in, but the quietness makes him hesitate, and he contents himself with running his hands over the fine carving on the gate. The wood is already warm from the sun and giving to the touch.

The temple street is in full sun, broader, and more open. He soon understands the reason for the openness. He's walking beside a cemetery. The gate here is open, too, and he takes a few steps inside.

The stone monuments, on plots neatly railed or edged in smaller stones, are not like the ones he's used to. There are characters deeply incised in them, and they're backed by clusters of tall wooden sticks, like fence palings, painted in black with more characters. Names? Prayers? There are fresh flowers on some of the graves, and often something more. He looks closer. On one grave there's a packet of cigarettes, on another a bottle he recognises from the refrigerator in his room, a mini-bottle of sake. Have vandals left them? No, they're too precisely placed for that. Here's a small carton of milk with a straw in it, here an orange and a candy bar. On the step before the gravestone in a well-swept enclosure with its own magnolia tree, there's a pretty blue-and-white plate, and on it a soft, fresh white rice cake. A sound makes him look up, and and he sees in the tree an enormous crow. Its eyes seem to move from the cake to Lew and back again, and impatiently it shifts its claws on the branch.

These must be gifts to the dead, things that they liked, to give them pleasure. Joanne's grave isn't like this. It's a plaque in a lawn. He wishes he could bring her something, but the lawn cemetery has rules against it. Chocolates. French perfume from the duty-free.

He hears voices. At a grave nearby there are two women. They have a wooden bucket, and the elder woman is ladling water from it, with a bamboo ladle, over the stone. Her daughter, it must be, is watching her, holding a bouquet of flowers. As Lew approaches, he sees that they have a brush, and dusters, in a basket. The younger woman gives him a little bow as he passes, and he nods in reply.

He has been thinking that he is lost, but he isn't. Facing in this direction he can see the hotel among the other tall buildings not far away. Now the lanes are full of delivery vans and housewives in their aprons, and young mothers on bikes, with children perched on little seats in front or behind. He has to dodge all the time, and once he almost trips over a box of squid outside a fish shop, but he makes it back. It's getting very hot.

Frank is in the lobby. "Sonny Boy was asking for you. He says he's got you a ticket for the kabuki. He's coming back. Did you say you wanted to go to the kabuki or what? What got into you?"

Lew tries to think. "I said—I think I said my daughter said I had to go. I didn't say I wanted to."

"A wink's as good as a nod to Sonny Boy. Now you've let yourself in for it."

"I don't know anything about it."

"All I know is, it's men dressed up as women. Not my kind of show, mate."

"When did he say?"

"This afternoon. I thought you wanted to come to the cheap electrical goods place."

"I didn't think—"

"Here he comes. There's that smile."

Tommy Yamamoto displays the ticket in its bright envelope. "The performance already started," he says.

"Oh, look, I'm sorry I'm late," says Lew, floundering.

"No, no. All right. It's too long, the whole performance, three plays. Maybe even one is enough. We have time for lunch. I will attend you to there."

Lew follows him helplessly. He looks over his shoulder at

Frank, miming bewilderment. Frank shakes his head in irritation, and mouths, "Have a good time."

Over a lacquer tray on which Lew doesn't recognise anything except the rice, a single prawn, and a carrot slice cut like a flower, Tommy says, "Very sorry, I can't see the kabuki with you. I must work."

"That's all right. Don't worry."

"This tells the plays," says Tommy, taking a glossy sheet from his pocket and pointing to a picture of a young man with a narrow face and large eyes. "This is a very famous actor. He acts a woman. Don't you think this is strange?"

"Well—I've heard about it," says Lew cautiously.

"I've seen him only on TV," admits Tommy. "He has many fans."

"I see. Good."

At the entrance to the theatre, Tommy consults his watch. "First play ends in five minutes. Then intermission. English programme there at desk. Earphone translation available too, turn left. If you wish."

"You've got me pretty well organised."

"This evening I will attend you with Mr. Suzuki.

"Thanks." Lew is resigned.

"My pleasure. Please enjoy." He stands bowing conscientiously till Lew is out of sight.

Lew sits down on a bench in the lobby and has a cigarette. Every time he smokes he remembers how much Joanne nagged him to give it up. She was worried about cancer. He smokes it defiantly right down to the butt.

People start coming out, and through the open doors he can

hear drumming, wails, whistles, rattles, and a burst of applause that fades away rapidly with the music. Women with lunch-boxes squeeze onto both ends of his bench, so he hurriedly gets up to find his seat.

It must be an expensive one, so close to the stage. He looks around. The theatre is hung with paper lanterns. Quite a few women are wearing kimono, but otherwise the crowd looks like a weekday matinee crowd anywhere, middle-aged and at ease. This is okay, he thinks, and opens his programme.

The second play is really a dance. That's good, no words. No doubt Tommy's thought of this, as he's thought, too, of putting Lew in an aisle seat so he can stretch his legs out. Otherwise his knees would be up around his ears.

The programme says the spirit of a heron maiden is seen as a lovely young woman. Presumably that's the lovely young man. What's a heron maiden? The dance depicts nuances of love, the agony of death, and the torments of fiery hell. Maybe it's lucky that the plot, such as it is—surely they've left something out?—doesn't really make sense. It's not the kind of story he would have chosen to see. These days he can't bear sadness and suffering, and turns his face away often from the television news, and even from the police dramas he used to like.

An urgent clattering sound, and the curtain is pulled aside. Lew leans forward. There's the maiden, in white kimono in the snow, and she dances.

He has never seen such grace. He has been to the ballet with Joanne, but this—this has existed all along and he never knew. This transfiguration of man into woman, woman into bird, of living being into pure pain, he never could have envisaged.

There is a point where the actor's costume is being changed

on stage, by black-hooded men, and Lew becomes aware of himself again. He takes a breath, lets it out, bites his lip, swallows, and all these small natural actions he performs as if remembering gestures of great intricacy he used to know how to do, noting them as he does so. His whole body feels sensitive. He clasps and unclasps his hands. Still he feels it. He begins to worry, but the actor moves again and he forgets all this, failing to notice the moment when the strange feeling passes.

That on the stage there is a story to be told, that there are certain steps to be danced, cannot matter. He has no key to the meaning of it. The dancer is unbelievably beautiful. The whitened neck turns, long hands weave upwards, the back bends till it must break. There is nothing that is not possible.

Lew sits, bewildered, as people applaud, rise. He turns his legs to the side to let them get to the aisle. The embroidered fire curtain slides down. It isn't until it rises again, the lights dim, and actors appear behind him on a walkway that runs through the audience that he realises he doesn't want to see anything else, he can't take it in. He gets up and walks quickly out of the theatre, into the street. Almost blinded by the afternoon glare, he manages to get a taxi back to the hotel.

He has a shower, puts on the fresh cotton kimono that is folded on his bed, and lies down. He doesn't sleep, but he thinks, as he has often these past months wished desperately to do, of nothing.

It's hard to know what to say when they ask him about it. "It was very interesting," he says to Tommy, and to Frank, "Amazing performance. You never would have known."

Tommy seems satisfied. Frank says, "Their voices always give them away, female impersonators."

"I didn't hear his voice."

"Anyway, better you than me."

They're all quiet in the taxi on the way to meet Mr. Suzuki. The streets, now it's dark, are as busy as at midday, and men in dark business suits seem so likely to wander out of brightly lit doorways and straight under the wheels of the car that even being a passenger seems to require concentration. The driver never slackens his speed, so maybe they do all know what they're doing, but Lew keeps one hand on the back of the seat in front, just in case.

Mr. Suzuki is waiting for them outside the restaurant, and leads the way up the stairs. Tommy, relinquishing responsibility for them, deferentially brings up the rear.

"I've never seen so many waiters around one table, and just get a gander at this," mutters Frank, as the chef, a Frenchman in full regalia, emerges to greet Mr. Suzuki and bow to them all. "What d'you make of it? Does it mean we're doing all right after all?"

"You're asking the wrong bloke," says Lew.

The wine is one he's heard of, but never expected to drink. They have a toast. "Kampai, cheers," says Mr. Suzuki heartily.

"Bottoms up," adds Tommy.

"Not a bad drop," concedes Frank.

"A very famous wine," says Mr. Suzuki.

By the end of the soup, he and Tommy are both flushed from the wine, and Mr. Suzuki becomes expansive. He has lived in California, where the company sent him for several years, and he speaks with nostalgia of martinis and cheap golf. Then, mid-sentence, he breaks off and leans towards Lew. "Over there," he says, "Look. There is a geisha."

All three follow his eyes. At a table slightly to the side, two people are sitting over coffee. Lew can see the man, who is about his own and Suzuki's age, also red-faced.

He can't see the woman's face. Her head is bent. A pale cheek, hair in a low sleek roll above a powdered neck—not a sturdy freckled neck like those of the women he knows, like Joanne's, but a slender one rising in a curve from the low-dipping collar of a silk kimono that is a subdued and impeccable dark blue. In the brocade knot at her waist there is a glimmer of gold threads.

"Where's the geisha costume?" asks Frank.

"She is relaxing,"says Mr. Suzuki. Not exactly the word, thinks Lew.

"Then how do you know?"

"The elegance. The hair. The mannerism. How she wears the kimono, see, it's low at the back."

"You sound like a bit of an authority."

"No," says Mr. Suzuki. "Unfortunately." He smiles and adjusts his glasses. "I'm not a company president. I'm a salaryman."

There is a silence.

"It's the neck," says Frank. "Am I right?"

"Sure," agrees Mr. Suzuki. "Back of the neck is very erotic." The word hangs in the air for an instant. Not a word we use, thinks Lew. "For us it is. For you, always the—" He gestures briefly with his hands in front of his chest. "Am I right?" They all laugh. "Naturally, we appreciate this, too."

He calls for another bottle, and the conversation returns to California. "I was mugged once only," says Mr. Suzuki, "While jogging. I had prepared fifty dollars for that, in my shirt pocket. I gave it to them, no problem."

"That's the know-how," says Tommy.

"Exactly," says Mr. Suzuki.

Lew cannot keep his eyes off the geisha. He has heard that sometimes visiting businessmen are invited to parties where they dance and sing. Obviously he and Frank don't rate that. He didn't expect they'd even rate dinner in a restaurant like this one. He doesn't want to go to a geisha party. He just wants to look at this woman.

Frank is showing them a watch he bought this afternoon. It does everything. If you enter in your birthdate it tells you your biorhythms. What are biorhythms?

She is more animated now. He can't hear her voice. He wishes he could, though he'd understand nothing. As he watches, she raises her hand, palm upward, towards the man. There is a sugar cube on her palm, and she feeds it to him, like that. Lew feels a stab of desire so frantic and shocking that it stops his breath in his chest. It might have stopped his heart. He is dazed with it. He fixes his gaze on the stem of his own hand twisted round the stem of his wine glass, and concentrates on holding it still.

He senses the couple move, stand, sees the waiters hurry to pull back their chairs, but he doesn't look up to see them go. He can't. He wonders if today is the day he cracks.

Mr. Suzuki is looking past him to the door. "Not so young," he says. "They don't have to be young."

It comes to Lew what Joanne would have said about a woman who fed sugar cubes to a man in a restaurant. It almost makes him smile, but it doesn't help.

When dinner is over, it is over rather abruptly. Mr. Suzuki manages to bring it to an end with a maximum of politeness and a minimum of delay. Apparently, they're skipping dessert. Both Mr. Suzuki and Tommy opt only for coffee. Frank asks, "Don't you like dessert?" His own sweet tooth is notorious in the office. Toss him a doughnut, they'll quip after a tongue-lashing, shut him up for a while.

Tommy says, "I only eat sweet things when I'm with a lady."

"Obviously it's only for sissies, Frank," says Lew maliciously. He himself has not been eating well for a long time, and wants nothing now.

"Please have dessert," begs Mr. Suzuki with great sincerity. Frank has coffee.

Nothing is said, but it becomes apparent that Mr. Suzuki has a train to catch. His final bows and handshakes outside the restaurant are unhurried, but when Lew looks again he's running towards a taxi.

Tommy's in charge again now. "Shall we go another place?" he asks. He looks tired. Poor little bastard, thinks Lew. All this attending can't be much fun.

"Hey, let's do that!" cries Frank.

"Listen, it's all right," says Lew.

Frank gives him a look. "Just for a drink."

"If it's okay with Tommy—"

"Somewhere ordinary," says Frank, with exasperated emphasis. "You know, see what it's like."

Tommy steps in front of a taxi and holds up his hand.

They end up in a narrow street behind a railway station. There are little bars with blue-and-white curtains over their doors, and red paper lanterns. Lew thinks he would like to try one. They look friendly.

But Tommy leads them down some chipped tile steps with a dark glass door at the bottom. As Lew's eyes adjust to the dark of the room they enter, he makes out that it's lined with red plush and black mirrors. There's a piano, and someone groaning off-key. The air is dense with smoke and whisky fumes. This is the kind of place that in the morning must look terrible and smell worse.

A woman in a long black dress appears. With a show of graciousness, Western-style, she shakes their hands. "Please . . . ." she says, "Please . . . ." for the benefit of Lew and Frank, and they all follow her.

As she leads them to their table, the people they pass notice them. Drunken voices from out of the gloom say, "*Herro, Herro.*" Lew isn't sure he likes their tone. There are no other foreigners here. But once they sit down on a semicircular velvet banquette, he looks around and sees that people are smiling, if not exactly in welcome, at least as if—could it be this?—he and Frank might, by their presence, offer some entertainment. He notices, too, that the faces he sees are mostly those of young women and middle-aged men. Doubtless there are places young Tommy would rather be, but he's doing his best for them.

The groaning pauses and then resumes. The singer, squinting at a songbook held up to him by a girl who smiles and nods at the audience, has taken his friends' applause as encouragement and decided to give an encore.

"Amateur night down the pub," says Frank disgustedly. "Not even carry-oaky."

"You said, ordinary," points out Lew, adding under his breath, "Karaoke."

A girl in red satin comes and sits beside Tommy. Another, in red sequins, sits beside Lew. Frank, trapped in the middle, shifts irritably in his seat. A bottle of Japanese whisky has appeared on the table, and an ice bucket. The girl next to Lew pours.

Tommy leans his head back against the red velvet and very briefly closes his eyes. The last stop of the day. Then he sits up, bright and ready for them again.

"What's your name?" asks Lew.

At this, however, Tommy seems mildly confused. "Yamamoto," he replies, after a pause.

"No, I know that. I mean, it's not Tommy, is it?"

"My name is difficult to say. It is Tomokazu."

"That's not so difficult."

"Foreign friends call me Tommy."

"What do your Japanese friends call you?"

"Yamamoto. With friendly suffix."

"Friendly suffix, eh? Well, who calls you Tomokazu?"

"For example, my mother."

"I see," says Lew.

"That's put you in your place," says Frank. With a watch-me air, he leans forward. "Got a girlfriend? A looker, I'll bet!"

A shadow crosses Tommy's face. Could be an unhappy thought, or it could just mean fuck off. But he only presses his lips together, and smiles. He lifts his glass. "Bottoms up," he says. "Is that King's English or American English?"

Frank raises his eyebrows at Lew, as if this is the response he meant to elicit. "Not saying, see?" In an undertone he adds, "Sonny Boy's secret life? What do you reckon?"

It's Lew's turn to pretend not to hear. Fortunately, Frank gets busy clinking glasses.

"I speak American English," says the girl next to Lew. He peers down at her. She looks very young. Her shoulders above the strapless dress are the skinniest he has seen on a grown-up woman. Her hair is long and curled, and, as far as he can see in the darkness, dyed red. She has thin-penciled eyebrows and her lips are lined in heavy pencil, inside their full natural shape. It's hard to say if she's pretty or not. She lifts a hand to adjust a red sequinned earring. Her nails are sequinned too.

She looks up at him coquettishly. "Do you like here?"

"Yes, I do," he says. He doesn't know if this is true.

"He went to the Kabuki-za today," Tommy tells her, as if speaking of a child who has done something clever.

"Oh! Which play did he see?"

"It was a dance about a heron," says Lew. "Er, a white bird."

"*Sagi Musume*," explains Tommy. "He saw Tamasaburo."

She gives an excited squeak. "Oh! Tamasaburo is so famous! He is beautiful, isn't he?"

"Yes. He is beautiful."

Frank raises his eyebrows.

"He is more than me! More like woman!"

What should Lew say to this?

"He plays traditional Japanese woman," says Tommy earnestly.

"Should be standing like a shakuyaku," says the girl. "Right? It is a flower with long stem."

"Sitting, like a botan, isn't it? What is botan?" asks Tommy.

"Peony! Sitting like a peony, with the head—" she lets her head fall a little, and with a thin, sequinned hand sweeps aside her hair so as to look at Lew. "You see, I'm not graceful like him."

"You are graceful," says Lew politely.

"Walking," says Tommy, "like yuri—that is—"

"I don't know," she laughs, covering her mouth with her hand. "I don't know vocabulary—another flower!"

"Oh, lily!" exclaims Tommy, "Yes, walking like a lily!"

At the table next to them a fat man lurches from his seat. He seems to want to sing, but he's too drunk to make it to the stage. The hostess next to him pulls at his sleeve, and pats his chair, saying his name over and over in a sort of sweet whine. He tumbles back, and she pats his knee. Someone else gets up, and sings "My Way," in Japanese, breathing loudly into the microphone, drowning out the piano.

"Very popular!" yells Tommy over the noise.

"What else is popular?"

"For singing? John Denver, 'Country Roads,' everyone likes."

"Paul Anka," says the girl. "Oldest ones are popular."

With this crowd, I'll bet they are, thinks Lew.

"Now you're talking!" says Frank.

The girl gazes up at Lew, and then, when he has nothing to say, remarks, out of the blue, "You look like Clint Eastwood." Only she says "Crint."

He laughs at the silliness of it. "Really?"

"You do! But also—Crark Gable! If you had a moustache."

She places her finger across his upper lip and giggles at the effect. Ancient history. Old songs, old movies, too. They must be in the video shops. Or she's never actually seen Clark Gable, it's just a name handed down in the trade. Or—she really thinks that's his generation. "Clint Eastwood *and* Clark Gable? I'm doing well."

"Who do I look like?" demands Frank.

"Gene Hackman."

"Gene Hackman?"

"Very good actor," she says firmly.

Frank looks uncertain. Then, after a moment, he declares, changing the subject, "Think I'll have a go."

He struggles past Lew, and marches up to the microphone with the girl skittering after him. They all applaud, and the people at the other tables sit up. Frank has a conference with the pianist, wagging his hand to illustrate some point. Then he steps forward and launches into "Diana."

Lew is amazed. Frank's not bad! He even puts an "uh! oh!" in! The only thing is, no one back at the office will ever believe it if he tells them, and he can't imagine Frank telling.

Frank is a big success. He waves, he blows kisses! He stumbles down the dark steps from the stage, and the girl navigates him back to the table. He beams all around and wipes his glasses with his handkerchief. People from the next table offer him drinks, all of which he accepts.

Everyone says to Lew, "Sing! Sing!" But Lew spoils it. He cannot, will not, sing. He senses the atmosphere becoming heavy with embarrassment around him as he presses back into the seat shaking his head, with a smile that he knows is stiff and miserable. Gradually it becomes clear that he's not just being modest, and the chorus dies down and people turn away in disappointment.

Diplomatically, the woman in black steps into the spotlight by the piano. The light doesn't flatter her, but she has a perfect smile. She draws her skirt forward with an air of professional calm, and everyone looks towards her, Lew most gratefully of all. She starts to sing an old Patsy Cline song Lew hasn't heard for years, "Crazy." Strange, he thinks, how familiar, simple words in a foreign accent sometimes seem to mean more—maybe it's only because you have to listen. This song is about lost love. Well, he never lost the love, but he lost the lover, and sometimes crazy is just how it feels.

Someone's shaking his arm. It's the girl, of course. She's taken hold of his sleeve, and she seems to be trying to say something. He bends down to catch what she's saying amidst the noise of conversation that bursts out all around them as the applause fades.

She's asking, "Do you think I am typical Japanese girl?"

Lew wonders wearily how he could be expected to know, but before he decides on the answer, she adds quickly, "To tell the truth, I am haafu." It takes a moment before he realises the word is "half."

"Half what?" he asks stupidly.

"My father is American," she says proudly, and waits for his reaction.

"Is that so?" What else can he say?

Her gaze slides away, and he thinks, R&R? The age would be about right. The mother a bar-girl, too.

"I want to go to America," she says. "Maybe I can meet him there."

Cautiously, he asks, "You know where he lives?"

She doesn't answer. Instead, she giggles, and puts her hand on his knee. "I think he is like you. You are very tall and handsome."

"He wouldn't be as old as me," says Lew. Looking at her again, it occurs to him that her father is probably black, too. Yes, he sees it now. He has no idea what that might be like, here.

"Oh, no," she says, laughing nervously. "You are too young!"

She thinks she's made a mistake. As if she could make him feel any older than he does already. "It's all right," he says. God, what does he care?

He takes her hand. It's all bones, like a bird's claw.

"You're a tiny lass," he says. The word is wrong. If he and Joanne had been speaking of her, that is what he would have called her, a little lass. And he knows what an old goat he must look. He has both his hands tight around hers.

"What time do you finish work?" he asks.

"Three o'clock," she says.

"Three o'clock?" He turns his wrist to look at his watch. It's only just eleven. Four more hours of this?

"It's a late time, isn't it?"

He holds on to her hand. "You work a long night."

"Yes. And the trains are finished then."

"How do you get home? By taxi?"

"A taxi is very expensive every night. I live quite far. We wait for the first train, at five."

"You mean, after a whole night here"—he looks around at the tired plush and smeary mirrors—"You have to wait till five to go home? You must be dog-tired."

"We are tired, but we kill the time."

"What do you do? Lie down somewhere?"

"We study," she says.

"You study?"

"We are studying English."

Lew is stopped cold. Finally he asks, "Who's 'we'?"

"Me, my friends—" she nods at the girl beside Tommy—"and the piano player."

He takes this in. "How do you learn?"

"We don't have a teacher, of course not, in the midnight. We have a textbook. And tapes, with useful dialogues. We are now intermediate level."

"Are you? I see."

"We have a plan!" she says. "Will I tell you our plan?"

"Yes, tell me."

"It is this: we are going to the Newport Jazz Festival! Some day. That is our dream. And I want to meet my father at that time." She looks down. "If possible."

"I see," says Lew again.

"Then, what do you think?"

"Think?"

She gives a little impatient jump. "My English! Is it good enough?"

Lew lets go of her. "It's good enough," he says. "It's good already. Intermediate. That's good."

"Thank you. I hope so!" She strokes his hand—from the perfunctory touch of her fingertips, she's just recalled her duties—and then reaches for the ice tongs and his glass.

"No," says Lew. "Look, no—" He stands up.

Frank has no intention of leaving. Tommy looks from one to the other, not knowing what to do.

"Don't worry," says Lew. "I won't get lost."

Frank hardly bothers to say goodnight. The girl and Tommy escort Lew to the door, where the woman in black joins them, and they all troop up the stairs and out into the lane. The humid air is like soup.

Tommy puts him in a taxi and gives lengthy instructions to the driver. They all shake his hand, and stand in the street bowing and bowing until the car reaches the corner.

After a while, Lew realises where he is. This is the little shopping street where he walked this morning. Isn't that the fish shop? Its metal shutters are closed, but he remembers a sign with a silver fish leaping out of a bright blue wave, and there it is, right under a street light.

"Stop!" he cries. The driver stops, but he doesn't want to let Lew out, and the doors are automatic. He looks worriedly back in the direction they've come from, as if for further instructions.

Lew tries to pay.

"No," says the driver. "Company pay." He waves a chit that Tommy must have given him.

"Walk!" shouts Lew. He makes walking motions with his fingers.

"I will walk! Hotel—that way! I know! Okay!"

"Okay," says the driver. He opens the door. Lew walks.

He's tired, but somehow the walking is good. He leaves the shops behind. Here's a narrower street. Small apartment buildings and houses close together, some above shuttered workshops, and bikes propped up everywhere. As he passes each house with its row of potted plants outside, the scent of gardenias comes to him in gentle waves.

From one house he hears splashing sounds, as if someone's taking a bath. In another, through a window, he can see men in floppy white underwear sitting on the floor around a low table and playing a game he thinks must be mahjongg. He can hear the clatter of the tiles as they're gathered up.

He thought he knew the way. Now he realises that already he's going around in a circle, but he doesn't feel lost. He turns into another lane, which could be the one where this morning he saw the young mothers talking. Or perhaps not.

Coming towards him down the lane is what he at first imagines to be a big animal of some kind, a dog. It moves with a slight swaying motion, from side to side. But there's something funny about it. He pauses, uncertain.

It comes closer, out of the darkness, and he realises that it is not an animal. It is a woman. A little old woman in grey kimono, her back bent almost double, so that her arms are held low in front of her. As they pass under a light, he can't help trying to see her better, and in the same moment she lifts her head and glances sideways up at him. She gives him a small courteous nod, and her look is sharp and warm.

5

White Kurisumasu

JANET HAS BEEN OUT IN the bright, bitter, winter sunlight, making her erratic way along crowded narrow streets, her list crumpled in her pocket, the sharp-edged handles of her laden shopping bags nipping through her gloves. And through the clamouring of fish vendors, the urgent bells of darting bikes, the electronic tinkle of the notes that alert the blind to the green light, threaded like tinsel through all these everyday sounds, she's been pursued by "White Christmas." Bing Crosby, naturally, from the supermarket. A heavy rock arrangement reverberating from a toy shop bristling with robots. Whiny strings from the bakery, where approximations of Christmas cakes, decorated with cream and giant strawberries and plastic miniature alpine scenes, have almost edged out the thin citron-scented cookies that she sometimes takes home to have with tea. All this has made her feel disoriented. It is Christmas and yet not Christmas. It will be a relief when, in a few days' time, the whole thing is over, and the pine, plum and bamboo come out for the New Year.

She's told herself that this plundering of Christmas isn't done altogether cynically, but out of a sort of rapacious innocence, a feeling that any festival is all to the good and good for business. Nevertheless, she's come home with a headache.

All the bags of food and paper cups and red napkins that she's bought are lying on the tatami floor where she dumped them when she came in. She's pulled back the paper shoji inside the glass sliding door leading to the sliver of verandah, which is not much wider than her feet are long, and is standing there massaging her temples and looking out at the garden, her eyes screwed up against the light. The garden's only about half the size of her eight-mat room, but it accommodates a magnolia tree and a daphne bush and a mossy rock with a water-filled hollow in it, across which, in imitation of more elegant arrangements, she has rested a long-handled bamboo cup.

As she moves her fingertips in circles, the irritation of "White Christmas" fades out of her consciousness, and another sound drifts in, a familiar one, a drone she thinks of as something like "myoommyoommyoom," although she knows there are words to it, and Elaine probably knows what they are. The people next door belong to one of the new Buddhist sects, and several times a day they chant sutras. Generally Janet likes it, just as she likes the smell of incense that floats across the road from the neighbourhood temple. She thinks sutras are how Japan should sound, and incense is how Japan should smell, and she sometimes mentions these aspects of her environment in her letters home, to add colour. But somehow today she doesn't want to hear sutras either. She reaches for her radio and turns the dial to the American forces' Far East Network. They're playing "The Little Drummer Boy."

Again. They probably like it because it's military. She leaves it on, and says aloud to herself, "Get moving!"

Cleaning up doesn't take long. She transfers the shopping bags to the kitchen floor, shuffles through some magazines and piles them on the bottom shelf of the bookcase, slides open the paper-covered door of the closet where she keeps her bedding, picks up various bits and pieces that are lying around, sweaters and socks and a bra, stuffs them in on top of the quilts, and holds them there with one hand while she slides the door across with the other. "Ta rum pa pum pum," she sings.

She takes more pleasure than she ever would have expected in this rough housekeeping. Shouldn't she miss having dinner parties in a proper house with chairs, and china in sets? Not only does she not miss it, but the memory of it, though it isn't really long ago, seems obscure. The crystal and candlesticks and all the rest of it, things she used to be fond of, still exist. Some of them Ron got custody of —that's how she said it to everyone, keeping it light—and some are in tea-chests in various garages, waiting for her return, but she has nearly forgotten what they are.

She almost never entertains now, and in fact no-one seriously expects to be entertained much in these tiny Tokyo apartments. It's a long time since she cooked anything, even for herself. At night, after class, she picks up some yakitori at a stall down the street, standing by the brazier while the man patiently turns the sticks of chicken over the coals, or she buys a box of sushi, the translucent raw fish laid on white pillows of rice or wrapped in papery seaweed, the colours arranged in careful contrast, a twist of pink ginger tucked in a corner and a bright plastic leaf on top. All this beautiful work done by other, more skillful hands than hers, and she has only to bring it home, make a pot of green tea, take an apple from the old blue-and-white bowl she got at the temple market (how Ron hated anything old) and there's dinner.

So why are all these people coming here tonight? She can't imagine where she's going to put everyone she had to invite, once she got started. Maybe, she thinks, she just wanted Christmas after all, and wanted it her way. And she does owe the students something for all the times they've taken her out and plied her with unfamiliar morsels, and treated her, too, because she doesn't know how not to let them.

Well, she's made sandwiches, and put crackers and such in bowls. There are drinks in the tiny refrigerator. And there's the cake, the real thing, studded with cherries and almonds, glossy, fragrant.

At the last minute she's found a real tree that's big enough to be credible but small enough to fit into a corner of the room, standing on a pile of textbooks covered in red paper. It isn't quite straight, and it clearly means to be a bonsai, bending in imitation of a full-size tree, wind-torn on some rocky shore.

When Janet bought its white ceramic pot, the woman at the shop asked her, "What's it for?"

"A pine tree."

"Oh no, not that one!" said the woman, shocked. "You can't put a pine tree in that!" She began pulling out flat brown and grey dishes with little feet, in which a Japanese pine tree could gracefully lean.

"A Christmas tree," said Janet, pronouncing it carefully, "Kurisumasu torii."

"Ah." The woman smiled. "Of course." Her smile might have

said, "Now, isn't that nice?" or it might have said, "Philistine!" These are things Janet has no way of knowing.

Turning the tree so that it inclines in the right direction, she drapes it with shiny red ribbon and hangs on it some small things she's been collecting: gold and silver bells, paper lanterns, balls made of wound silk, clay monkeys that swing from the branches. She's made some origami cranes, from a book, and she hangs them on, too. Singly, the little birds look festive, but she's seen them at temples, joined in strings of hundreds together, there to demonstrate the sincerity of someone's prayers.

This is different from any other tree she's ever had. If Ron has a tree—and he has a baby, so he must have a tree—it isn't like this. Letters from friends, too gently phrased, have told her about the baby. Perhaps they're thinking how late it almost is for her.

It's getting dark outside. Janet opens the glass doors and icy air floods into the room. Quickly she reaches out to pull across the metal shutters, then the glass doors again, and finally the white paper shoji. The room looks bright, it looks pretty.

She has just time to wash her face in freezing water in her dark little bathroom, to put on a red blouse and some lipstick. She peers into the mirror she keeps on a lacquered stand on a shelf in the bookcase. Here, in her room, she looks at herself with a tolerant eye, forgets that outside she's too tall, too heavy, too everything.

Janet believes that some aspects of her life would be different if she were short and slim, and maybe blond. Surrounded as she is by small men, so that in a rush-hour train she sometimes imagines herself a volcanic island risen out of a dark sea, she hasn't yet had many of what she generally calls, even to herself, social opportunities. On the other hand, so many men ogle her breasts, which also exceed the local norm, that she's given up T-shirts for the duration. She believes she gets the worst of it all.

The very worst: One night, out jogging, she panted up a dark lane behind a slight, sedate man in a business suit, walking home from the station. Hearing her gaining on him, he gave a single alarmed glance over his shoulder and broke into a trot, and then a run, his briefcase banging against his knees, Janet in astonished pursuit. She had to stop and lean against a wall, and she giggled till she got a stitch in her side, and was too weak to jog anymore. Later, when she thought about it, it was very depressing.

In the coffee shop between classes, Elaine said, wiping her eyes, "Maybe you should make friends with a sumo wrestler. Seriously. A hundred fifty kilos doesn't scare so easy, and if you like the simple country-boy type, some of them are very cute." Janet, as it happens, has developed a passion for sumo, and thinks some of them are more than cute, but this doesn't seem to be the answer. What would she say to a sumo wrestler? They're supposed to be men of few words, grunting modestly in response to praise, but even so, she doesn't think her vocabulary would be up to it.

Now she smiles at herself in the mirror. She tucks in her blouse and goes into the narrow entrance hall. She stoops to pick up the shoes littering the space just inside the door, and places them out of sight in the shoe cupboard, all without stepping down from the clean tatami in her stockinged feet. She observes this taboo as religiously as any Japanese, because it pleases her, even when there's no-one to see.

She reaches over to unlock the door for the guests. Almost at the same moment, it opens away from her, and hastily she jumps back. Larry's face appears, inches from her own. He's already half out of his shoes as he falls in, as startled as she is and off-balance. Janet catches him, and for a moment they sway together.

"Thank God!" he says, looking past her into the empty room. "Not my best entrance. Just slightly undignified!"

"Is that it?" asks Janet, gesturing at his large canvas bag. He takes it from his shoulder, upends it, and draws out folds of red fabric.

"Hora!" It's a Santa costume he's borrowed from the master of a bar in Shinjuku where he's a regular. He scrambles into it, over his jeans and shirt. It's voluminous, widthways, and only slightly short in the leg. He adjusts the white beard. "What do you think?"

"Brilliant!" And then, doubtfully, "I hope they don't think it's silly."

"They'll love it." He brings out a flat packet wrapped in Christmas paper. "This is a silk scarf from Bangkok, el cheapo, but it's pretty. I'll try to make sure you get it. I am Santa."

"Sounds like corruption," says Janet, putting it under the tree. "But how can I refuse? Cheap's okay. I told everyone five hundred yen."

"I haven't seen that blouse before. You look terrific in red."

"So do you." She pours two beers, then hesitates. "Is it all right? Before they come?"

"Why not? We need a head start. It's the gaijin metabolism. A scientific fact. You know we'd drink them under the table if it was more than ten inches high."

"Well, try not to disarrange the food."

"Oh, quit fussing," he says. "Kampai! Merry Christmas!"

"Kampai!" They touch glasses. "It's nothing fancy, except for the cake. And that Al, he's such a gourmet! Did you hear him talking about squid the other day? He goes down to the fish market at dawn to get it fresh, and then he even knows what to do with it."

"Gourmet!" scoffs Larry. "The guy's a faggot's faggot, so what could he be but a gourmet?"

Janet is shocked. "What a thing to say!"

"Listen, Jan-chan," says Larry sternly. "Just because Al and I share the same affective orientation, I don't want you to think we've got anything in common. If I thought I was ever going to get like Al, I'd—" He draws his clenched fist across his belly. "He knows it, too. He always pretends not to see me in bars or wherever. I saw him at the bath, and he looked right through me. To me he's nothing but a caricature, that's all. Gross."

"He's not young, Larry."

"He doesn't take care of himself. The one place I never see him is the gym. Gourmet!" Larry picks up a cushion and stuffs it down his trim front. "That's better. You should have got Al to be Santa, he's a natural," he adds complacently.

"Al goes to the bath-house as well?"

"Used to. Before they got it into their heads that all gaijin have AIDS. Canadian guy I know was still going, but I heard he was asked to leave. That scene's finished. Who do they think they're kidding? Oh God, don't let's talk about that." He fishes a small whole crab from a bowl of nuts and rice crackers and such, and munches it. "Interesting. But not like Mom used to make."

"I didn't know there were crabs in there."

"Put your glasses on. You never know what's in anything."

Janet has heard a lot from Larry about the bath-house. Men go there and have sex with each other right in front of other people, around the bath. He says it's just like an ordinary bath, otherwise. With soap? She doesn't like to ask. She's amazed that she hears such things at all. Certainly, when she was married, before she came to Tokyo, no-one ever told her anything like the things Larry tells her. She wonders if she's led a particularly sheltered life. Sometimes, when they go drinking after work, she tells Larry about her own experiences, but she tends to exaggerate somewhat to make it worth telling, whereas she has the feeling Larry never does.

Larry strokes his Santa beard. "¥ou ever wonder—why no Easter?"

"Here, you mean?"

"Where else? We're having Christmas! Don't you think they'd love Easter? Chocolate bunnies! Fluffy chickens! What's stopping them?" For answer, he puts on a mournful expression, and spreads his scarlet arms wide, head lolling.

Janet's laughing, but she cries, "Oh, Larry, don't!"

"See? Easter's hard core," he says.

The room's getting hot, or else it's the beer. When the students arrive together, obviously having arranged to meet at the station so as to make an entrance in a seemly group, she's afraid her cheeks are already red, gaijin metabolism notwithstanding.

Larry ho-ho-hos at them as they take off their shoes, and come into the room one by one, half-bowing. Some of them look nervous, even when they recognise him.

He ho-ho-hos at Elaine and Nigel when they come, and at

Al, who slaps him hard on the back and yells, "Don't call us, we'll call you!" He doesn't ho-ho at Gwyneth Plummer. Well, you wouldn't, not even Larry.

Boxes of gift-wrapped food and cookies are heaped on the kitchen counter. The space around the table is hopelessly crammed with bodies. There aren't enough cushions to go round. The guests sit neatly, each folded up into as small a space as possible, shoulders forward, knees bent into positions that Janet knows would cripple her. She hears herself saying, "Sorry! Oh, sorry!" as she fails to control her elbows while handing round plates of food. She inadvertently kicks Miss Watanabe, and is the more humiliated when Miss Watanabe overapologises with every appearance of sincerity.

She notices Elaine squirming back towards the corner of the bookcase, looking for something to rest against. Elaine has been in Japan a long time, and she has ways of knowing what's going to make things easier. Janet has learned a number of useful ploys from her.

Only Gwyneth sits as straight-backed as the Japanese women, her pleated skirt smoothed under her, but she doesn't look poised, she looks prim.

Al, his maroon cravat already loosened around his sweating neck, leans towards Janet. "I have to make a fast getaway tonight," he says in a deep-toned whisper, rolling his eyes to convey, she supposes, regret. "I have a dress rehearsal." Al's playing piano for a gaijin Christmas revue, as he has for the last twenty years or so. He takes out a folded handkerchief and dabs his brow, the way he does at the piano. Janet gets up and goes to the door. She props it open with one of Larry's sneakers to let in some fresh air. It was a mistake to close the shutters on the garden window, but now she'd have to tread all over people to get to them.

Nigel's "forgotten" to bring a present. And as soon as he sits down, the other guests shuffling on their bottoms around the table to make room for him, Janet discovers that his feet stink. She should have known. Nigel's feet are as famous as Al's cologne. By the look on Gwyneth's face, she's noticed, too, and identified the source. Janet, next to him, surreptitiously covers the offending extremities with the edge of the tablecloth, but he flings it off, mumbling, "It's bloody hot in here!" She feels sorry for the student on his other side, but Miss Nakamura gives no sign of unease. On the contrary, she smiles at him more sweetly than is strictly necessary, refills his glass, and holds out to him with both hands a plate of rice crackers, a fistful of which he snuffles down so fast that Janet has to look away.

She and Elaine exchange glances. Elaine's thin face looks grey beside the smooth peaches-and-olive of the women on either side of her. Miss Watanabe and Miss Ogura are both "office ladies." Perhaps they need English for their jobs, welcoming foreign clients, but that's not all.

Miss Watanabe, in class, has hinted—no, has let it be known—that she has a gaijin boyfriend. But this boyfriend's not a boy. Janet has seen him more than once waiting for Ms. Watanabe by the school gate, in the darkness, has noted the expensive dark overcoat, the combination-locked briefcase, Ms. Watanabe's needlessly proprietary hand on his arm, and the lowered gaze and turned shoulder that avoid the necessity of introduction. A married man from the bank, more like it, thinks Janet. It's hard to feel friendly towards Miss Watanabe, remembering what she remembers from her own past. Indeed, looking at Ms. Watanabe's soft face, and the smile that she'd have to describe as smug, she feels for a moment almost ferocious. But the moment passes. What do I know, she reminds herself. Poor girl, she's in love, and his wife might be a bitch.

Miss Ogura's honeymoon is going to be in Hawaii. The very fact of Miss Ogura's wedding has been causing Janet some anxiety. It's the fashion to have one's English teacher make a speech at the reception in amusingly imperfect Japanese, and Janet's pretty sure her turn's coming up. Now Miss Ogura sits with her pristine handkerchief spread upon her knees, and nibbles at the smallest possible piece of Christmas cake. She looks up.

"Oh! My mother sent me that cake," says Janet. "She makes it every year. It's traditional. We have many kinds of dried fruits where I come from." She hears the way she's talking, that awful teacherspeak, and stops.

Miss Ogura beams. "Yes, how delicious it is! There is a Japanese saying, perhaps you know, about the taste of one's mother. It remembers us our childhood."

"Beats store-bought every time," smiles Al, his mouth full, holding up a fat slice.

"My mother also sends me many things from our home in each season. Ah! Do you like grapes, the big purple ones? That's our famous product, she always sends me. Next year I will present you. Please receive them."

"Thank you." Janet is being bribed, but what can she do? Those grapes are expensive, and such presents are placed with care. She'd better start preparing her speech now.

"Wish someone'd send me grapes," mutters Nigel, but Miss Ogura has prudently turned away.

"Put your feet under the table, Nigel," whispers Janet.

"Why?" he demands loudly.

There's a break in the conversation. Janet, confused by the unexpected silence, fails to answer, and he grins into his beer.

Mr. Sato is talking about the koalas at the zoo. It is agreed that they're extremely sweet, but somewhat lacking in vivacity, and therefore disappointing when you've queued up with the kids to see them. ("I saw them mating on TV the other night," says Al in an undertone to Elaine. "On one of those nature shows. They moved pretty damn quick then. For koalas. This was in the wild, naturally. They don't make koala porn at the zoo.")

"And they live in luxury," says Mr. Sato. "Their apartment is much bigger than my rabbit house."

"Rabbit hutch," smiles Janet, the teacher. She looks around her own room meaningfully.

Mr. Sato won't let her get away with this. "But your house in your country, it's wide, isn't it?"

"I haven't got a house."

"Your parents' house," he insists.

"Oh, my parents' house, yes, I suppose so."

Elaine is drinking sake from a paper cup. Janet offers her a glass, but she waves it away and allows Miss Watanabe to fill the paper cup to the brim again. Miss Watanabe and Miss Ogura look at each other. "Waa!" they murmur.

Miss Ogura turns to Elaine. "Miss Walters, you are a lady, but you are very strong against the alcohol!"

"You think so?"

"Oh, yes! You really like Japanese sake?"

"I like it."

"Do you like beer?"

"Mm."

"Whisky too?"

"Sure." A wary look has come into Elaine's pale eyes.

Miss Watanabe leans forward. A double act. "Miss Walters, do you drink alone in your room?"

"For God's sake!" cries Elaine, stung. "Do I look like I drink alone in my room?"

Janet can't help laughing at Elaine, usually so cool, sitting in her corner, her legs crossed in front of her, with an expression of outrage on her clever face.

"Ah," says Miss Watanabe. "I am sorry."

Like hell, thinks Janet.

"Don't mention it," says Elaine.

Mr. Sato is quizzing Al. Where is he from? Where did he study? Al seems to be hedging. "The school of life is the best school," he says, brushing cake crumbs from his trousers with large sweeps of his hand. He wears a silver cat's-eye ring. Mr. Sato considers this answer gravely. "No, seriously, folks," says Al. "Columbia Daigaku. That's in New York, you know?"

"A very famous school," confirms Mr. Sato.

Janet doubts that Al has ever graduated from anywhere, but he's been working in Japan so long that it's hardly an issue. She's heard it said of Al, as of other Americans of his generation, that he first came soon after the Occupation, with the CIA. It seems to Janet that a person would have to be smarter than Al to have been in the CIA, but she's not sure. These days, anyway, he teaches here and there, tends bar in a jazz club, and sometimes writes reminiscences for the English-language papers, in which he mentions all his old friends of the fifties and the Mama-sans they used to know.

"I'm not primarily a teacher," he now confides to Mr. Sato. "I am a musician and *litterateur*. Teaching is my avocation. Know what I mean? Sort of a hobby. But I love it, I really do. I meet such wonderful people."

Larry stifles a snicker. Elaine raises her eyes to the ceiling, where Janet has hung chains of origami paper.

Nigel leans over Miss Nakamura. Janet hears him say, in an accent that's just slightly off, "In some ways, yes, perhaps I am a typical Englishman."

Monty Python, thinks Janet.

"It means you are an English gentleman?"

Gwyneth, cradling demurely between her palms the same small glass of beer she's had from the beginning (it must be almost warm enough by now) permits herself a faint smile. Seeing it, Janet thinks: she and I will never be friends. There's something so stiff about her. She's got that nice pale skin, I just—it's her expression. She must be older than me, but surely not as old as she seems. Isn't she ever going home to England?

Nigel's reciting what could be lines from Gilbert and Sullivan. He does that, and nobody else has the faintest idea what it's about. He really thinks it's funny.

Enough! Janet sits up and claps her hands loudly. "Let's have the presents! Santa!"

Unfortunately, Larry, who has been mixing sake and whisky, is now in the mood to play the part chiefly for his own amusement. "Have you been very good?" he booms at the guests. "Have you studied English hard? Have you been kind to gaijin? If you haven't, nooo present! Oh no ho-ho! Do you know what happens? I punish you!" He strikes a kabuki pose. "I take you back to the North Pole in my sleigh and make you slave elves!"

Someone giggles uncertainly. Janet tries to get Larry's attention by tugging at the hem of his Santa jacket. "Get on with it!" she begs, "Please, Larry!" The cushion falls out, and this creates a diversion while he replaces it with much mugging.

And then Mr. Komata, a small, balding young man, who speaks hardly at all, in or out of class, wipes his shiny brow with a folded handkerchief, and begins to sing. "... Treetops glisten," he sings, "and children listen, to the sound of slave elves in the snow..." Is Janet hearing right? She doesn't care. Other people join in, grateful to know what to do. Even Gwyneth hums along.

Larry is overcome with glee at his success. He attempts another pose and knocks over the tree.

When the song ends, everybody claps. Janet picks up the tree and helps him give out the presents. Because they're a present short, she goes without. Nigel ends up with Larry's scarf. He looks at it and says, "What's this? Not exactly me, is it?" He tosses the pretty thing casually in Miss Nakamura's direction. It floats into her lap.

"There's a real gentleman for you," remarks Elaine to Miss Nakamura, who only smiles.

In the kitchen, Janet dumps orange slices and a stick of cinnamon into a pot with the wine, which no-one has been drinking. Elaine slouches out to join her.

"Larry can be so damn campy," she says crossly.

"It doesn't matter." Janet's headache has come back. She opens the window above the sink and puts her face out into the cold.

Behind her, Elaine asks, "Janet, you know how long I've been working on this thesis?"

Elaine was a Fulbright scholar, once. Her research, which seems to be going on forever, long after her fellowship has ended, is about some monk who brought a particular kind of Buddhism to Japan. Janet, who loves temples but knows nothing of Buddhism except what she sees, is not even certain which century he was in. Elaine knows Japanese, Chinese and Sanskrit. In her apartment, which is the same size as Janet's, dictionaries fill the bookshelves, and boxes and boxes of notes cover the floor, except for the space where she lays out her futon at night. Janet sometimes imagines her, stretched out on her quilts, walled in by boxes, at the end of each day spent teaching how to ask the way to the post office, or the use of modal verbs.

"Sometimes," says Elaine, "I think about waking up one morning and finding myself forty. Still here. Telling people I'm really a scholar and teaching's only my avocation."

Janet turns around. She hasn't known Elaine very long, but she thinks of her as always, at least, being sure of what she's doing and of the value of it, however long it might take. "But your work," she begins. "Not that I—"

Elaine takes no notice. She crushes her cup, picks up a fresh one. "Have I told you why I started to study religion? It was war. Conflict. Vietnam. I was a kid. Northern Ireland. I wanted to find out—you know, why people believe what they believe."

"Well, that was bound to take a while," says Janet drily.

"Yes. I thought I had the time."

Larry and Mr. Komata are leading the guests in "Silent Night." Mr. Komata is singing it in German.

"You wouldn't give up?" asks Janet uncertainly.

"No! God, I've come this far! No—what I have to do is, cut back my teaching hours, live on tofu if I have to. Try to get done."

"Well then, you should," says Janet, trying to put some energy into her voice. In fact, she has no idea of what it will take for Elaine to get done, but it all sounds terribly daunting. No wonder Elaine looks tired.

"Sorry Janet, you don't want to hear about it at your party," says Elaine, shaking her head as if to clear it. She holds out her cup. "Let me taste that." Janet pours her a half cup of punch and slops the rest into a bowl.

As she places the punch on the table, rather shakily, amidst a jumble of empty plates and crumpled paper napkins, Miss Kita asks her, "Miss Harris, do you have any brothers and sisters? We are talking about our family."

"No," says Janet, "I haven't." She lifts the ladle. "Would you like some punch?"

"What is punch?"

"This is punch."

"Thank you, I have juice.... Then why your parents don't call you home? They must be lonely with just themselves."

There's no answer to this one. Being a grown-up woman, already married and divorced, that certainly isn't it. All the more reason to go home, Miss Kita would think. Anyhow, Janet has learned the hard way never to mention divorce.

She turns to Larry. "Why don't your parents call you home, Mr. Anderson?"

"You're kidding!" cries Larry. "When I left home, they turned cartwheels!"

Mistake, thinks Janet, seeing the looks on the students' faces as they search their vocabularies. But Larry still has some of his wits about him, and he sees, too, and backs away in time. "Al?"

"No doubt I will be called to the place where my parents are, all in due course, and it's a better place than this one, terrific as this is, believe me," says Al heavily. "But I'm in no great rush."

Miss Kita catches his meaning and nods sympathetically behind her hand.

"Is this some kind of a parlour game?" Elaine's voice is sharp. "Leave me out of it, will you?"

As far as Janet can make out, Elaine barely speaks to her parents, but she occasionally gets letters from them enclosing pamphlets with titles like, "The Liberal Betrayal," and "Abortion Holocaust," whatever they think will help. One day, when Janet arrived at Elaine's just after the postman, Elaine showed her an example. Then she tore it up. "If you weren't here I might jump on it," she said, but Janet doesn't believe she meant that.

And then she sees that Gwyneth's eyes have filled with tears, and Gwyneth's pale nose has turned red, and Gwyneth is fumbling, trying to be inconspicuous, but still fumbling, in the neat leather handbag placed precisely by her knee, for a tissue.

Janet looks around, but no-one's noticed, least of all Nigel.

"Dad did call me home, more or less, when Mum died," he volunteers. "I mean, he wanted me to come home, he made that pretty clear. But bloody hell, what could I do there?"

"So much for filial piety," remarks Larry.

"Well, it's different for us from what it is for them, isn't it? If you can't you can't, that's it."

"Oh, sure. Right. Who am I to say?"

"Right." Nigel stares angrily.

Gwyneth leans forward, the tissue hidden in her clenched hand. "You can't," she says clearly.

Nigel looks at her. Gratitude and suspicion mixed, the belligerence still there, too.

The guests are quiet. Janet wonders: What must they think of us? We're so careless, it must seem to them. We must look so foolish in their eyes.

She tries to think of a way to change the subject, but nothing comes. Then, suddenly, though it doesn't quite follow, she's filled with emotion. She feels an affection for all gaijin, even Nigel. Well, not necessarily all, not IBM executives or diplomats or people like that, they don't need it, or the young with their backpacks, on the way to somewhere else. The real gaijin, she thinks. The ones who can't go home, not just yet. The ones still here, still fumbling for the right words in a language made for not explaining, still searching for lovers whose embraces bring to mind no pain, still hopefully clapping hands before the shrines of gods who will never know them but whose indifference itself seems sweet. The uncertain, the messy, the screwed-up, her own kind, though how long she'll be among them she can't tell—no, she's not a forever person, but she's grateful for whatever chances, quarrels, passions or refusals have brought them here, to be with her, to find out what it is to be irrevocably other, and to be able to call it, most of the time, peace.

Janet is drunk.

She reaches out and hugs Larry, and in her eagerness, somehow, she falls into his lap. "You're such a lovely Santa!" she burbles. Startled and awkward, he hugs her, too, and she tweaks his beard, and tickles him under his pillow. He tumbles back, laughing, and Janet with him. Their feet fly up under the table and people grab for glasses and bottles. Christmas paper crackles under them.

Janet struggles up. The students wait a decent moment, and

then they look at each other, murmur, "Ja, soro soro," hand around coats and scarves and handbags, rise to their knees and then to their feet, bow, say thank you. A real Christmas party! Thank you so much!

She follows them to the door and bows and gives them little waves, as one by one they put on their shoes and leave. Gwyneth is among them, balancing on one foot getting into her sensible pumps, and with them alone is already different, smiling, not that thin superior smile of hers, but one that's warm and has brought colour to her cheeks. They release her, thinks Janet, astonished, watching her go.

When the last of them has bowed for the last time, quietly shutting the door behind him, she turns and bursts out, "Was it because of that?"

"You know they always leave together," says Larry, already out of his Santa suit and bundling it up.

"Oh, God! How—" Her head throbs—"How humiliating! Now they probably think we're in love or something!"

"Not only that, they think we're engaged."

Elaine, lying on the floor stretching, says, "Certainly they do. And they think you have no sense of propriety."

"Propriety!" yells Larry, rolling over with his bundle in his arms and waving his legs in the air. "I love it!"

Al lights a cigar. Janet hates smoke, but she lets it go. She leans against the wall, and then, feeling it's too fragile to hold her, lets her knees buckle and slides down gratefully onto the tatami.

Nigel reaches over the table for a beer bottle, finishes it in one swallow, and stands up, bending to rub the backs of his long calves.

"Nigel! Your feet!" says Elaine.

"Miss Nakamura says I need new socks. They are a bit holey."

"Holey! Dear God! If Miss Nakamura wants to get involved with your socks she's more of a baka than I thought!"

"You're right there," says Nigel smugly. "A big mistake, poor girl. A hardened old ruffian like me. But you know, they can't help it. I'm an exotic, aren't I?"

"Nigel. Give us a break."

He picks up his jacket. "Well, a Merry Christmas to all. Happy New Year!" He bows elaborately, again and again, doing a silly walk backwards all the way to the door.

"Asshole," says Larry.

"Janet," says Elaine, "New Year's day, you want to go to Meiji Shrine and see all the people, say a prayer, buy an arrow?"

"Buy an arrow for me," says Larry. "I need it to fly away with my next year's sins. I plan to commit a few."

"It's not really sin in the sense you might think," Elaine starts to explain to Janet. "The concept—"

"Honey, when I says sin, I means sin. I need that arrow!"

Al is pulling on his lambskin jacket. "Like the poet," he says. "'Wilt thou forgive those sins through which I run / And do them still, though still I do deplore?'" He gives the cigar in the corner of his mouth a chew. "Uh . . . 'When thou hast done, thou hast not done / For I have more.' That it?"

Larry only shrugs, but Elaine sits up. "Good God, Al! Where'd you get that from?"

"Gotta rush. Great cake, Janet. Tell your mom."

After a while, Larry gets to his knees, shuffles nearer to Janet. He puts his arm around her. "Now don't forget, Jan-chan, no more promiscuous public hugging!"

"Someone might call the hug police," says Elaine.

"It's not a joking matter," says Larry severely. "Believe me, they can pull your gaijin card for less than that! And then where are you?"

When they've gone, Janet pushes back the shoji and the doors to the garden, and flaps a cushion to get rid of the smoke. She steps out onto the verandah, resting her eyes in the darkness. After a few minutes, great big snowflakes start floating down, at first slowly, but then thicker and faster, as she watches.

She stands there with her hand outstretched to catch the flakes. They're enormous and melt in splotches on her palm.

Then, far away, she hears a sound. A cry. Although the words are still a distant blur, the cadence is all: "Sweet potato! Roast potato! Hot, baked sweet potato!"

This sweet-potato man has a small open truck instead of an old handcart, and his cry is an amplified recording, but still. All at once she realises she's eaten nothing at her own party. She runs to the closet. As she opens it, a lot of things fall out, but she kicks them aside and grabs a sweater. She scrabbles for money in her purse, finds her clogs in the shoe box, and dashes down the side passage, leaving the door swinging. There he is, at the end of the road, going slowly away from her. She can see through the snow the fire in the brazier glowing red on the back of the truck, and clumsily, slipping and sliding on the icy road, she runs after it, just managing to keep it in view.

6

Salted Blossoms

THIS CITY IS A MESS. Power lines crisscross narrow lanes crammed with houses whose walls are webbed with earthquake cracks; a gaudy postmodern office block pops up overnight beside a rickety sweet shop presided over by an old woman in a grey striped kimono; the priest can't find anywhere to park except in the temple garden, with no regard for aesthetic values whatsoever; and whenever there's an election on, which there usually is, vans mounted with loudspeakers are allowed to drive around the streets so that people waving white-gloved hands can scream slogans in the windows. What if you had an invalid, or a baby, in the house? How is it that everyone isn't raving mad? Sometimes Gwyneth thinks she is living in a madhouse. But then something good happens. She slogs up the steps of the pedestrian bridge on a windy morning, and there on the horizon is Mount Fuji, hovering in the limpid air, poised as if for takeoff. She is invited to a tea ceremony, and goes, and remembers to hold the bowl properly and to turn it in a clockwise direction before sipping the bitter green tea, and doesn't drop or spill anything, and actually feels tranquil. The cherry blossoms come out.

How could she have known, before she saw them for the first time, what they would be like? She'd supposed they were just for tourists, that all the glossy photos she'd seen in guidebooks would turn out to have been half a dozen famous trees somewhere. How could she have known the way the blossoms creep slowly up towards Tokyo, following the warmth, how the pink arrows of the blossom front move from day to day across the TV weather map, how the buds begin to open and everyone starts to calculate, "Half open today, maybe full bloom Thursday, we could have our party Friday night, or if there's no wind, if it doesn't rain—will they still be there on Sunday?" And then the first sight of them, around the school fence, in the shrine, in the cemetery, along the railway line, by the moat; more thickly clustered on the bough, deeper against the blue of the sky, paler against the grey of stone lanterns, more astonishing than she had ever thought possible. No matter how long she stays here, they will never fail to astonish her, in their bursting out, in their all-enveloping lightness, and in the violence of their fall. The office boy is sent out to sit on a rug (his shoes set neatly beside it) to keep a place, there's a night of drinking and silliness, and even Gwyneth joins in bawling out the songs. Mounds of garbage pile up but no-one looks at the ground, no-one cares, one must look up at the masses of blossom, let them fill one's eyes. If it rains, the blossoms only become more luminous, and the drunks sodden, but the next day there'll probably be a wind, and the day after, and the petals will swirl from the trees in a great storm that goes on and on, until the children scuffle through heaps of them in the playground, and kick them up in clouds from the swings.

Once Gwyneth had tea made from last year's cherry blossoms, salted down to soft, pink lumps that floated in the cup, in the tea-room of a museum, with a man she quite liked, and it tasted like tears.

Gwyneth puts on her clothes, pulling on her thick black tights and her skirt and her sweater, because it's still cold, looking out the window at the cherry blossoms. When she took this apartment, several years ago, they were just in bud, and nothing, not the northerly aspect, or the sight of a cockroach scuttling under the bath, or even the fact that it's next door to a cemetery, could have stopped her taking it, or could persuade her now to move somewhere better. The blossoms are the whole point.

Anyway, she doesn't really mind living next door to a cemetery, except for the ferocious mosquitoes that lurk in the water jars in which people leave flowers. It's better than a scrap-metal yard or something like that. There are trees. And besides, she thinks of it as her refuge from the fire that everyone says will follow the Big One. She would have minded very much living next to an English cemetery, but when someone asked her, "Aren't you afraid that a spirit will get lost at O-Bon and come into your room?" she laughed. She knows that the only spirits that get lost are those whose families fail to care for them, and there don't seem to be many of those. Every grave is regularly weeded, there are flowers everywhere at the appropriate times of year, and the dead seem well supplied with treats. Gwyneth is fascinated by the ceremonies. Looking down from her kitchen window, while washing up or making a cup of tea, she learns things. A few weeks ago, at the spring equinox, she spent most of a morning gazing down at all the people who came to tend the graves. This was just before her mother died.

She didn't go back for the funeral. It was, as she explained to people who wondered, the beginning of the term, and she'd been home not long before, after all. It wasn't as if she hadn't more or less said goodbye. But these were not the real reasons. Of course she had only to say, and she could have got the time off. She could certainly have afforded to go again. She's earning more money than her mother would ever have thought possible.

The real reason was that her sister-in-law said on the phone, "There's absolutely no need to come back. Robert has taken care of everything." And she realised it was true. Her brother would have taken care of everything, and he wouldn't give a tinker's damn if she came or not. Her sister-in-law's voice was chill with reproaches, and why not? It was she who had traipsed back and forth to the hospital and washed her mother's nightgowns, while Gwyneth, the unmarried daughter, the rightful performer of these tasks, got off scot free. It was no use thinking it would make any difference to her mother now, if she went or not. The Japanese might think they can talk to a gravestone and be heard, but Gwyneth cannot.

Only yesterday the doorbell rang and she heard the postman shout. She went to open the door, standing on top of a pair of shoes in the entranceway, rather than taking time to slip into them properly, because she didn't want to hold up the postman—he always sounds so urgent. He handed her a bundle of English magazines that wouldn't fit in her box downstairs, the *Guardian Weekly* and a letter. Gwyneth turned it over. It was a fat letter, more of a small packet, and it was addressed to Gwyneth, in her sister-in-law's writing, from her mother. There was no airmail sticker and the date stamp was more than two months old. She knew what it would be. Her birthday present. Her mother would have remembered it at the last minute and given it to her sister-in-law to post, because she wasn't really able to get about much herself, even before the stroke. Although it was bound to be too late, she would have said, counting out the exact change, "Send it by sea now, the airmail's too dear these days." And her sister-in-law wouldn't have cared, certainly not enough to add a few stamps. This was the last thing Gwyneth would ever receive from her mother, a gift from beyond the grave, but she felt hurt and resentment rising up in her. Her mother would not go out of her way to give pleasure to her. She would send this tiny, light thing in the hold of some filthy ship, to be held up at a dozen ports along the way, to arrive too late, too late for everything, rather than part with a penny more than she had to. It was not that she was ill. There was something small and narrow in her. Nor did she take pleasure in anything Gwyneth ever sent her. Gwyneth knows that the little purse of Nishijin silk, the cashmere scarf, the miniature gold leaf screen with irises on it, are stuck in a drawer somewhere—no, they are now in her sister-in-law's drawer—have never been used, never been taken out and lovingly touched. Then again, how could Gwyneth have hoped to touch her mother with expensive, too-pretty things from far away? Her mother saw through that.

She opened the envelope. In it was a card hastily signed, a broken celluloid box of three handkerchiefs, and a ten-pound note. Gwyneth looked at the money and thought, I shall never know if this means forgiveness.

Last night, for the first time, she failed to go to the blossom-viewing party the teachers and students organised in the park near the school. Even today she feels tired, unwilling to go out. But she is even more unwilling to stay home. She has never before felt like this, here. Generally, she has only to think of the contrast between life in her mother's house and her every-day life in this place, and the effect is of a brief touching together of two wires in her brain: a tingling, but of joy, rather than pain. It's not only the things that most gaijin love that she can draw on in this way, though she does love them, the festivals and all that. It's everything. Everything interests her. Her students, as conventional a lot of young persons, in their own terms, as one could expect to meet, interest her. Going to the post office interests her, for heaven's sake.

Perhaps she's a little strange. She can't overlook this possibility. She hasn't turned out the way she was supposed to. Her mother, all those years, assumed that she would teach at a local school, and marry, finally (better late than never), another teacher, or someone who worked in an office, a man mild and plain, with harmless hobbies and a mother, faintly jealous, of his own. They would live not far away and make themselves useful. It could certainly have happened like that.

Her mother had a boarder for a while, a Japanese student, and Gwyneth would go into her room sometimes for green tea, and rice crackers wrapped in crisp seaweed. She would watch this girl make little things of bright paper with slim, precise fingers. Cranes and boats and flowers were the currency of communication. The girl gave her presents. A miniature tea ceremony set nested in a brocade bag, a fan with a drawing on it of a grasshopper clinging to a stem, a red fake-lacquer box. These things led Gwyneth down the rabbit hole as surely as if they had been labeled EAT ME.

She started to go to all the Japanese films at the National Film Theatre. She saw *Rashomon* and *Tokyo Story*, she saw ghost stories, B-grade samurai epics, proletarian dramas and tragedies about fallen geisha. She saw a lot of things the Japanese girl had never heard of.

She enrolled in an evening class in Japanese that was held in the dim, smelly depths of a school in Pimlico. It was a relief to see that there were enough other people to make up a class. Some of the faces were familiar from the NFT.

Her mother and the Japanese girl were united in one thing, in thinking her absolutely cracked.

She learned characters, more and more each week. She put white cards with characters on them around her room, indicating the desk and the chair and everything else, as in kindergarten. She bought a pen that had a brush instead of a nib, and squared Japanese manuscript paper from a shop near the British Museum, and copied characters from her book every night, following the stroke order exactly, one character to a square. Sometimes she asked the Japanese girl, Fumiko, to help her, but Fumiko had found an English boyfriend, a mousy youth she described as "tall and blond," at a performance of *The Tempest*, and soon went to live with him in a bedsit in Highgate. Gwyneth persevered.

All this time, she was reading translations of Japanese literature. She read all of Mishima. She read Kawabata. She read *The Tale of Genji* by Lady Murasaki, and Murasaki's diary, and *The*

Pillow Book of Sei Shonagon, a Penguin Classic, and everything else that was written by the ladies of the court of Heian Kyo and survived to be translated.

She read about Arthur Waley, the great translator, who so loved the vision of ancient Japan he held in his head that he did not wish to see the place in the twentieth century, fearing disappointment. Gwyneth, though no scholar, had her own vision, but no such fears. She did wish it.

Only today, for the first time, she feels that the attainment of her wish may have used up more strength than she had. Or is it that the exhilaration of the escape has ended in the loss of what she was escaping from, and, with it, of the surge of energy that sustained her flight? Why did she not anticipate that loss? What made her think that in her absence everything would go on just as before? Now her ties to home—which turn out to have been only one tie, really—have been dissolved, while she wasn't looking. Her mother is gone, and she has no reason to go home again, and nobody to mind if she stays away. And she doesn't even feel like going out to look at cherry blossoms. No thought impels her in any direction at all. Yet she has to think.

The future. Tentatively, she considers it. Strange that she's hardly given it a thought until now. What will it be like for her when she's old and, as seems likely, alone? Where will she be? Here? Why not? In a little place like this one? But will she be able to afford it? A very small place then, a six-mat room, with a cat—no, that will never be allowed, and anyhow Japanese cats are different, nervous and suspicious when she tries to make friends with them in the street. Still, that's the idea. She'll be a nice old lady, still rather British, waylaying cats, worrying about dogs. Perhaps she'll write long, crotchety letters to the *Japan Times*. She'll do her calligraphy, too. She might do ikebana or that art where you make pictures in pebbles and sand on lacquer trays. She might take up Zen, and spend her last days in a temple. She wouldn't be very good at it, because already she has a trick knee that would interfere with meditation, but it would be nice to hear visitors say, "Who's that old gaijin lady? What a lovely old face, so serene." It could be worse.

It's funny that the contemplation of her impoverished old age should be a comfort, but it is. She decides to go out after all, and buy books, to assuage the craving for English that has replaced her craving for Japanese. She puts on her coat, winds her muffler around her throat, scrabbles around at the door for her shoes, and gets herself downstairs.

There's a breeze, rather sharp, but no threat to the blossoms, yet. They are full out, refusing to relinquish a single petal, ravishing, defiant. Gwyneth walks slowly beneath them.

As she passes the cemetery, she sees a family gathered round the priest in the new plot by the fence. The priest's brocade robes move slightly in the breeze. Everyone else is dressed with elaborate casualness. The father of the family is wearing a golf shirt, loud checked jacket, white trousers and white shoes, and his hair is permed in tight curls. Gangsters! thinks Gwyneth. She has a quarrel with this family, because a tree was cut down to make way for their plot. One morning, she woke to a crashing sound, and the whine of a chainsaw, and when she opened her eyes a strange brightness flooded the room. Running to the window, she saw that the tree was already being cut into neat lengths, and she wanted to shout at the men who were doing it. But how could she? It's their temple. In the next few days she watched helplessly the creation of this splendid plot where the tree used to be. An iron railing, a marble monument, a quantity of new wooden prayer sticks bunched behind it, and two mature camellia bushes, one on each side. The family must be coming up in the world. What it must have cost to persuade the priest to cut down that tree! Gwyneth glares at them as she passes.

Turning into the shopping street that leads to the station, she jumps aside to avoid a little boy on a bike. The boy is dressed in his kendo uniform, and his bamboo sword, wrapped in dark blue cloth, is slung across his back. His head is down and he is standing on his pedals, kimono flying, as he rounds the corner. Gwyneth almost cries, "Watch where you're going!" but he's already out of range by the time she's pulled herself together. His bike is bumping over the railway crossing where the bell is clanging for the approach of a train, and he has to duck as the barrier comes down. He looks like a young samurai, with the samurai's sternness of purpose.

All the way down the street, as far as the station, green plastic branches of artificial cherry blossoms flutter from the telegraph poles. It's odd, but Gwyneth can't find it in herself to resent them. They're commercial, they're crass, she ought to find them a repellent manifestation of something or other, but she doesn't. There's the real thing, back in the distance, a faint pink cloud; here are the plastic cherry blossoms, a kind of resonance. She hurries under them, alert now, dodging all the hazards.

She takes the train to Shinjuku, threads her way briskly through the station where once she was lost for a whole hour, but where she now knows all the exits and shortcuts, plunges into a crowded pedestrian tunnel, follows it at the trotting pace of the people around her, breaks away from the stream and darts up some stairs, and keeps on going till the smell of curry rice from a basement food stall gives way to the cool smell of books.

The place is packed, with Japanese and gaijin. Gwyneth hopes she won't meet anyone she knows. She starts at A in the paperback fiction, and has got as far as F (here at least they understand the alphabet, which she's found not always to be the case), with two books in her hand, before she hears a soft voice behind her. "Miss Plummer? Hello."

Reluctantly, she turns. "Mr. Yamamoto. Fancy seeing you here."

"I come here quite often," he says. "Today I bought this." It's a book on English letter-writing. "Can you recommend it?"

She flicks through it. The model letters aren't as old-fashioned as some. No humble servants. She hands it back. "It seems all right. Are you writing English letters in your work now?"

He hesitates. "Yes, sometimes I do so."

"I haven't seen you for a while."

"I've been very busy. It's a busy time, the end of the fiscal year. And I was rotated in my job."

"Is that good?"

"It's busy."

"Do you still have to attend foreign guests?"

"Recently, not so often."

"Fortunately for you." She smiles.

He doesn't reply. This aspect of his job must bore him to sobs, but he'd never admit it to her.

"Would you like a cup of coffee?" he asks. "Can you make time?"

There's a small coffee shop in a corner of the bookstore, a couple of floors down, and they manage to squeeze in just as someone else is leaving. "Have you been busy, Miss Plummer?"

"Yes, very," she lies. She's never heard anyone in Tokyo admit to not being busy. Why be the first?

"I heard you couldn't return to your country because of your work."

"No. It was all very sudden. My elder brother took care of everything." That sounds right.

He nods, as if in confirmation. "I am very sorry for you."

"Thank you."

"My uncle's mother has also been lost."

"She died? Oh, I'm sorry."

"Thank you. She was very old."

"Yes, but still . . . Then I'll go and see your aunt soon."

"She will appreciate."

There is a pause. Gwyneth casts around for something to say.

When she used to give him private lessons, at his aunt's request—that was when he was nervous about the foreign businessmen—then, she never had any trouble talking to him. Now, he seems to have come over all quiet. She looks with pleasure at his smooth forehead and dark eyebrows, as he studies his coffee. She has always had the awkward feeling that he thinks of her as a fairly old lady, though there are not all that many years between them. It's probably because of the connection with his aunt, who, reflects Gwyneth morosely, seems to her to be merely middle aged. He looks even younger than he is, whereas she—well, who knows what impression one is making?

"May I change the subject?" he asks politely.

"Oh, do!"

"To tell the truth," he says, "I didn't buy this book for business." He places it on the table between them.

"No?"

"No. I bought it because I have a friend who is possible to be more than a friend, maybe."

"Maybe?"

"I want to marry her!"

"Oh!"

"But she says she might return to her country."

"Oh, dear."

"I am not happy. But if she goes, I want to write to her. And I will go to there."

Gwyneth sighs. "It sounds very difficult for you." Marriage again. It often comes up with one's students. Well, it comes up everywhere. She doesn't understand much of the conversations she overhears on the train, but she understands very well the word she seems to hear all the time: "kekkon . . . kekkon . . ." She is marrying soon; he doesn't want to marry yet; her parents are against it; his are very happy. So it goes. Gwyneth has been to her share of weddings. Her students are always getting married, and sometimes to each other. She's always placed at a front table at the reception, with the other sensei (the bridegroom's old professor, the bride's kindergarten teacher), and she always has to stumble over a speech. One of her students married a music teacher, and every one of the bride's pupils played. There were about twenty-five little pieces for violin.

"Will you meet her?"

"What?"

"Please, if you can make the time, will you meet her?"

"I don't know. Why?" That sounds rude, but Gwyneth is starting to feel cross. The things people ask! Why should she meet this girl? What is meeting her supposed to accomplish?

"You are my friend," he says. An ordinary sort of young man, she's always thought, but she notices now that his eyes are very deep brown, and long-lashed. This only makes her crosser. She is not his friend. Not in any serious sense of the word, surely? But she has been his teacher. She knows his aunt. Worse, his aunt is her landlady. Does this make her responsible? What does he want? He wants to make her part of his net, probably, his strategy. Show the girl he is to be trusted. He understands gaijin. He has Gwyneth in his background. A respectable older lady, too. A gaijin aunt. No, really! It's too silly. Probably he wants her to say nice things about him.

His head is lowered. He looks absolutely miserable.

"Are you sure?" asks Gwyneth, leaning forward. "I mean, are you sure this is the right thing for you?"

He looks up and nods wordlessly.

She does have a responsibility. She has talked to him. He has told her, when they used to meet for his lessons on Saturday mornings at his aunt's house, while his aunt stayed in the kitchen, about his omiai, about how he's met this girl and that girl, at his mother's and his aunt's urging. He laughed about it, but once her curiosity got the better of her, and she asked some direct question like, "What was wrong with her?" and immediately he turned chivalrous and declined to answer, and made her feel embarrassed, and angry at herself. Obviously he doesn't hold it against her. He's confided in her now. And he's asked her to do something really quite simple, to meet this girl, whatever good he thinks it will do.

"All right," she says. "If you want me to."

"Tomorrow? Do you have time tomorrow?"

"Tomorrow? Tomorrow I wanted to look at cherry blossoms."

"You have a plan already with your friends?"

"No, I mean, I thought I'd walk . . ."

"Oh, with yourself! That's great! Then let's go together, you and me, and Liz!"

"Wouldn't it be more romantic, just the two of you?" she asks craftily.

"Cherry blossoms can't help me," he says. "Honestly I don't think so. She is not romantic."

"Oh, dear," says Gwyneth again.

On the way home, she buys a pot of white cyclamen and makes for her landlady's house. No time like the present. She means just to hand them over and express condolences to the family.

However, when she gets there, she finds Mrs. Shiba alone and eager for company, and allows herself to be ushered into the sitting room, which has been transformed by the installation of a shrine to old Mrs. Shiba. It's an old-fashioned room, with a wide alcove in one wall, formerly set austerely with a hanging picture scroll and a vase containing a flower or two. Now the shrine, very grand in black lacquer, fills the alcove. Incense burns before it, candles glow, white and yellow flowers are massed all around, and a colour portrait of the old lady surmounts it. Gwyneth eyes it with alarm as she kneels on the tatami. She bows and tries to say the right thing, with some difficulty as to the correct level of politeness. For all she knows, there are special verbs to refer to dead people, but she manages as best she can. There's no way out.

The fears aroused in her by the shrine are about to be justified. Mrs. Shiba is moving to the side and motioning Gwyneth forward.

"Would you perhaps like to pay your respects to Mother?" she asks, properly diffident.

Gwyneth shuffles on her knees towards the shrine, places her palms together, bows her head. Heavens, what to do next? The little bell! She taps it and it gives a lovely ting! Encouraged, she reaches for a stick of incense, holds it in the flame of a candle, remembers to fan it with her hand till it starts to glow, stands it with the other sticks in a bed of ash in a ceramic bowl, and bows her head again. Is that it? Out of the corner of her eye she sees that Mrs. Shiba is sitting quietly, making no move. Is she waiting for more? Gwyneth thinks rapidly. A lot of things are done in threes, aren't they? The right number will be one, or it will be three. If it is three and she stops now, it will be awful. If she does three and it turns out to have been one, she will have overdone it and that will be awful, too. She steals another glance at Mrs. Shiba. Mrs. Shiba looks meditative. What to do? Go for three? Gwyneth seizes another stick. Mrs. Shiba stirs, her eyes widen slightly in surprise. Wrong! But too late. She has to go through with it. Probably three would be all right if you'd known the old lady intimately for fifty years, and Gwyneth is only a gaijin who has bowed to her in passing, and here she is labouring over the incense: light incense, wave hand, place in bowl, pray. If only she could compromise at two, but what use is two? The third seems to take forever. Finally, it's done, and Gwyneth backs away from the shrine on her knees.

Mrs. Shiba thanks her gently. Gwyneth begins to recover. Maybe it wasn't so bad. She didn't do anything so very terrible, she didn't knock anything over, the sticks didn't fall down. This is not one of her worst moments, is it, not like when she smudged the guests' book at a wedding, in spite of being so proud of her brush writing, and ruined it forever? Or, if it is, Mrs. Shiba will never let her know.

Mrs. Shiba is taking teacups from the round lacquered box she keeps by the table, shaking green tea leaves into the pot, pouring in hot water from the flask. "We understand each other," she says, "since you have lost your dear mother, too, so far away." She looks down at the cups. "Of course, Mother was my mother-in-law. But she was like a mother to me since I entered the house as a bride. She taught me everything. You hear a lot of stories about mothers-in-law, and no doubt some of them are true. But she was always kind. I hope my daughter will find such a good mother-in-law."

Gwyneth looks at the portrait of Mr. Shiba's mother. She thinks about her own mother's spirit. No doubt thoroughly cleaned out the day after the funeral by her daughter-in-law, it will have vanished utterly from the room where she used to sit through the winter evenings knitting fine, fine, sweaters in all the wrong colours. Nothing can be changed now, nothing can be solved.

"It's Mother's favourite time of the year," says Mrs. Shiba, placing before Gwyneth a sugar cake moulded in the shape of a blossom, on a small celadon plate.

"I'm going to see the blossoms tomorrow," says Gwyneth, after a pause, "With your nephew and"—something stops her just in time—" a friend."

"A friend?" There's nothing wrong with Mrs. Shiba's antennae. "A gaijin friend."

"Oh," says Mrs. Shiba, pleased. "A friend of yours, Gwyneth-san?"

Gwyneth smiles and sips her tea. "I met your nephew in Kinokuniya this afternoon."

"Really? Tomokazu's been so busy! His mother says he comes home late every night." She slides a cup towards Gwyneth with the tips of her fingers. "He's using English all the time in his work. He always says how much he owes to Miss Plummer's good teaching. Maybe they'll send him abroad, later."

"I expect they will. He'd bought a book on English letter writing."

"Is that so?" Mrs. Shiba is impressed.

"Oh, yes."

"He should be married soon," says Mrs. Shiba.

"Is there someone?"

"Not exactly. He's so busy, you see. But his mother is giving it a lot of thought. Mothers are like that! Hours on the telephone! So far . . . he's very hard to please!"

"Are you helping her look?"

"My daughter Shizuko has several college friends," replies Mrs. Shiba musingly. "Intellectual girls who speak English very well, and would like to live abroad if the opportunity comes up. His mother has asked for my help, of course, but with Mother ill, and then . . . but perhaps later I may be of use . . . ."

A breathing space for Tomokazu, thinks Gwyneth. Then she thinks, but what do I care? Is this how I ought to be spending my time, gossiping about other people's marriage arrangements?

As soon as she can, she makes her excuses and leaves. She sends her sympathy to Mr. Shiba. Mrs. Shiba thanks her for coming, and bows and waves from the doorway until Gwyneth is outside the garden gate.

What if I had someone like Mrs. Shiba to make arrangements for me, Gwyneth wonders, walking home. How would I feel? I might like to feel that someone was taking the trouble, that someone was willing to make herself responsible for my happiness, as she saw it. It does all depend on everyone's agreeing what happiness is, though. They do seem to be able to agree on the whole. They're not always left floundering about finding their own way, like we are. On the other hand . . . but she's tired of this argument already. She knows it just goes round and round.

The memory comes to her of something that happened not long before she left England. On an impulse, she'd picked up a cheap single ticket to the opera at the Coliseum, and gone by herself. Sometimes she really enjoyed doing this, reading her programme over a sandwich and a gin and tonic in the bar, getting involved in the music without having to discuss it with anyone, being able to cry at the end without feeling embarrassed. She was standing on a bus queue afterwards when the man next to her began to talk. He'd been to the same performance, also alone. He was a bit older than herself, and he wore a grey muffler tucked in the front of his coat as she remembers her father used to do. At first, she thought he was pleasant enough. He knew a lot about music. Then she noticed a disquieting urgency about him, and at the same time something not quite clean, a sort of bedsit aura. She began to realise, by the increasing confidence of his manner, that he believed there was a chance she might end up in the bedsit bed with him, if not on this night, then on some other. The flush created by this realisation seemed to spread outwards through her body. Just thinking about it makes her feel mortified all over again. She couldn't wait to get away, even politeness couldn't hinder her. She took off for the underground. It wasn't that the man might have been the kind who looked out for women alone and preyed on them, she didn't think that. It was that he must have thought her, Gwyneth, alone and clutching her programme on the bus queue, as pathetic as she thought him.

She escaped! She escaped from everything! From grubby men on bus queues, from headscarves, and gravy, and Tories!

She has felt herself blossoming. To be a foreigner has turned out, after all, to be her destiny! Gwyneth, mousy Gwyneth, in this place is now truly fair. Thin, gangly Gwyneth, her mother's streak of misery, is now "our elegant teacher"—that's what one of her students wrote in an essay, and if it's Oriental flattery, who cares? She likes it. Her mother used to say, "Be polite to everyone, because you never know who they might be." The Japanese know who she is, a gaijin teacher, a sort of upper servant of the economic miracle, and still they say kind things to her, things she never heard at home.

On a train journey recently, she found herself a seat in the crowded dining car. A serious-looking man took the seat opposite her. He asked her, of course, where she was from. He ordered beer, and poured her one, and they talked. In the dark, they passed Mount Fuji, and he said, "Some day, let's climb Mount Fuji together." He gave her his card. She didn't give him hers, but it didn't matter. It was only an encounter, the kind of thing that leaves you with a sense of the possibilities.

❖ ❖ ❖

When she meets Tomokazu and Liz by the entrance to the park, there are a few petals swirling in the air, and a few on the ground. Tomokazu comes forward eagerly, but Liz holds back. She barely smiles as he introduces them. A sullen-looking girl, with droopy light-brown hair and some inadequately concealed spots, she is so unlike Gwyneth's preconception of her that Gwyneth can't help looking her up and down. A mistake. But Liz is Australian, and Australian girls are supposed to be bouncy, aren't they, and young Japanese men are supposed to go for sweetness, and this one seems to be neither bouncy nor sweet. What can have got into Tomokazu?

They walk by the lake. Tomokazu suggests they hire a boat, and he will row. It does look rather like fun, thinks Gwyneth, but the people doing it seem to be couples or families, not threesomes, and although she's known the girl hardly five minutes, she is quite sure Liz won't do it. She is right. "Look at the queue!" says Liz. "What a drag. It's even crowded on the water. People are bumping each other!"

Two boats collide right in front of them, under an overhanging bough of blossoms, as if to prove her point. The people in both boats are laughing as they push away. A charming scene, actually, but Liz folds her arms across the front of her baggy sweater and walks on, with Tomokazu and Gwyneth following rather too fast in order to keep up with her.

Right, thinks Gwyneth. Conversation. "Isn't it amazing," she offers, "the cherry blossoms are such a dreadful cliché, but they are amazing, aren't they?" The words fall into a silence.

"Mount Fuji, cherry blossoms, geisha," says Tomokazu. "That's the image, isn't it? Now all the kids are dying their hair orange."

Liz pays no attention to him. "They are pretty," she says to Gwyneth, grudgingly. "There's more than I thought."

"Yes!" enthuses Gwyneth, all too glad of a response. "That's the thing, the profusion!" This glum girl is making her talk drivel.

However, it seems Liz is willing to talk, in her own way. Here they are, strolling beneath the blossoms, and she starts to go on about Japanese politics. How shockingly corrupt it is, and so on.

"Um, I don't know," says Gwyneth foolishly. "I mean, it is, of course, though I'm not sure it's really more than anywhere else, different kinds perhaps, and then where do you draw the line? There's money at weddings, money at funerals, all those little envelopes, our students bring us cookies all the time—"

"I'm not talking about cookies!" says Liz scornfully.

"No, well, obviously—"

"There's so much more that warrants concern. The Right, the militarism, it's there you know, just under the surface, and then there's China. If you don't think the possibilities for the next century are grim—"

"Oh, surely—"

"They don't know a lot about history, about how it happened before. You ask anyone! Ask him!" She tosses her head in the direction of Tomokazu. "At high school they do the first two thousand years in incredible detail, the Battle of This, the Battle of That, but guess what, they're not so big on the twentieth century!"

Gwyneth glances at Tomokazu. He doesn't meet her eyes. "Let's hope—" she begins again. The truth is, she has enjoyed not thinking about politics since she came to Japan. She chooses to ignore the rightists in their blaring sound trucks, just as she ignores the ghosts in the cemetery. They're not her rightists, not her ghosts. As for the war, Gwyneth herself, remembering her mother's distressingly often-expressed nostalgia for a mythologized version of the Blitz, would much rather not hear any more about it, so she can hardly blame the Japanese for feeling the same, especially as their memories are made up of both suffering and shame—in varying proportions, no doubt, but incapable of transformation into something more bearable. Perhaps I'm wrong, thinks Gwyneth, but surely it's more important to care about keeping the peace now, and as far as I can see they do. In any case, it's hardly Tomokazu's responsibility, and this is just sheer bad manners on Liz's part. And furthermore, she thinks, getting rather hot under the collar, it's not about politics at all, it's about them, and I wish I were a million miles away.

"On the other hand," Liz is saying, "the Americans. Everyone forgets about their responsibility. They let themselves off the hook every chance they get! The discriminatory laws against the Japanese in the 1920s. Pure racism. Now, look at the trade dispute—they need a new enemy, there always has to be someone to blame—yet at the same time—"

"See!" exclaims Tomokazu. "Isn't she cute?" A young father is taking a picture of his wife and baby by the side of the path. The baby in its mother's arms is reaching up towards a spray of blossoms, its hands spread out as if to embrace them.

Gwyneth laughs. "There you are. You can't go wrong with cherry blossoms and a baby."

Liz bites her lip.

"I do agree—" ventures Gwyneth. The silly girl, are her feelings hurt that her exposition has been interrupted?

Tomokazu has walked away from them, towards the water's edge.

"It doesn't matter," says Liz, cutting her off. Her face is screwed up and she's staring past him, out into the middle of the lake somewhere.

Gwyneth sticks her hands in her pockets and stares in roughly the same direction. Probably she should try to make some remark to Liz about Tomokazu, what a nice person he is, or something of the sort, that's presumably her role here, but she can imagine the rebuff she'll receive, so she's damned if she will. It's not her problem. Whatever it is.

In any case, she thinks bitterly, to Liz I'm practically elderly, so I don't know anything. And there's something about me—something she doesn't like. I give the wrong impression, I know I do. I'm not natural, not easygoing. She'd like me if I could smooth her way. Well, I can't help that.

Tomokazu's head is bowed, as he pretends to see something interesting in the murky water. Watching him, affected in spite of herself by his evident unhappiness, Gwyneth is taken unawares by a sickening attack of envy of this girl, Liz. To be loved as Liz is loved—to have done so little to deserve it! It does really make her sick, although the feeling lasts only for one horrible moment. It passes, she overcomes it, but the brief struggle leaves her dizzy with shame.

Tomokazu comes back to them. "There are lots of small fish down there," he announces cheerfully, "but I had to leave my hand from the water. I started thinking of piranhas."

Amazingly, Liz smiles at this modest effort. "Piranhas are

medium-size fish, not little ones like everyone thinks," she says. She turns to Gwyneth. "Did you hear someone's running pack tours to the Amazon for Japanese gourmets, so-called, so they can eat piranha sashimi?"

"Oh, no. Really?" responds Gwyneth. "Too silly!"

"It's decadent," says Tomokazu, whose English vocabulary is improving all the time.

So they continue. They walk all the way round the lake in something like companionship. Gwyneth takes her camera out of her bag and offers, hesitantly, to take a picture. Liz and Tomokazu stand by the red rail of a bridge. The lake and the blossoms make a perfect background. They look rather self-conscious, but you can't go wrong with this picture either. Tomokazu takes a picture of Liz and Gwyneth, then gives the camera to Liz so she can take a picture of himself and Gwyneth, something Gwyneth is fairly certain Liz would not have offered to do, left to herself.

That done, Gwyneth says she will go home. At the station, Tomokazu takes her hand. His is soft. "You are so kind and considerable," he says. Liz looks slightly put out at this, but as Gwyneth turns to wave a final goodbye, she sees that the wretched girl is already a good deal brighter, and is actually hanging on to Tomokazu's arm. He nudges her, and they both wave.

Well, thinks Gwyneth. If she does come round, she's going to be quite a challenge to the Yamamotos and the Shibas. And then she thinks, Oh God, I wish I'd been as young as she is when I made my escape.

As she nears home, a strong wind gets up. The blossoms are falling, and there are enough on the ground for the neighbourhood children, playing house on a mat spread out in the lane, to fill their rice bowls with.

The wind doesn't let up, and in the morning, when Gwyneth wakes and stands shivering by the window, it's raining. The blossoms are being torn apart, and the petals blow over the road in wild gusts.

Gwyneth thinks of the old lady's portrait, secure on the shrine in her daughter-in-law's quiet front room. She remembers now that there were cherry trees in the background. Probably there were other people in the picture, before. They're gone from it now, leaving only the blossoms in view.

The wind blows a flurry of petals towards Gwyneth's window. One sticks wetly to the glass. She bends to look. It's about the size of her fingernail, and flushed at the base. Fine pink veins fan out from the centre. All the colour is in those veins! The petal is quite translucent, and through it Gwyneth can see a cluster of miniature raindrops on its underside. She is transfixed. She has never seen anything so wonderful. Then something outside moves into her field of vision, and she lifts her eyes to focus. It is the boy with the kendo sword, on his bike and followed by a dog, riding hard through a storm of blossoms.

7

Buddha's Birthday

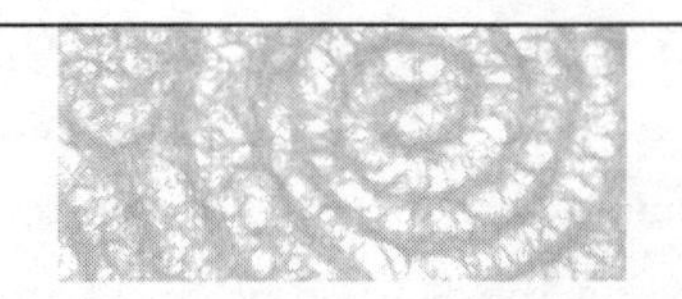

ON HER WAY TO Miyoko's place, trying to decide whether to call in at Cathy's first, Elaine walks by the temple kindergarten. She's just before been cursing it, as it happens. Its loudspeakers, blaring out that damn Mickey Mouse song, have wakened her three mornings this week at eight thirty, when she'd planned to sleep much later after working most of the night on her dissertation, and her body still begged for sleep. This morning included.

She has a lot on her mind, too, so at first it doesn't register that something's going on. The children sound excited, and they're all clustered together in their pink and blue smocks. The group's moving, in a hesitant way. They're having a parade of some kind. She stops in the shade of a cherry tree, new-leaved after the blossoms. Above the heads of the children she glimpses something white sticking up. A trunk! They're pulling a miniature wheeled float, a papier-mâché white elephant, only slightly taller than themselves. Now she sees that on its back there's a little shrine, decorated with arches of paper flowers, and inside the shrine is the baby Buddha, standing on a lotus blossom, one hand pointing up towards heaven, the other towards the earth. Of course. It's Buddha's Birthday. Right after he was born in a grove of trees in the Lumbini Garden, the new baby stood up and took seven steps, and said in a lordly voice, "In heaven and on earth I am the honoured one. I shall end the sufferings of the world." This is the scene, and this is the first time Elaine has happened to pass the kindergarten at exactly the right moment on the right day. In all the time she's lived here, she's never seen them doing this before.

Elaine stands for a while watching. They're going to pour hydrangea-leaf tea three times on the head of the Buddha. There's quite a crowd. Kids, teachers, mothers. She almost forgives them Mickey Mouse.

She finds herself thinking about the offer, as if she hasn't gone over and over it in her mind a hundred times since the letter came yesterday. Not the best offer in the world. Freshman Chinese, Eastern Religions 1A, maybe some Japanese, maybe some history. The salary's poor, though they want a lot for their money, and it's not such a prestigious place at that. But isn't this what she wants? She's not going to marry, like Liz. She's not like Cathy, in love with pots and things. She certainly isn't needed to teach Eastern Religions here. So isn't this job, or something like it, what she's done it all for? Hasn't she worked this hard so as to be able to go home in the end? If she took it, she'd work hard, publish, find herself a better job in a few years. Buy herself a professor suit.

She's been talking about finally finishing her thesis and going home for so long now. She's tired; she knows she looks tired because people tell her she does, though she's trying to drink less and eat better. Everyone's probably bored to death by her talk.

She wouldn't be so tired if she didn't hate teaching English so much. It's not only the teaching, it's changing trains. Running all over Tokyo from college to college, huge classes of fifty or so students waiting when she gets there, hardly one of them really interested. The freshmen are playful and shy, like puppies, and they drive her crazy. She's not a real English teacher, and she's not good at it. She does what's required, that's all. It's a wonderful day when she wakes up and thinks, I don't have to teach a word of English to anybody today.

Especially not to Miyoko. "A nice little thing," Larry said when he unloaded her on Elaine before he went to Osaka that time, "but she's not playing with a full deck." Probably that's why he refused to take her back later, and Elaine was stuck with her. So every week she traipses over to Miyoko's place, up to the top floor of that huge apartment building with its rows and rows of regulation metal fireproof doors. She sits at Miyoko's lace-covered table and they work through the textbook very, very slowly. The wedding pix look down. There's Miyoko in a white crinoline, her husband in a white tuxedo, someone playing a white piano, both of them cutting a cake taller than themselves. They have a big, fat candle they brought home from the wedding hall to burn on every anniversary. Each time it gets shorter. Elaine feels depressed whenever she looks at it, covered the rest of the year in plastic wrap, squatting at the back of the china cabinet. Whose idea was it that this would be a nice ersatz custom, to watch your life burn away? There are honeymoon pictures, too. They all show Miyoko and her husband, in identical sweaters, at sites connected with James Dean.

Poor little Miyoko. The funny thing is, though, Elaine thinks Miyoko probably pities her! This is completely the wrong way round, but it's very likely. For a start, Miyoko knows how old Elaine is. It's hard to go wrong with animal signs, since the cycle is twelve years. Though the Japanese have a hard time telling the ages of gaijin by appearance, anyone can see the difference between twenty-four and thirty-six. So she knows that Elaine, born in the Year of the Rat, is on the shelf, "left-over goods," as they say. At least Miyoko is a married lady.

Miyoko's husband has decorated one wall with a James Dean poster, the one where Dean is holding the rifle like the cross-piece of a crucifix, arms draped over it. And there's a picture of himself, plump and pouty, squinting through the sights of a large gun, taken at one of those places in America where young Japanese male tourists pay to pose holding guns, so they can bring the photos home to a country where this particular thrill is forbidden by a law they almost certainly agree with. Odd. Anyway, Miyoko's husband is just a big kid, with his James Dean obsession, his pictures of Porsches and oil wells, and his devotion to blue jeans, when all around him have graduated to golf clothes.

Then again, Miyoko has her dolls. Half a dozen beautiful doll children in kimono, with thick black pudding-basin hair, like real children, amazingly real, with childlike expressions and long-lashed brown eyes. They cost a fortune because they're handmade, but Miyoko can afford them. Every day she puts doll-size cups of juice in front of them, and miniature bowls of rice. Elaine has often looked up and found them watching her from the top of a chest of drawers as Miyoko bends obsessively over her textbook, or laboriously writes down a word she's just learned. Miyoko doesn't need English, not that Elaine can see, but she trembles with the effort to get it in her head.

Sometimes Elaine can't stand it anymore, cooped up in there with the dolls, and so they go for a walk, and "have conversation," practicing expressions from the book, theoretically at least, along the way. The only place to go is the local shrine, and they walk up the flagstone path, around in front of the Noh stage, and back again. Miyoko always breaks off to pray, nothing unusual about that, but she stands there, head bowed, for a long time after clapping her hands, sometimes for so long that Elaine has started to worry.

"Don't you want to know what I pray for?" she said the last time. "I pray for a baby." Elaine was not surprised, but when she looked at Miyoko she thought she saw a strange expression on the girl's soft, round face, and the spring wind was whipping strands of black hair across her eyes and mouth, that she didn't bother to brush away.

If Miyoko gets pregnant she'll go home to her family to have the baby, just as the Buddha's mother was on her way back to her own parents when she gave birth. That must seem a very natural part of the story to Japanese people, thinks Elaine, watching the baby Buddha.

Babies. A lot of people who are more together than Miyoko seem to want them very badly. This desire is something of a mystery to Elaine. She's grateful she doesn't suffer from it, though she likes babies well enough, and in different circumstances might have been glad to have one, she supposes, though it's not really easy to imagine what those circumstances might be, when she thinks about it. She has certainly never wanted to get married.

She has had an abortion, in fact, and not so long ago. The whole thing has a dramatic aspect in her mind, for though it ended very undramatically, it started last September, in the typhoon season. One afternoon she made love with someone in a dark apartment, dark as the middle of the night, with the electricity out, and the typhoon getting nearer as the TV had forecast, zooming up on the white swirls on the weather map before it flickered off. Later they got up naked and peered down into the street, saw the trees bending over, and branches and trash cans and pieces off people's houses leaping and whirling. Where they were, high up in this apartment, all they could hear was a sort of dull roar, and the walls of the building quivered, and Elaine began to be afraid to stand near the window. Then a boy who must have been crazy came round the corner on a motorbike, and, as they watched, the wind picked him up off it. They saw him fly, really fly, tumbling high through the air, and finally fall to the ground. The man with her—well, he was very young, too—said in English, "Shit!" as they like to do, having heard it at the movies, and Elaine couldn't say a thing, just stood there with a quilt around her shoulders and stared down. Some people ran out of the door in a shuttered shop front and carried the boy inside. Then Elaine and this other boy went back to bed.

When she had the abortion, Cathy went with her. She remembers what they talked about in the waiting room, though she was so nervous—they talked about Murasaki Shikibu having had no real name, or those other great women writers of the Heian period either. "But to have been Murasaki!" cried

Cathy, becoming impassioned even under the critical eye of the nurse in reception. "To have written *Genji!* If your work lives for a thousand years, does it matter what you were called? The men all had names, but who remembers them? So what are their names worth?" Anyhow, it turned out to be all right, good treatment, no problem.

What would her mother say if she knew? She couldn't be any more shocked and ashamed than Elaine was when once, years ago—she was still in high school—she saw her mother on a right-to-life demonstration outside the county court. It was one of the things that divided them absolutely.

And nothing that has happened since Elaine grew up has made them more comprehensible to each other. Her mother thinks there's one right answer to each of life's questions. Only one, and that's that. Elaine seems to her to have no values whatsoever.

Other people have stopped along the fence to watch the children and their elephant. On one side of Elaine there's an old lady with a shopping cart, a bunch of leeks sticking out the top, and on the other a dark-suited salesman carrying a briefcase and his order book.

Interesting how the Japanese always say they aren't religious, she thinks. It's probably because they know what being religious means to us. You sit in church, you fight over interpretation and doctrine and practice, you lapse and recant and convert—and they know what they do isn't that. It isn't even necessary to choose any one religion, Shinto or Buddhism. The gods were on the scene eons before the Buddha, but they get on, they're all still here.

Elaine arrived with her notecards and dictionaries a long time ago, the dispassionate scholar. She has never relinquished the methodology of the scholar, but she is no longer all that dispassionate. She had to admit this to herself after she came back from Zenkoji. Something had changed.

She went not because she needed to, but just to see the great temple. She thought she should. In the Nagano countryside, the buckwheat was in bloom, and strings of persimmons hung drying under the eaves of farmhouses. Even in the town, walking up the road from the station to the temple, there was a sense of harvest richness wherever she looked. Black grapes the size of plums, nashi pears, red clover honey, deep barrels of miso. She stopped to watch a chef rolling out dough for buckwheat noodles in the window of a restaurant, admiring the deftness of his floury hands, lingering till he noticed her and grinned. The path leading from the temple gate was crowded with tourists and pilgrims, pretty much like it must have been in medieval times, and has been ever since. Only now, among the souvenirs, you can buy a Buddhist rosary with microfiche prayers embedded in the beads.

What she really wanted to see was the dawn ceremony, so the next morning she got up before sunrise with the other people staying in the cheap guesthouse of one of the side temples, and staggered out just as the light was breaking. The place was already buzzing. Young monks darted around on errands. Hundreds of people were already lined up, waiting for the abbess to approach in procession, on her way to conduct the service. Elaine waited, too, yawning by the lotus pond. It had rained overnight, and every now and then a huge lotus leaf would give way under the weight of rainwater collected in its centre, and bow down, and the water would pour into the pond. The leaves glinted with raindrops and with coins in the pale first rays of the sun. Elaine began to walk back and forth on the bridge over the pond, hugging herself, and wishing she'd remembered how high it was here and how cold it would be at this hour, and that she'd brought her heavy jacket.

When she saw the procession coming, the big red lacquered umbrella held by young nuns over the head of the abbess, she went to meet it. The abbess, she knew, was very old. An aristocratic child, given to the temple in the early years of the century, who'd survived to become a living saint at its end. But the person she saw coming towards her was no frail, saintly old lady. Rosy-cheeked and gorgeously androgynous in purple silk robes—amazing how hard it is to tell the sex of a bald old person, thought Elaine, and amazing what a life of early to bed and early to rise and fresh vegetables and meditation does for the complexion—she moved briskly and with purpose. The people waiting by the side of the path sank to their knees in a wave as she passed, to receive her blessing. Elaine, the observer, momentarily inattentive, found herself next in line, and, so swiftly did it happen, with no choice but to kneel. So she knelt, and was blessed, more or less by accident. Somehow she still feels glad of the touch of the abbess's hand, placed just barely, but at the same time with surprising firmness, on her head. She could call it research, but it wouldn't be true. She feels she was really blessed.

Not only does Elaine understand how easily the Japanese take religion, mostly, but she's also been around monks quite a lot, the more scholarly kind. She smiles to think of the time—this was in the early years, when she'd just arrived, fresh, with her scholarship—she was invited to a meeting to hear a report from a Buddhist studies conference in Hawaii, and was astonished to see that it was prefaced by slide shots of Waikiki, and a goodly number of those had girls in bikinis well to the fore. Since then, she's gotten used to the monks. So all in all, she was rather unprepared for the way she felt when the abbess passed by.

The crowd of kids parts for a moment and Elaine gets a better look at the elephant. They've given it a gentle face. It reminds her of something. Not Buddha's birth, though he was conceived from the symbolic union of his mother and a white elephant, and born out of her side—a sort of virgin birth, in fact—no, not that, but Buddha's deathbed.

A fourteenth-century picture: Buddha, dying, leaning on his elbow, the way Japanese men like to lie drowsing. There are people and birds and animals there, all together around him, no distinction made between them. An angel with wings and feet like a bird. Horses and tigers and monkeys and ducks, weeping quietly. A crane, reaching out its long neck, and the elephant, its trunk raised to heaven in a bellow of grief.

Her thoughts return to death even on this sunny day, watching pink-and-white paper flowers fluttering over the baby Buddha, feeling the warmth of the sun dappled through the cherry leaves, and the breeze lifting the collar of her shirt.

The other night by the station she saw a kid, a freshman—she knew because of the university nearby, and because of the dumb way the seniors have of making kids drink themselves into a stupor by way of initiation—this kid was lying under the stairs of the pedestrian crossing and he looked so bad, so pale and cold when she bent over him, that she thought he was dead. She went to the police box and asked the policeman to call an ambulance, and the policeman said, "He'll be all right. His friends have gone to get a car."

"People can die from alcohol poisoning," said Elaine. "He looks just awful."

"Don't worry about it," said the policeman.

The boy didn't die. It would have been in the papers next morning if he had, along with the ritual lament about what's wrong with the education system, and how parents don't have time for their children anymore. Elaine looked carefully, she couldn't have missed it. So she was not responsible.

She knows what's going on in her head here, but she doesn't understand why it should be, when what happened—that's how she always seems to say it, to think it: what happened, as if nothing else ever had—is in the past, and utterly irrevocable. Then, it was a matter of just a second. Not even that. If only she'd looked up, if only she'd been paying attention. The man was right by her, and yet she hadn't noticed a thing about him until the moment when he threw himself—no, moved quietly to the edge and let himself fall—he simply let himself fall off the platform as the green train came in. Then there was that terrible, long silence, until at last she heard a voice, and it was her own voice, "Oh, God!" If only she could have stepped forward and grabbed his sleeve, he wasn't a big man, she could have held him. There, in that moment, there were people all around, looking across the line at billboards for love hotels and salary loans, looking at their feet, thinking about God knows what, there was the man, there was Elaine herself reading the blurb on the cover of a new book, till she looked up and saw the man step forward as the train came whining in, so fast. She could have reached out her hand.

To have been able to see just one second into the future: It would have changed everything.

Yet isn't this one of the things religion is for, to deal with the impossibility of ever knowing what even that one second holds, which cell may divide in that second, which cable snap? To deal with the fear.

And the fortunetellers in their red velvet caps, sitting beside their lanterns among the Saturday-night crowds in Shinjuku—who could blame their customers?

Nevertheless, the other day Elaine listened crossly while Miyoko explained how she and her husband can't have a house built for them by her in-laws after all, not anytime soon. "Because my mother-in-law went to the fortune-teller and he told her it's wrong for this year. Wrong direction, too. It can't be helped, Elaine-san." The trouble is, anything Miyoko says makes her impatient and irritated and concerned in about equal proportions. Perhaps it's the fact that they're so rich. Miyoko and her husband are both second children, and therefore without any particular responsibilities, of families linked somehow in the construction subcontracting business in the same provincial town. (Big in local politics, too, no doubt, their noses deep in the pork barrel.) She got a red sports car for a wedding present from her parents, a ladies' model that tinkles a warning tune when she exceeds the speed limit, and a huge emerald ring for her little bony finger from his. Their city apartment, simple and neat as it is, was only ever meant to be temporary.

Elaine has been invited to dinner there, and gone, seeing no way out. They were so sweet, she has to admit it, so grateful. Miyoko's husband thanked her for teaching his wife, and showed her his James Dean photo collection. They pressed food on her, and lots of whisky out of various weird-shaped bottles. But there's something wrong. It's not only that they seem to know less about anything real than anyone Elaine has ever met before. She had the impression then that Miyoko's husband was home on her account, but that it didn't happen very often. Where does he go, what does he do? Miyoko was even more nervous than usual. Elaine thinks perhaps he's growing out of James Dean after all, but into what other obsession?

They made conversation. Of course Miyoko asked her the old question, "Don't you have to go home sometime, Elaine-san, and take care of your mother?" It's strange, perhaps she's heard this one too often, but it seems to be taking on more meaning. It seems not to matter so much to her now that she and her mother provide less than shining examples of maternal devotion or of filial piety. What's more, they didn't fight much last time she was home. There are a lot of things they never mention now. There doesn't seem to be much point anymore. Her mother looks smaller than she used to, is smaller, Elaine could swear to it, a small woman in a diminished environment, now she's moved from the house she shared with Elaine's father into a two-room apartment. Mother no longer has the advantage, without Dad there to back her up, nor are they evenly matched. Elaine finds herself bending over so as not to tower, softening her voice so as not to intimidate. She even likes it somehow, now, that her mother calls her "Lainie," whereas when she was a teenager it used to drive her wild. Her mother is still a fascist, but it's possible they've fought themselves to a standstill. And since there's no one else, the responsibility for at least looking out for her mother's wellbeing in old age will certainly be hers. What she said to Miyoko was, "Fortunately, my mother is still in good health." No reason to tell Miyoko how near she is to making her decision. If only going home didn't feel so much like visiting a foreign country. There, people come out in the morning to the smell of dew on lawns and think of mowing them. Lawns. Mowing. These are foreign ways.

Then again, in a few years' time, she might come back to Tokyo and see all the now familiar things and feel that same shiver of strangeness. The thought makes her uneasy. She's given so much to knowing this city. She has a feeling, too, that life here might well have unfitted her for the realities of home. There, last time, she got stuck in her mother's car in the middle of a crossing, and someone walking around her banged hard on the roof of the car with his fist. Inside, Elaine was so shocked that she wasn't able to move when the lights changed. She sat there until someone blew his horn behind her. Another time, her mother, dropping her off at the station, told her in strict and anxious detail where to stand until the train came—the safest place. Here, she stands where she wants at any time of day or night, and fears nothing.

The little procession has receded. Way over the other side of the schoolyard, she can just see the top of the shrine and the tip of the elephant's trunk, caught by the sun. People are picking up their things and going on their way.

The old lady says to her, "Do you know what that was all about?"

"Yes," says Elaine. "I'm glad I saw it."

"When I was little I used to go to a kindergarten in a temple, in my hometown. We always had Buddha's birthday. It was so much fun. My, that was a long time ago. You can't imagine how long. You really know all about it?"

"I study Japanese religion."

"*Maa!*" exclaims the old lady. "How clever you must be! But it's incredible, all these foreign people who know things about us. I see them on TV all the time, chattering away. Have you been on TV?"

"No, no-one's ever asked me."

"Oh, what a pity, but I'm sure they will, sooner or later, and when they do I'll know who you are! I'll know I met you right here. I'd like to see someone I know on TV. You just keep on studying! If I were younger I'd go to some foreign country and study everything. Maybe I'd go to your country and study you! Can you believe I'm eighty-seven?"

"Not a bit," says Elaine sincerely. Sometimes these old ladies with all their joie de vivre make her feel quite exhausted.

But then, so many things do. Even Larry. Last night he called her just to say, "Elaine! You have to see this! It's 'Wonderful Children From All Around the World Who Do Very Strange Things,' or something like that! There's this little Chinese boy and there's these stairs like a xylophone, each one makes a note—he goes upstairs jumping on his head! See? Wow!" By the time she found the channel the boy was gone. She talked to Larry with one eye on the screen. On the next segment up, a gaijin talento showed how he made a cocktail cabinet out of a household shrine, and the studio audience laughed indulgently.

"Larry, what can I say? An all-time low. Should I be grateful to you for bringing it to my attention?"

"I can tell you're not in the mood," said Larry. "Let's switch channels. Hey, just a minute! Channel twelve! Isn't that whatsisface? That old boyfriend of yours from graduate school? With a beard? He's a Russian!" Yes, it was whatsisface, the shithead, now playing a bit part in a B movie about the Russo-Japanese War of 1904. "It's the assault on Hill Two-o-three!" said Larry. "You know, when General Nogi led wave upon wave— Oh, my God, that was a shell! He's in about a million pieces! Happy now? Maybe you can get the video?"

"That's more like it," admitted Elaine. They talked for a while, looking at this and that. "How's that dippy little Miyoko?" asked Larry.

"I'm not sure . . . ." said Elaine hesitantly. "Oh, she's probably missing you. I think you should take her back."

"Dream on, sweetheart. She's all yours." He'd switched to a news chat show. "Look who's on now!" A sumo wrestler, one they've been taking an interest in, was being invited by an interviewer to demonstrate a winning throw: Come on, show me. Shyly, he obliged. Elaine and Larry laughed as the interviewer was picked up and dusted down by the flustered young giant, and limped back to his chair.

"Great potential," says Larry. "Remember, I said it first, far back as Osaka."

"Soon as he learns his own strength," says Elaine. "He has to quit flinging people into the third row."

"I admit that. A little less exuberance, a little more control. Hey, did I tell you, he's an old school buddy of the younger brother of Teruko's older brother's wife?"

"Really? That's pretty close. Brother's brother-in-law's brother's friend."

"You do better. Anyhow, her brother's promised to take Teruko with the baby to meet him. So he can hold it for luck, give it health and strength and all, you know. It's all arranged."

"She's had the baby?"

"Didn't I say? I've seen it! Him. Funny thing, her husband's not much to look at, right?"

"As I recall, his omiai picture betrayed a certain resemblance to a frog."

"Toad. She was kind of taken aback. And I have to say, at the wedding, even in kimono, and you know how I am about men in kimono—"

"I know, Larry."

"Well, I don't think Terry's kiss is going to do it for him. Let me put it that way. But now she says he's a good person, he's got a sense of humour. Almost every time I see her she tells me that. I think she feels guilty. And the baby—it's just as cute as a button! No, it's beautiful. And she looks so happy."

"Is she really?"

"You're the one who said it'd be okay! You know, I think she really is."

"Good," said Elaine. "Then I'm happy for her."

"And you know that friend of hers, Hiromi? The one that always wears Chanel shoes, even on a picnic? She got passed over at the bank, after she made herself the big Brazil expert! They sent someone else to the branch in Rio. At first she was all, like, the injustice of it, etcetera, but then you know what she did? She quit, cashed in some investments—"

"A bank employee?"

"Nothing illegal, it's just that her money works. She knows where it is, what it's doing every fucking minute. It's not hanging out in bookstores, forgetting to eat lunch. *Your* money's plain feckless! Let me finish. A resort apartment in Izu. Her sister bought her out. And then she went anyhow. By herself. She said she'd learned the language and all, she didn't want to waste it. And she already knew this wealthy older guy, a Brazilian, and now he's backing her in an export-import business. She saw a niche, wouldn't you know it? How about that?"

"I'm happy for her, too."

"You're really not in the mood, are you?" said Larry.

After he'd hung up, she realised she hadn't said anything about the job offer. She stayed there, lying on the floor in front of the TV, too tired to move.

That was a mistake, because then there was a story about someone who'd jumped off a building in Marunouchi towards the end of the day and fallen on a young man who was on his way home to his mother with his first pay envelope, killing him. It showed the place where he landed, where the two bodies lay entangled, outlined with chalk. Elaine covered her face. Suicide stories seem to lie in wait for her. Stories about girls leaping from the roofs of apartment buildings in emulation of pop stars; about a police sweep of the lower slopes of Mount Fuji looking for bodies, finding watches and wallets for identification of people who've crept into the woods there to die; about mothers who gas themselves, walk into the sea, step in front of trains, taking their children with them, because they think it's the right thing to do. Ever since that moment on the station, over the years, these stories have been looking for her, or she's been looking for them. More so, lately.

❖ ❖ ❖

She decides she will go to Cathy's after all. It's not far out of her way. She notices, turning the corner, that the building opposite Cathy's place is being pulled down. There's a heap of rubble, and on the back of a truck several workmen are lying sprawled, on their break. Elaine thinks Cathy's cheap little two-room apartment, like her own, is probably not long for this world either. This kind of accommodation, washing strung outside every window, is disappearing, making way for something that will bring in rents commensurate with the value of the land. Where will they go, though, the students, and the old people that you can see through the open windows watching TV or playing go in their long white underwear on summer evenings? She should try not to care so much about these things—she's not going to stay, is she? Only she knows, as well, it's the scenes of her own youth she's mourning.

Cathy is sitting just inside the door catching the sun and combing out her wet hair. "So what are you up to?" she asks.

"Nothing much. I'm on my way to Miyoko's."

"Do you have a lesson today?"

"No, I just thought I'd check her out."

"Why, is she sick?"

"No, not really. I don't know."

Cathy makes an exasperated sound. "What is that woman's problem? Besides the big movie star."

"She wants a baby."

"She's a baby herself, from what I hear. Look, I know Larry palmed her off on you, but you're not supposed to be totally responsible for her. Don't . . . " She stops. Elaine knows the next words were going to be "try to mother her."

"It's just a funny feeling. I want to make sure she's all right, that's all."

"Well." Cathy holds her comb in the palm of her hand and runs a finger lovingly along it. It's made of silky boxwood by a craftsman in Ueno, an eighteenth-generation comb maker. It's been sanded with sharkskin, and smoothed with the bone of a deer, Cathy says. She's given one to Elaine, too. "Do you oil your comb?" she asks. "You know, I told you, with use and oiling, the colour deepens and it gets more and more beautiful. Do it, you'll see."

"Yeah, sure," lies Elaine. She does love the comb, it is beautiful, and it slips right through her hair. It's just that she forgets. She never seems to be able to remember to water potted plants either, they always die, and then she feels guilty, whereas Cathy has a miniature azalea sitting on the windowsill in the sun that looks as if it will bloom forever. "I saw the kids at the kindergarten doing Buddha's birthday on my way here," she says.

"Oh? Did you see that? Isn't it cute, with the elephant?"

She leaves without saying anything to Cathy about the job offer.

When she steps out of the claustrophobic little elevator, she sees Miyoko's neighbour outside on the open walkway sprinkling water and sweeping the concrete. It smells clean, water on dust, like a village street nine floors up. The woman gives Elaine a hard, clear, peasant look, watches her ring the bell, wait, and ring again. There's no answer. Elaine moves aside and catches sight of the James Dean poster through the barred kitchen window.

"You're the English conversation teacher, aren't you?"

"Yes."

There is no smile. "You don't know?"

"What?" Elaine hears her own voice rising.

The picture is there in her head already: Miyoko, falling, and a doll in her arms. Black hair streaming upwards.

"She returned to her parents in the country. By herself, and she isn't coming back."

Thank God.

The woman is waiting for a response, but Elaine can hardly speak. Finally, she manages, "Is that so?" then abruptly turns her head and and looks out, over the railing, over the grey roofs, the roads, the train line, the shrines and temples marked by patches of dark green treetops. You can see as far as the tall buildings of Shinjuku, clustered together in the distance. It's very high here.

She feels weak. Looks away.

This woman is asking questions, wanting to know if Elaine has any inside information. She hasn't, and if she had she wouldn't tell the neighbours.

She doesn't expect ever to hear from Miyoko again. There will be too much shame. Starting with shame at running out on their lessons, and working up from there. As if it matters. It's all right, Miyoko. The past is gone, and the future is not yet.

At home, she strips off her clothes and has a shower. She washes her hair, combs it out and carefully oils the comb. This once, at least.

She sits in the middle of her room and looks around at her

books, her boxes of notes. If I took that job, I'd never have to teach English again. But I have so much more to do here. Dwell in the present moment.

She pulls out a file, and out of the file a photocopy of a difficult translation she's been working on for ages. She thinks she'll take a quick look at it, now she feels fresh, but soon she's absorbed in it.

It's hours before she notices anything else again, and that's because it's getting dark, and the old monk's words are fading from the page.

8

The Foxes' Wedding

THE TRAIN COMES AROUND the side of a wooded hill, through a tunnel, and out into a valley of fairytale lushness. The rice shoots stand in glistening rows in the flooded fields, against the perfect, mirrored shapes of mountains, of clouds. The vermilion gate of a shrine, half-hidden by young bamboo, the silver-brown tiled roof of a farmhouse, the bent, sun-bonneted figure of a woman working up to her knees in water, are brilliant flickers against the tender, translucent green of the rice. The light, heavy with all the colours of unseen rainbows, shimmers between sky and fields, lies like silk on the surface of the stream that runs by the side of the line.

Cathy, who has sometimes disparaged the Japanese landscape for its lack of scale and grandeur, fumbles in her bag for her sunglasses, the better to take in the loveliness of the scene, but in so doing she allows her lunchbox to slide off her knees onto the floor. Fortunately, she's finished eating the neat cylinders of rice sprinkled with black sesame seeds, the fried tofu and glazed fish, and the vinegared ginger and pickled plum, and she's rewrapped the box in its original paper and string as she has learned to do, so it's no disaster, but she's annoyed at herself all the same. When do you ever stop being a clumsy gaijin? The schoolboy opposite her hasn't looked up from his robot monster comic book, but his grandmother, a tiny woman sitting with her legs tucked up under her on the seat and her shoes placed precisely on the floor in front of her, gazes at Cathy with open curiosity as she stoops down to retrieve the box.

By the time she rights herself, the train has rounded a bend and the enchanted valley has taken on a more familiar aspect. Cathy sees vinyl greenhouses, power pylons, a boy riding a motorbike along the bank of a rice field.

They're coming into the station. There's a family waiting, squatting on the platform surrounded by packages knotted in faded cloths, for the train to take them back the way it has come.

The arriving passengers disappear quickly across the dusty station square. There's one taxi, and the driver is heading back from the noodle shop across the way. Cathy is in luck.

On the way to Matsuno—she gives only the name of the village and of the family she's staying with, but this is enough—the driver asks her, "Where are you from?"

"Tokyo," says Cathy.

"You've come a long way all alone," he says seriously.

She relents. "I'm Australian."

"Australia? Isn't that near Germany?"

"No. It's in the south."

"Oh, Australia! Where the seasons are opposite?"

"Yes, that's right." Impossible to escape this conversation. How many times can she have had it?

"What language do you speak there?"

"English."

They are passing over a river, perhaps the same one that ran through the beautiful valley. Here, the river is wide, and its bed of smooth grey stones wider still. On a rock in the distance sits the small figure of an old man in a straw hat, and a child plays with a red bucket in a pool at his feet. Behind them rises a conical mountain, hazy as in an old ink painting.

"I never met a foreign person before," says the taxi driver shyly. "To tell the truth, I didn't know what you were. You speak Japanese differently from anyone I know, so I thought you might be some kind of strange Japanese I didn't know about."

God, am I in the backwoods or what! thinks Cathy, but she takes this as a compliment to her Japanese, which has never before been mistaken for any variety of the real thing.

"I learned English at school," he says, "but I never had a chance to speak it. We had, 'This is a pen.' That's about all I remember."

"Of course, you can't really speak unless you get the chance," agrees Cathy.

"That's it," says the driver. "You need to meet people. But there are no gaijin here, though I hear they had some staying at the inn, near Omori-san, the potter's." He turns in his seat. "Have you heard of Omori-san?"

"Yes. I'm interested in pottery."

"Oh. Well then, these gaijin that came to see Omori-san, I heard they were Americans, one of them let the water out of the bath at the inn! Takes hours to fill that big bath! No-one else had a bath that night." He laughs. "The lady at the inn told me that."

"Some people don't know any better," says Cathy.

"Well, that's natural. If I went to a foreign country I wouldn't know what to do. You wear shoes in the house over there, don't you? Is it true you lie on the bed with your shoes on?"

"No. No. It isn't. Not usually."

"Oh, well, you see, I wouldn't know that."

They're climbing now, up the side of a conical mountain. Looking out, Cathy sees a small mud-and-brick kiln under a sagging lean-to beside a farmer's house. Above the kiln hangs a string of onions, drying.

"Do you have pottery in your country?"

"Yes, we have."

"Can you do it?"

"I've been learning."

"It takes a long time."

"I know."

"I did a bit at school, but I wasn't good at it. My family aren't potters, I suppose that's why. Some families around here, they've been potters since the Edo period, at least. People like that know the clay. You know what they say, a frog's child is always a frog."

"Omori-san's family are potters too?"

"Oh, yes. They used to make the same as everybody, sesame seed roasters, mortars, kitchen things. But Omori-san went to art school in Kyoto. So did his wife. She's a friend of my wife's from junior high."

"Maybe I'll be able to learn something from Omori-san," says Cathy. "I don't know yet, but I'm going to teach English to

Hayashi-san's children. She's a friend of my teacher's in Tokyo, and she's a friend of Omori-san's, so perhaps I'll be able to meet him, and . . ."

"Really?"cried the taxi driver. "You want to be his deshi?"

"Oh, no! Not exactly!" Immediately Cathy regrets having said anything. She feels a fool. A deshi is an apprentice, no, more than that, a disciple. She doesn't want to be anybody's disciple, though she's seen Omori's work, and it's terrific.

The driver is delighted. "A gaijin deshi! That's amazing! Omori-san will be your sensei, well, well. But I'll bet you don't know how hard it is to be the deshi of a real craftsman! They're tough, I'll tell you! A deshi has to sweep the floor of the workshop for seven years, you know? And after that, mix clay for seven years, and only then . . ."

Cathy knows he's kidding her, but she also knows there's something in what he says. She's heard stories. "I'm not going to be a deshi," she says. "I'm going to teach English. If I get the chance to learn something, too, fine."

"There's no use going into it halfhearted," says the driver severely. Cathy feels he's getting to be a bore, and doesn't reply.

The road broadens to go through a village. A candy shop, with a sign saying it sells stamps. A grocer's shop, with a few boxes of fruit in the shade of an awning. An open-fronted fish shop. They stop for an old man to cross the road, and Cathy sees, on top of a refrigerated fish counter, a bunch of purple irises thrust casually into a cylindrical black-glazed vase, similar to one she's seen in a picture. As the taxi moves again, she turns to look back, not wanting to lose sight of it. Omori's vase on a fish-shop counter, above the rows of silver fish, its shape as pure as theirs.

Mrs. Hayashi is a round-cheeked country housewife in apron and white ankle-socks, but she has the ambitious Japanese mother's fanatic gleam in her eye. Her elder son, Kinichiro, failed his university entrance exam the first time, and is studying for a second try, she explains to Cathy over green tea and bean jelly. He is a lazy boy, perhaps too fond of his motor scooter, but he is looking forward to improving his English under Cathy-san's guidance. Cathy thinks it unlikely that both parts of this statement are true. Jiro, the younger brother, doesn't care for English at all, and is really rather stupid, but doubtless just being in close proximity with Cathy-san will do him good. At this point, both brothers slouch in, Kinichiro blushing and tongue-tied in either language, Jiro a bright-eyed little imp. They all bow, Mrs. Hayashi right down to the floor.

Cathy is to sleep in the back room, which contains nothing but an old-fashioned dressing-table whose mirror, now covered with a brocade cloth, she would almost have to lie on the floor to see herself in, and a vast, lacquered, Buddhist shrine, which occupies the whole of one wall and fully a quarter of the room. However, when Mrs. Hayashi opens the sliding door of the wall closet, Cathy sees that the quilts on which she will lie look fat and comfortable. Even the tiny pillow stuffed with buckwheat husks, which will certainly be as hard as a brick, looks welcoming now in a crisp, white-lace-edged cover.

Cathy thinks how much she would like to take a nap after her long journey, but Mrs. Hayashi is talking to her. "Now, about your pottery," she's saying. "Omori-sensei's family and our family have always been close. Very close," she adds, meaningfully. God knows what it does mean. Probably they've been screwing each other for centuries, thinks Cathy. She's got a good idea what's coming next. "I explained to him that you're Ikeda-san's student in Tokyo, and because Ikeda-san went to college with my sister's husband—and with Mrs. Omori's younger uncle, as it happens—Omori-sensei wouldn't have just anyone in his workshop, Cathy-san—he's kindly agreed to take you on. Isn't that wonderful?" She doesn't wait for an answer. "I don't want to make it sound easy. We had to do a lot of talking. At first he wasn't at all sure. But there you are. You must do everything you can to show him you're sincere. Well! I don't suppose you ever thought you'd get the chance to study with such a famous potter," she concludes triumphantly. "Aren't you lucky?"

Cathy thinks, I should have listened to the taxi driver. She's tired and exasperated. The whole thing is obviously out of control. She's not unfamiliar with the way this happens, and it isn't the first time that she's found herself manoeuvred into the centre of a web of obligations. She should have realised that in the negotiations that have taken place around her since she was first suggested as a tutor for the Hayashi boys, the various elements of her situation, which is really quite simple, would have got all out of proportion. The most important thing, as far as she herself is concerned, is that for a long time she's been fed up with the mediocre teaching jobs she's had since her scholarship ran out, and has been thinking about leaving Tokyo for a while. She loves pottery, but she doesn't yet know if she's dedicated, or even if she has talent, and she has not been longing to study with Omori, who is not nearly as famous as Mrs. Hayashi thinks. Still, she did express interest, and here she is, so it serves her right. If only she could have just got to him first, though! Now it's too late. There's nothing to be done, and if it doesn't work out she'll have to think of something very convincing, or there'll be loss of face and hurt feelings all round.

She sighs and begins to root around in her bag for the presents she's brought. Omori-sensei will have to have a present. She's come loaded with gifts, boxes of cookies, one of which she's already given to Mrs. Hayashi, and two bottles of good Australian wine, from a department store in Tokyo, gorgeously wrapped. One of these she pulls out, and, holding it carefully so as not to shake it anymore than it has already been shaken, follows Mrs. Hayashi.

Follows her out the gate and up the hill, Mrs. Hayashi still in her apron, to what is obviously a potter's place. A five-chamber climbing kiln, a magnificent thing, stretches up the slope towards the house, under the roof of an open-sided shed. Wood is stacked in great piles in the shed too. Several smaller, connected buildings behind must be workshops and storerooms, and maybe the newer one facing them is a gallery.

The house, higher up the hill, is a traditional farmhouse, heavily thatched, with grasses growing out of the thatch in places. It is surrounded by narrow verandahs, with wooden shutters pushed aside to let in the breeze this summer day, and, like a delicate inner shell, paper shoji screens open into its dim rooms.

There's an orchard behind the house, where an old woman in sunbonnet and baggy indigo-dyed pants is wielding a bamboo rake.

The usual farm mess—discarded baskets, plastic buckets, empty fertilizer bags—is compounded by the workshop mess, but there is no sense of disorder. Several women are squatting beside racks of drying pots, pale ochre, turning them to catch the sun. They nod to Mrs. Hayashi and stare at Cathy. A child, a little girl of four or so, stands for a moment in Cathy's path, and then turns and runs up to the orchard.

A man comes towards them from around the corner of one of the workshops. He is thin, fairly tall for a Japanese, and he is wearing stained khaki pants and a T-shirt with the word MUDMAN printed across the chest. He moves with a swinging litheness, and as he comes, he pauses without stopping to scoop up from behind a woodpile another, smaller child, who clings to his neck.

Cathy knows what she thinks of him almost the moment she sets eyes on him. By the time he's in front of her, bowing to her, talking to Mrs. Hayashi, putting down the child, who grabs hold of his pants leg, she knows she wants him. That's all there is to it, she thinks. She doesn't know yet that in some sense that has no logic to it she will always want him, that whatever happens and whoever else she may be with, there will always be times when, perhaps lying in bed in the morning, she will open her eyes and stare at the ceiling and think of him. She doesn't know it, and yet the beginning of that knowledge is in the way she must force herself to take her eyes from his face and look down at the child, who, to the delight of his father and Mrs. Hayashi, is making swipes with his one free hand at a white cabbage moth that flutters just out of reach. The child, afraid while Cathy is there to let go of his grip on his father in order to chase it, bursts into wails of frustration, and is hoisted up onto his father's shoulders, where he sits clutching at handfuls of black hair.

"Oh, sweet, sweet!" cries Mrs Hayashi.

Cathy may look again at the potter, and gratefully she takes in the smooth brown narrowness of his face, traces the shape of the black brows above the long, dark-glinting eyes, of the deep downward lines that appear at the corners of his mouth when he smiles, as he is now, though not at her.

It's all decided. Cathy will help out in the workshop every day except Sunday, and "learn what she can." Mrs. Hayashi is volubly appreciative of the honor, on her behalf. Maybe she will also teach him a little English?

He tries it out. "I will have the exhibition in San Francisco later," he explains, slowly. "I must go to there."

Mrs. Hayashi wants to know if the exhibition has anything to do with the Americans who let the water out of the bath, and, since it does, the whole story is gone over again.

Holding the child's feet, he turns and leads them up to the buildings beside the kiln. In one of them, in a sunny, untidy, earth-floored room, two old men sit on cushions on a wooden platform, before handwheels. They don't look up. On the wheels the clay spreads, rises, bends back upon itself. At the end of the room, apart, is an empty wheel which Cathy assumes is his.

Ducking so the child doesn't bump his head, he takes them into the gallery. Here, on a platform inlaid with tatami mats, are his pots. A tea bowl with a milk-white glaze gathering at the curve in droplets, so that the foot finishes in a plain, unglazed band. A water container, also for the tea ceremony, whose austere grey glaze slips over the rim into a green as deep as a well. A brown bowl which Cathy takes up and holds. Its surface is covered with tiny pores, as if it breathed. Her fingers meet around it, and it seems to have been made for her hands.

There's a sound at the open doorway. A young woman in

apron and white socks, like Mrs. Hayashi's, comes in carrying a tray, which she places on a table, making room for it by pushing aside a jumble of papers and ashtrays.

"My wife," says the potter.

"This is Cathy-san," says Mrs. Hayashi, bowing deeply. "Please be good to her." The words are a formality. Cathy bows, too.

The sensei's wife bows not quite so low.

She's ordinary, thinks Cathy, taking her in from her short permed hair down to her plastic mesh scuffs. Her face is round, flat and pretty. Her bare legs, like millions of other legs, like her husband's in fact, are slightly bandy. Those socks!

As the potter's wife is handing around glasses of cold barley tea, a telephone rings in the distance, back at the house. She looks across to the orchard. "Mother can't hear it," she says. She takes the child from her husband, and, murmuring apologies, backs out of the room. Once outside, she turns and shuffles rapidly down the slope, followed by the little girl, who has been hovering by the door.

"Forgive us for bothering you, sensei, when you're so busy," says Mrs. Hayashi. "Cathy-san will come tomorrow."

"I'll come tomorrow," echoes Cathy, wanting to speak for herself. "And I like your T-shirt," she adds in English.

He looks down, as if he hasn't seen it before. "My American friends presented me. It is a joke." He says this quite seriously, but then he smiles directly at her. Cathy thinks he really looks at her for the first time.

Still, he is the sensei. Cathy starts work on menial tasks. She does sweep the floor, and she keeps the clay from drying out, and she makes tea.

His wife doesn't come up to the workshop again while Cathy is there. Cathy sees her sometimes, walking up and down with the baby on her back to soothe him, beating the bed-quilts that she hangs out of the upstairs windows to air in the morning, or gossiping with the women. Their conversation is animated, but when Cathy overhears it, it always seems to be about somebody's wedding, or about vegetables. Cathy can hardly believe this is the woman who went to art school in Kyoto. And yet she knows, too, that the potter's wife must take most of the practical responsibility for the running of the kiln, the business side. That's how it is in craftsmen's families.

Cathy spends all the time she has between tasks sitting near the potter's wheel. She watches his hands wet with creamy clay, moving up the ridged walls of the pot, forming, smoothing, pinching. He works fast, with absolute concentration. He seldom speaks to her, except to ask her the name of something in English.

Even her orders come mostly from the old men, who worked for his father. They make the pots that are sold in the shops on the highway, and in Takanaka, the nearest town. These are sturdy pieces with simple ash glazes. The sensei's work is something different. It, too, is made under the gaze of his father, whose picture hangs on the workshop wall beside the shelf that holds the Shinto shrine, and under the protection of the gods of the workshop, to whom the sensei makes offerings of sake and lighted candles each morning, but beside the other pots it seems to sing.

In the evenings, Cathy sits with Kinichiro and Jiro at the kitchen table, for the agreed hour and a half. It is a trial to them all. Kinichiro is stolid and silent. Jiro kneels on his chair and bounces up and down and yells "Iya da!" I hate this! When the time, strictly monitored by their mother, is finally up, they fling themselves in front of the television and wrestle in a frenzy of relief.

Cathy sometimes watches a soap opera with Mrs. Hayashi, but she becomes impatient with the long weeping scenes. Generally, she goes to her room and writes letters. She writes to Elaine in Tokyo about the sensei. Night after night, sitting on the floor in front of the shrine, she writes, but most of the letters she tears up the next morning. She's used to talking to Elaine about practically anything, but this is different.

The sensei lets her throw pots. She struggles with the clay, which is of an unfamiliar texture. It seems to have no plasticity. It has a life and will of its own. The old men give her amused glances. She is humiliated.

The sensei laughs. "This is good clay," he says, "but you have to be bold with it. You have to know it well. It comes from this mountain, you know, this mountain we're sitting on." He looks at her hands. "Yes, maybe you should get to know the clay." The old men have been listening, and he says to the younger of them, "Gen-san, let's go!"

The old man shoves his feet into his wooden geta, and Cathy grabs her sneakers. The three of them walk out into the sunshine, the old man stretching. "I'm stiff, Kiyoshi-san," he complains. Cathy envies him for that. It would be unthinkable for her to call this man she wants so much anything but "Sensei." She has never before heard anyone call him by his given name. The sensei stands behind the old man and massages his neck, his shoulders. He presses his thumbs part-way down the sides of the old man's spine, and the old man straightens, giving little sounds of pleasure. The sensei pats his shoulders one last time, and they set off up the stony path that runs behind the house.

Just above the orchard, they meet the sensei's mother coming down, with a basket of roots and herbs on her hip. She bows politely to Cathy and sidles past, averting her face.

They walk up into the shade of the mountain, the sensei going first, and the old man, exhorting himself at every step, "Yoisho! Yoisho!" bringing up the rear. Cathy watches the way the sensei walks. The path gets steeper. It is cold. Cathy looks up and is dazzled by the height of the trees and the glare of the patch of sky at the top. She has to stop for a moment and is disappointed to see that the old man is catching her up. She begins to climb again.

The feeling of the path changes. The undergrowth crowds in, but the path is now defined by rocks. Sometimes she has to clutch at roots and branches. The sensei never looks back, and the old man is tougher than he seems.

They pass under a square wooden arch, and then they're in a clearing, dark and damp, and there is a shrine built into the side of the mountain. In front of it are the stone guardian foxes, a male with a key in his mouth and a female with a cub nestled under her. Offerings have been placed on the ledge in front of the shrine: a handful of rice, some fried tofu, which foxes are said to like, a cup of sake.

The sensei takes some coins from his pocket. Cathy has none, and he gives her a five-yen piece. They throw the coins into the box behind the ledge, ring the bell and clap their hands to attract the attention of the god of the shrine, and bend their heads to pray.

Cathy, who rarely prays, prays: Let me have him.

"Foxes are the messengers of the gods," he tells her.

"I know. I like them."

"They've got magic powers, but they're not always good. They love to torment people. Isn't that right, Gen-san?"

"Yes, indeed," agrees the old man. "You never know where you are with foxes." He sits on a rock, still puffing, and takes out his fan. Cathy's heart lifts when she realises he doesn't want to go any further. He grins at her and says, "I know the clay."

There isn't really very much to see at the clay pit, which is cut into the mountain just off the path that leads from the shrine and down into the village. The sensei is still using a store of clay that was cut a long time ago, and the pit is overgrown, but the striations in the earth where the side of the mountain has been sliced away are clearly visible. He clears a way through the brush and they clamber into the pit.

"Here," he says, "this is the clay." He lays his thin brown hand flat against it, fingers spread, and Cathy does the same. The weight of the mountain presses against her palm. He takes away his hand and thoughtfully rubs his palms together, though the clay is not wet, only heavy with damp. Cathy puts her finger to her nose and breathes in the cold, damp smell of the mountain.

As they walk back, she hears a birdcall she's never heard before, high up in the trees. Gently she touches his arm, just above the elbow. She touches him for a fraction of a second, but she has felt, before her hand moves to point upwards, a reaction in him, a sharp sideways glance from his narrow eyes. He tells her the name of the bird, which she doesn't register. Her mind is numb with hope. They return to the old man and go quite quickly down the mountain.

The clay is still not easy, but she's learning. He sets her to making cylindrical cups for ordinary green tea, and maybe one in ten is all right. She works on the same thing every day, and by evening she's so exhausted that the boys' textbooks seem to float before her unfocused eyes.

"It's the only way," says the sensei. "The hand remembers."

On Sundays Cathy takes her sketchbook out onto the paths around the village. She is filling it with drawings of rice plants and pine branches and red-headed dragon-flies. She draws stone wayside statues, a row of blue-and-white cotton kimono hanging on drying poles at the inn, a tricycle abandoned under a bridge. The people she meets know who she is and bow to her. Sometimes she comes across little gangs of children, who shout "Herro!" and follow her around, giggling and pushing. Once she recognises the potter's daughter, but the child hangs back, sucking her fingers and staring. These Sundays seem very long.

The sensei and his old assistants are working all hours now. Drying pots lie everywhere, lined up in the sun. If there's a sudden shower of rain, everyone runs out and carries the loaded drying boards into the shed. The pots are to be glazed, and the preparation of the glazes is a matter of great complexity. Cathy sieves what she is told to sieve and stirs what she is told to stir. The sensei dips the pots. He twists each one to let the glaze run, or to stop its flow. Watching the swift movement of his wrists, Cathy is mesmerized.

The night firing begins. Mrs. Hayashi lets her off the lessons. The kiln has been packed, with incredible speed, in a rhythm that seems natural to the men and women there, through the late afternoon, finishing by the light of lamps. A small altar has been made on a ledge above the firemouth of the kiln, and offerings of sake and salt, and a branch of leaves from the sacred tree, are laid there. The sensei is worried about damp in the kiln walls, and consults with the old men for a long time. Cathy listens, but she doesn't always understand the accents of the old country people. The potter's wife stands among the women in their baggy trousers, holding the baby. Cathy realises that she will probably be up all night, organising food for the workers who will watch and stoke the kiln. A tide of jealousy rises in her, and it spoils her excitement in the firing. At about midnight she leaves the circle of light and smoke, and the kiln, now panting like a living thing, and feels her way through the darkness to the Hayashis', and quietly lets herself in. She lies absolutely wide awake on her futon all night.

For the next few days there is nothing for Cathy to do. Everything centres around the kiln. The sensei stands quietly for hours, arms folded, staring calmly at it. Once he motions her closer, and stands behind her as she looks through the spy-hole at the fire inside. In spite of the fearsome noise, it seems strangely peaceful. Flames ripple around the stacked pots in translucent waves. The pots glow, miraculously unmoved.

For days more the kiln must cool. Cathy does odd jobs around the workshop. The old men nap under the trees. The sensei chain-smokes. Nobody is thinking of anything but the pots, of their transformation.

On Saturday the kiln is opened. As the pots are brought out, the sensei examines them. Cathy sits on a box and watches. The fire has destroyed some of the pots that could have been most beautiful, and others it has given a beauty that Cathy, at least, could not have anticipated. He hands her a pot of her own. "This is not bad," he says. But Cathy is bitterly dissatisfied. He looks at his own work coolly for the most part, but when Cathy puts out her hand to touch a bowl with a warm, flushed brown glaze, he laughs and says, "It's like a young country girl's sunburned cheek!" and sets it aside for the exhibition.

At the end of the day, Cathy sees him a little way up the hill behind the workshop, breaking failed pots. There's no-one else around. She walks towards him, and stops a little way off. Shards of pottery lie in a heap between them.

He sinks down on his heels, pats his pockets, finds a cigarette. "Well, there's always some tragedy," he says. He smokes, looking up at the mountain. The late afternoon sunlight is caught on its top, and spills down the side like one of his own glazes, but the clearings where the fox shrine and the clay pit must be are completely in shadow.

There is a moment of stillness, and in that moment Cathy feels, for no reason, but with utter certainty, that he is concentrating on her. She thinks about it, then stops thinking and says, "Tomorrow morning I'm going to take my sketchbook up to the fox shrine." He nods, his eyes on the mountain.

Cathy goes home. She eats dinner with Mrs. Hayashi. The boys and their father are out, so she must keep Mrs. Hayashi company in front of the TV until they get back. The screams of the comedians on the Saturday-night variety shows are intolerable. Then they must all have baths in turn, and talk over green tea and fruit around the table together. In her room it's no better. She sits up and turns over the pages of books most of the night.

In the morning, she is at the fox shrine early. She has declined to tell Mrs. Hayashi when she'll be back, and Mrs. Hayashi has insisted she wait and take some rice balls with her, but even so the roof of the shrine still gleams with dew. She walks around for a while, then finds a tree trunk to sit on overlooking the clay pit, and takes out her sketchbook. She draws leaves, fungus, roots. She draws for hours.

She is beginning to be terribly afraid that he will not come, so afraid that it makes her feel sick, when she hears someone climbing the path from the house. She thinks of his mother and her basket, and stands up ready to fly, so she is standing when he comes. He picks up her book and box of pastels, and leads her further up the path to another clearing, where there is sunlight, and dry pine needles blanket the damp earth, and there they lie down and make love.

Cathy, for the whole summer, since the day she came to Matsuno, has known how it would be for her. What amazes her, and makes her cry out, is the emotion that now transforms his face, so that for the first time she sees him as the young man he really is. But he still has presence of mind enough to put his hand gently over her mouth. So, silently, she has him at last.

They straighten themselves up quickly afterwards, for the people who bring offerings to the foxes, and the children who play up and down the paths, are in both their minds. Then they rest against a tree trunk, and he kisses every part of her that he can reach, so she comes undone again. He kisses her fingers, and she his. Now she, too, has potters' fingers, the nails torn and stained. In between kisses, neither of them seems to be able to stop smiling.

This is beyond everything she has allowed herself to imagine, in these months of frantic imaginings.

Then, without warning, there's a rustling sound, a clattering in the trees above, and it starts to rain, hard. The raindrops slant down on them, glittering in the sunlight, and they scramble up, and stand holding each other against the tree till it stops.

"What do you call that?" he asks.

"A sunshower, I suppose."

"Such a simple word," he says, surprised. "In Japanese it's better. We say it's the foxes' wedding. You know, when the fox bride enters her husband's house for the first time, the weather is strange like this, the sun and rain together."

Cathy thinks of an old drawing she's seen of a fox bride, her muzzle demurely down-pointed beneath her bride's white headdress, the padded hem of her wedding kimono swirling around her fox feet. She laughs, and he kisses her.

This is the end. But when they go down to the fox shrine, Cathy throws in her coin and rings the bell and claps her hands and says, under her breath, "Thank you."

The rest of this day, after he has gone home, when she wanders the paths and fills her sketchbook with drawings of a few things done obsessively many times over, and the days of the week that follows, are worse than ever. She is shocked by the longing that overwhelms her, and she now knows how relatively easy to bear was what she felt before.

In the workshop, their eyes never meet when anyone else is there, but one day, as she is gazing at him, at his back, with what she realises, too late, must be an all too obvious intensity, she notices the old man, Gensuke, looking at her, and she puts her head down over her work, ashamed of her betrayal.

When they meet again, the next Sunday, he comes later than before, out of breath from hurrying. Their lovemaking is rougher, but the playing afterwards even more gentle. She strokes his slender body under his shirt, kisses the black hair that falls across her face.

He's brought something with him, wrapped in newspaper, and he retrieves it from between the roots of the tree and gives it to her. It is the brown bowl she held on the first day.

Standing in front of the fox shrine, she is dazed. There is nothing to say.

When she sees him in the workshop on Monday, the little girl is sitting by his side, dangling her legs over the platform where he bends at his wheel. He looks up and smiles, but the lines that emphasize the thinness of his face seem somehow longer, or deeper, than before. She sits at her wheel and tries to start work, but there is no strength in her hands, and they look at each other helplessly for a while, until he gets up and carries the child out.

She starts to write to Elaine again, but what she writes, when she reads it over, is barely coherent. She means to write afresh, but the next evening, when she gets home, Mrs. Hayashi says, "A letter came from your friend in Tokyo."

Elaine is going to Kyushu this coming Saturday to "tie up some ends," she says, of her endless research—and she can make a little detour on the way. Cathy takes the day off, and gets the early bus into Takanaka with the farm women.

In the coffee shop near the station, Elaine says, "Okay, I don't have much time. You want to just cut to where I tell you you're out of your mind?"

"I am, I think." It's difficult to form the words. And then the relief of saying them, of being able to speak about it at all, brings her near to losing control.

"My God, these sensei!" exclaims Elaine.

"I know, but he isn't like that!" He's done nothing to deserve Elaine's indignation.

"Where can it go, Cathy? Think! What about his wife? Is she a village girl?"

"I'm sure it was arranged. You know what these places are like, Elaine." What good is this pleading?

"So?" says Elaine. "That's neither here nor there, and you know it." She's silent for a while, and then she says, "Except it makes things worse. Can't you see that? Cathy, there's the ancestral kiln. The farm, the house. The wife, and don't forget she holds the purse strings. Her family. The little heir, the aged mother, the old retainers. For heaven's sake. Is this man going to divorce the whole village? Is he going to waste a single moment even thinking about it?"

"There are mistresses," says Cathy, trying to smile. "That's a tradition, too."

"You aren't a goddamn geisha."

"There are," she says stubbornly.

"Not gaijin mistresses, baka. Not in Matsuno there aren't. Not even in this metropolis." She looks around, to make the point. Everyone in the coffee shop is watching them, fascinated. "So, how often does he get up to Tokyo? Twice a year?"

Cathy puts her head in her hands. Useless to try to explain, even to Elaine, how far she would go.

"Get out of there," says Elaine softly.

After Elaine's train leaves, Cathy spends the rest of the day in Takanaka, sitting in the temple garden, walking in the grounds of the castle. She buys postcards, but later they will seem to be of places she has never been.

Before going back to Matsuno, she buys three boxes of the town's specialty, a kind of sponge cake filled with red bean paste. One for the Hayashis. One for Gensuke and the retainers; she can't help smiling at the word. One for the Omori household. These are obligatory.

It's late by the time the bus drops her off outside the fish shop in Matsuno. She walks up the hill to the Hayashis', and then, on an impulse, turns towards the pottery. She will just call in and hand over the cake. It is polite. She might not even see him.

The path up the slope is uneven, and she stubs her sandalled toe several times before she gets to the house. It's a hot night, and the shutters and paper screens are still open. Cathy realises she's never been inside this house, but tonight it's lit up like a stage. She stops. Now she's looking straight into the main room. He's there, sitting cross-legged on the tatami in a blue-and-white cotton kimono, his black obi slung low around his hips. Cathy has always wanted to see him like this. She has often lusted after slim men in kimono, especially on festival nights, when they stick fans in their obis at the back, and swagger. He looks wonderful. But what she feels now is so far beyond that old lust, that she experiences it as pain.

His wife comes into the room, carrying a bottle of sake and a glass on a tray, which she puts down in front of him. She is wearing, not a cotton kimono—that would become her—but what looks like a polyester calf-length robe, in some awful floral. Then, as Cathy watches, he reaches up, without raising his head, takes his wife's hand, and—tiredly, or so it seems to Cathy—holds it against his cheek. His wife looks down at him, with what expression Cathy cannot, does not want to, see.

Cathy stumbles back down the path, surrounded by darkness. Something is pounding in her chest and rising up in her throat. Somehow she makes it back to the Hayashis' house.

Inside, Mrs. Hayashi is waiting for her. Cathy gives her the cakes—not graciously, but she manages. Mrs. Hayashi accepts them with reserve. It is not Cathy's imagination that Mrs. Hayashi's manner towards her has become cooler. Cathy doesn't care. She goes to her room, shuts herself up with the shrine, falls to the floor and rocks herself back and forth, perhaps for hours.

The next morning, Sunday, before breakfast, her mother calls. Even Mrs. Hayashi leaves the room for this occasion. It's just an ordinary, "How are you, darling?" sort of phone call, but Cathy comes out of the room and says, "Mrs. Hayashi, my elder brother is very ill. I have to go home at once." Cathy has no elder brother, but she's said it now, and she can only hope Mrs. Hayashi has forgotten the details of her original interrogation on points relating to family.

The look on Mrs. Hayashi's face is very scrutable. It is one of unadorned relief. But Cathy feels herself trembling, and Mrs. Hayashi, seeing this, recovers herself. With exclamations of sympathy, she hurries off to make a lunchbox for Cathy to take on the train.

Cathy packs. The brown bowl, which she has had to keep wrapped, out of Mrs. Hayashi's sight, she places safely in the centre of her bag, but she does not look at it. Then she takes the boxes of cakes and once more walks up to the big house.

His wife is at an upstairs window, beating her futon with a rattan paddle. When she sees Cathy, she lays it down and disappears. Cathy hears her shuffling into her shoes in the entranceway, and then she comes out.

"Good morning," says Cathy. "Is the sensei here, or is he in the workshop?"

"Neither. He's away. He's in Takanaka, delivering pots."

Cathy feels her breath stop. Then she says, in a rush, "I have to go back to Tokyo and then home to my country. My elder brother is ill. Please tell the sensei this. Tell him I said thank you, and I will write a letter."

"I'm sorry you've had bad news. I will tell him."

Cathy thrusts the boxes into her hands. The sensei's wife, with smiles that convey a very proper degree of regret and concern, says all she ought to say, leaving nothing out: thank you for your helpfulness, take care of yourself, have a safe journey, give our best wishes to your family, and our prayers for your brother's health. Goodbye.

Cathy backs away, still bowing, then turns and walks as slowly as she can make herself down the slope. He is in Takanaka. Had she gone up the mountain later this morning, he would not have come. Whether this makes what she is doing easier or harder she does not know.

When she's about halfway, an outburst of beating begins, and the sound, ferocious, exultant, follows her down the hill.

9

The Mole Game

THIS IS A WORLD of high walls and camellia hedges. Tomokazu's favourite camellia is one called wabisuke, whose flowers do not fade, but drop upon the instant, like the heads of fallen warriors, he says. Little can be seen of the house. This is not even the house Tomokazu means when he says, "my house." That is the family and their business, not this place.

There are scents—plum blossom, daphne, or on summer evenings the headiness of gardenia, every flower in its season—and there are sounds—of morning sweeping and the tinkle of a glass windchime, which will be broken by the first typhoon of autumn—but of the house itself, there's only a glimpse of curved silver-grey tile above the clipped pine trees. This is where Liz's mother-in-law lives, she who sweeps the paths every morning and hangs out her washing before seven, while Liz, as she certainly suspects, is still in bed. And Liz's father-in-law, not yet retired but day by day more absorbed in his vases.

He shows Liz pictures in huge books with brocade covers.

The books are protected by boxes whose lids are held closed with ivory pegs. Here is a radish-shaped vase that came from the Dragon Fountain kiln in China eight hundred years ago, and its colour is the most perfect of all colours, "blue sky after rain." And here is a vase with phoenix-shaped ears that was owned by the Ashikaga and then the Tokugawa shoguns, the one that the Emperor Gosai called "A Thousand Voices." Liz thinks her father-in-law would give his life to own one of these transcendent objects, even for one day, but his own are pretty good, too, and he lets her hold them, not quite lifting them off the silk cloth spread on the tatami, turning them in her hands. She doesn't have to pretend to admire them, and she knows this pleases him. Tomokazu is proud that they are in the house, but he has no time to study them, and his younger sister, who worships only her tennis racket, couldn't care less. Liz likes being part of this paradox. There is nothing she can do, however, to surprise Tomokazu's grandmother, a tiny bundle of bones wrapped in grey kimono, to whom she takes care to bow deeply whenever they meet, but almost never dares to speak.

In earlier times, Liz would have lived in this house, too. She would have been "the bride of our house," and once she had entered that tall roofed cypress gate, with the family name in fine calligraphy on a wooden plate attached to one of its posts, that would have been it for her. Well, no, it wouldn't have happened like that. They wouldn't have let her in to begin with. It's only because this is today, and the Yamamotos of today are decent people with liberal ideas (though Liz is not sure about Grandmother), that she is permitted to exist at all as Tomokazu's wife, and to live with him in their own three-room rented apartment, a good twenty minutes' walk away.

Tomokazu has started his own family register, and Liz is entered in it. Not, it is true, in the space where a wife who had transferred from her father's register would be entered, but, being a foreigner, in a sort of footnote.

She doesn't feel like complaining about this, since she's so glad the Yamamotos have been unable to investigate her family background the way they would have if they could have got their hands on her father's register—that is, if such a thing had existed, if she had been Japanese. They would have ferreted out all the secrets her family had to hide, any whiff of bad blood. Bad blood! Genetic weakness! Alcoholism! Improvidence! Liz has to smile. They had to take her on trust, not a good idea, but what could they do? They had to deal with it, with what Tomokazu wanted, and take her in.

She has tried to play her part. The Yamamotos had the wedding the way they wanted it. Liz wore a frothy white dress chosen from a rental catalogue by Tomokazu's mother and aunt, with a little veiled white hat tilted coquettishly over one eye, in the manner of Empress Michiko, and even white lace mittens. Tomokazu's boss and his wife were official go-betweens, Tomokazu's old college classmates sang their school song, and there were dozens of speeches. It was rather restrained by some standards, as Tomokazu's parents are not the kind of people to go in for theatricality, coloured lights, electric organ music, clouds of dry ice, and that sort of thing. It's just as well. Liz has been to weddings where the life stories of bride and groom were projected on slides for everyone to see, starting with baby snaps. Liz has no pictures, as it happens, but she's seen them sometimes, stuffed into her mother's drawers, or fluttering from between the pages of books, and doubts they would have been suitable.

Visiting Dad, Roger that is, at the rehab unit, perhaps? (Why did they think of taking a picture there? Why did they think of anything?) Or sitting on his bony saronged knee with one of the inevitable sunburned bare-breasted women hanging over his shoulder, and all their eyes screwed up against the light out there in that godforsaken place where they were building the house of mud bricks that never got finished. Alternatively, her mother, Gill, on occasion known as Ranee, lying across that creep whose shifty and all too material hand between her legs Liz can still feel in her worst dreams, Liz herself sitting on the grass at their feet, spotty and limp-haired, her head sullenly bent so the camera can't see her eyes. So in touch with her feelings, as they always encouraged her to be, that she could barely speak. How to edit these rocky pictures into the smoothly flowing stream of remembrances that is Tomokazu's life? Tomokazu as a baby, on his first shrine visit, wrapped in brocade in his grandmother's arms; his earnest first day at school; his kendo club, with Tomokazu in kimono, lithe and confident; the family all in tweed knickerbockers, for God's sake, and climbing boots, on the top of some beautiful mountain. Impossible.

Yes, the wedding could have been a lot worse. At the end, they all stood in a row in front of a gold screen painted with cranes, for long life and happiness. Tomokazu's parents looked splendid, his mother in sleek black kimono embroidered in gold and silver at the hem, and Tomokazu couldn't stop smiling. Liz felt very hot and sticky, and the makeup they put on her seemed to be sliding off her face, but she thinks she did all right at the bowing and thanks, as all the guests filed past. She kissed Cathy and Elaine, because suddenly she just felt like it, and everyone thought that was sweet and lent an exotic touch.

She knows Tomokazu will never leave her. For one thing, Japanese men hardly ever do, no matter what. For another, he loves her. And the days when his parents could send you home with a three-and-a-half-line note saying you had failed to fit in with the ways of the house are fortunately over. Not that they would know where to send her. Gill wrote to them before the wedding, a letter dictated by Liz over the telephone, on fairly clean paper, but she isn't at that address anymore.

Anyway, Liz is getting on reasonably well with her mother-in-law. She doesn't always do as her mother-in-law would wish, but she never openly disagrees. This is the compromise she's worked out for herself, and she's stuck to it, somehow. It's one of the hardest things she's ever done. Also, she asks her mother-in-law for recipes. They all seem to have the same things in them, soy sauce, sake, and so forth, so it's hard to keep them straight, and she can never remember which end of the plate the head of the fish should point to, though there's definitely a right end and a wrong end, but the asking is the important thing, and she is learning. Sometimes she thinks her mother-in-law even takes a certain pride in her. After all, she was a research student at Tokyo University. The one indisputable fact they know about her, and it's a winner. Her mother-in-law always tells people that.

When Liz came to Japan, the last thing she imagined was that she would marry a Japanese. Or anyone. She wanted to study, in peace and quiet, far away from everything, that was all. She did study a lot, at first. She sat up late even on the coldest nights of her first winter, fingerless gloves on her hands, her feet warmed by the heater under the table, and her bent back (the chill air finding the gap where her sweater parted from her trousers) freezing. A man with a pair of wooden clappers and a boy with a lantern used to go by at the same time each night, chanting "Hi no Yojin!" Take care of your fires! She liked to think of the people around putting out their gas fires and retiring under their quilts. But she did not retire. She sat up till all hours, the kanji blurring on the page, but still steadily taking notes till she had finished what she had set out to do.

Once, in her first year, when Cathy and Elaine were going to the local festival, and you could actually hear the big drums in the distance, the sexiest sound in the world, said Elaine, she refused to go because she'd brought home a lot of photocopies from the library and promised herself she'd finish reading them over the weekend. They were astonished. "You can hear the taiko!" cried Cathy. "You can hear them! Those drums are being played by beautiful sweaty young men with almost no clothes on, for God's sake! Liz!"

But that only made her stubborn. She wanted to see the taiko players, and the men carrying the portable shrine, who'd be wearing little enough, too. Probably the same shy, long-muscled boys she liked to watch carrying boxes of squid at the market, or going into the bathhouse at night, and coming out pink-faced and scrubbed, their black hair damp and shiny. She wanted to see them very much. But it seemed very important to her then to deny herself what she wanted.

They all thought so much about sex in those days. That is, Liz thought and Cathy and Elaine acted. The three of them had rooms near each other—that was because Elaine had got there first and helped Cathy find hers, and then Cathy had helped Liz. On a Saturday or Sunday morning, if Liz dropped in on Cathy, say, she would often find her cooking breakfast for someone. It was usually someone polite and young, someone who was doing his doctorate and could expect to be at his professor's beck and call and very poor and unable to think of marriage for years, or taking his law exams for the third time and likely to fail again. He was always sweet-faced ("They're all completely out of it, these guys," said Elaine fondly) and very happy to be there having his breakfast cooked, Western-style, and he was usually sitting in the place Liz liked to sit and talk, in the morning sun, so she would just say hello and leave and go back home and do some hand-washing or something, and work.

Some of these boys really fell in love, and some of them hung around for ages. Liz couldn't help disapproving of the way Cathy and Elaine just let them do that. Some of them seemed to think they were engaged. One came back from studying in Europe looking for Cathy years later, when she was living in the country. He thought she had waited for him, though it had never occurred to him to send as much as a postcard to confirm. He was very upset, and he had found Liz and threatened suicide, and she had had to call his elder sister and get her to come and take him away.

If she hadn't promised herself that she'd work, Liz would sometimes go out with Cathy and Elaine. They liked to go on bar crawls in Shinjuku, and they knew lots of little bars all over. Cathy would say, "Let's go to that flamenco bar," or Elaine would say, "How about the one with the Mama-san from Kyushu who knows all the folksongs?" There was an Okinawan bar where the Mama-san sat with them and got terribly drunk one night on Okinawan liquor, and told them the story of her life, which was tragedy from start to finish, and cried all over Liz, to her horror. "But you are so young," she wept. Cathy and Elaine were amused. "She does that all the time," they said. "It's her thing." Liz hated it. There was a jazz bar where the woman wore a white flower behind her ear like Billie Holiday, and had no front teeth. There was a literary bar where all the customers wore black berets and men in women's kimono lingered in the shadows at the foot of the stairs. At all of these places, Cathy and Elaine had long conversations with people they met, and even seemed to understand the sort of jokes and puns and nonsense that people went on with, which left Liz gaping. Once she whispered to Elaine, "You understand all this?" And Elaine said, "Are you kidding? But it's the best way to improve your Japanese. You've got to stop sounding like a textbook, Liz!" They usually ended up with a trail of men following them through the dark lanes, and then tumbling, laughing and unconcerned, into a taxi on the main street, leaving the guys, sulking or disconsolate, behind on the pavement, in the neon glare. It was the boys from the library that they liked to bring home.

Liz began to go with them when they went they went dancing with Elaine's friend Larry and his friends, all Japanese gay guys. "I'm the original rice queen," said Larry, and Liz learned a new expression in her own language. She worried somewhat about the discos they went to, which might be on the fifth floor of some ramshackle sixties building that looked as if all the fire exits would be locked, and once you got inside, what with the darkness and the mirrors, you would never ever find your way out if there were an earthquake, say. But usually, after a while, she forgot to worry, because it was such fun to dance. Larry said she was a great dancer, which no-one had ever said before. One night, there was a sumo wrestler, in kimono and with straw zori on his huge feet. He danced solemnly with Liz, and made the flimsy floor shake. All sorts of things can happen, thought Liz.

Something changed her, and now she thinks she knows what it was. It was finding out about Elaine. It was finding out that Elaine was what she herself was supposed to be, and after all, was not: a scholar. A real scholar, a born scholar. It took time. How was Liz to know? There was nothing about Elaine of the bright child Liz found in herself, the child who had always clung to her A grades as evidence, if all else failed, that the gods loved her. Elaine loved her subject, her corner of Buddhist history, her thesis topic, her old monk. That was it. She didn't have to sacrifice anything for it, because it was part of her, she possessed it. None of the running around she did made any difference to that. When she turned to her work it was with a kind of grace, and then she worked long and hard. Longer and harder even than Liz.

Elaine introduced Liz to a foreign students' study group that met in someone's house out on the Toyoko line. Most of the members were American graduate students like Elaine, but very unlike her in one respect. Liz was appalled by their hunger. Each was desperate to stake a claim to one of the few jobs there would be for them back home, and they were so aggressive in debate that she was thankful her outsider status made her invisible to them. They were mostly men, from Harvard and Columbia and Stanford, and before the evening's paper was read they always talked excitedly about the late-night sex shows on TV. After the paper, they got down to tearing it apart. Their subjects were even more boring than her own, carefully chosen to fill the narrowest of gaps between the theses of their predecessors, and to avoid the complexity that risks failure. For example, the influence of minor bureaucrat X on the policy of the ministry of Y, during a five-year period of optimum inactivity. Liz was astonished at the savagery such innocent subjects could provoke in listeners intent on proving the hopeless stupidity of everyone else and the ineffable brilliance of themselves. Elaine didn't seem to mind the carnage. Liz loathed it.

"Why do you go?" asked Cathy. "I quit. Those guys are such a pain. You notice how many of them have Japanese girlfriends who do their translations and typing for them? How far do you think they'd get without that?"

"If I got a Japanese boyfriend, would he help?"

"What do you think?"

Elaine laughed, too, but without resentment, and said, "Who needs it?"

Well, when Liz met Tomokazu in the British Council library, where he was studying English and she was looking for a novel, to take her mind off the fact that her work was going very, very badly, she wasn't thinking about any of this. She just wanted to forget the whole thing for a while, and Tomokazu helped. She responded to his eager smile and attempts at conversation, and somehow, though she had no idea how to flirt with him, which was what Cathy would have done, her responses seemed to please him. He wouldn't go away, and she didn't want him to.

She realises now how deliberate and seriously considered was his courtship. She gave him a very hard time—she knows that, she even knew it then, while she was doing it—but he overcame her objections one by one, and somehow managed to get her through all the stages, and now she thinks of it as a wonderful time. She has a photo taken of them both in the Meiji shrine garden, when the irises were in bloom. She remembers how he set up the tripod and the timer, and ran towards her to get himself in position. He stood very straight beside her, looking at the camera, not even holding her hand. This was just after they had first slept together. It seemed incredible to her, this formality in public, after what they shared, beyond all expectation, in bed. It touched her, too. If she is to be honest, it excited her more than anything else ever had.

Gradually, she stopped fighting him. She began to understand that if she continued to see him, and there was no way she wouldn't, then she would end up marrying him. There was really no other possibility, given the kind of people they were. How could she have ever thought there was? She accepted it. Then she found she wanted it, and knew herself to be happy. And young. It was amazing!

She didn't stop being a very serious person, though. One thing she did was, she went to the bookshop and, not looking the clerk at the cash register in the eye, bought a mook—a magazine-book, a large, glossy thing—on sex. She thought she ought to familiarize herself with the vocabulary. There were pages and pages of positions, all with wonderful names: double camellia, floating bridge, return of the swallow, entwined pine needles. Her favourite was the disheveled peony, though it turned out to be not very easy to do. Tomokazu said not everyone knew those things now—maybe he hadn't, though he didn't say—and was very impressed.

She didn't stop worrying. She'd calmed down a lot, it's true, and wasn't so critical and touchy, but still, the worries were there in the background. Earthquakes. That was an old one, but now that it looked as if she might live here more or less forever, in for the long haul, as Elaine said, it returned full force. Could she live forever with earthquakes? And there were other things. Dying in Japan, for instance, and being cremated the way they do it, so that the bones are still there and the family has to pick them up with chopsticks. Could she pick over Tomokazu's bones? Oh, never! What about her own? The thought made her feel ill. She has never told anyone about this worry. For heaven's sake, plenty of time to think about that, they'd say. Young and in love and brooding over bones, over death. Liz! She has kept it to herself.

Other things seem to be somehow working themselves out. For instance, once upon a time she thought it wouldn't be possible for her to marry anyone with whom she didn't share a complete understanding of language. But it turns out to be better this way. There are some subjects she and Tomokazu can't fight about, because neither of them has the vocabulary, so they just have to give up. That's one thing. And there's never any point in saying, "But when you said that you really meant this." It would be ridiculously confusing. Which isn't to say they don't fight. Liz knows it's impossible for him not to fight with her sometimes. But the worst thing he has ever said to her is, "You're too logical!" He means it as a criticism. That's a laugh, after she's spent her life trying to be thought logical, as a woman. But here, mere logic is considered narrow and inhuman. It's a relief, in a way. If he's upset about something, he says, "Please understand me." This is irritating, because it puts her immediately in the wrong if she tries to argue, but it's certainly disarming, and she has even tried it herself once or twice. It seems to work. On the whole, they get along pretty well as long as she never says anything mean about his mother. He looks so hurt at that, and says, "But she is my mother. She borned me. She grew up me," and makes her feel really terrible.

Actually, she loves the way he speaks English, which he does quite often with her. She loves it when he calls toes "footfingers," and when she found out he thought "suite" was "sweet", as in "honeymoon sweet," she laughed, and he blushed, but really she liked his way much better.

They don't always think the same things are funny. The other day she was reading the TV programme. "Oh, listen to this!" she said. "There's this terrific drama! 'A housewife on vacation with her family meets her former lover. They had once attempted double suicide together, and now that their love has been rekindled, he suggests they attempt it again.' Great! I love it!"

"How is that funny?" asked Tomokazu.

They do cry at the same things, though.

Before she was married she thought it might be strange living with one other person, because she never had before. She thought it might not suit her. But it does. There are all sorts of sayings about husbands, such as that a good husband is healthy and absent. As a matter of fact, Tomokazu is often absent, and she has to try not to be upset when he comes home late. She hates it that he has to be out drinking so often, entertaining bloated, red-faced foreign businessmen (that's how she thinks of them, though it probably isn't fair). She hates it when he comes home drunk, even slightly. Sometimes he brings her things, and she doesn't know whether to be mad, or what. One night he brought her a soft toy, a pig, with KISS MY SNOUT on its T-shirt. Another time he brought her a boiled crab. It gave her a funny feeling to think of him as one of many drunks buying a crab from the back of a truck parked by the station late at night. Then there was the night she thought he wasn't coming home at all. He'd fallen asleep on the train and gone round and round the Yamanote line heaven knows how many times before he woke up. She looks at the older men on the train sometimes and thinks of how Tomokazu will inevitably take on that weary look they have, if he goes on like this.

He rather prides himself on being a modern husband, although he still has some way to go. One morning, helping her change the sheets, he said, reflectively, "I never knew this happened."

"You didn't?"

"No. Always just suddenly appeared the new sheets."

"Oh, really? Just appeared, did they?" Irony is always lost on Tomokazu, however, so she only shook her head and handed him a pillowcase.

He's not entirely unpractical. When she was packing their earthquake kit, and she asked him which flashlight to pack, he said, "The one with the heavy head, in case you have to kill." Liz had pinned her hopes on the official brochure, and she'd memorized the escape route to the nearest designated park, and taken comfort from the little cartoon figures showing how well everything would work there, carrying buckets to and from the water tap, and fanning fires with pots of rice cooking over them, but this gave her pause. She thought he might be joking, but she didn't want to go into it, so she obediently packed the flashlight with the heavy head. It's a really superior earthquake kit now, with everything in it, including changes of underwear and a compass.

It is also thanks to Tomokazu that she has grasped the function of the cockroach house, a cardboard box with drawings on the sides of happy little cockroaches waving from curtained windows. "See," he said, "They can't leave. The floor is covered with glue." Liz was horrified, but now she has to admit the effectiveness of it.

Husbands who spend too long in the kitchen are called "cockroach husbands," but in spite of this, Tomokazu likes to be there and to be useful. He does on occasion offer some interesting information, such as that mackerel are not so fatty in the summertime. He peers over her shoulder and says things like, "only a teardrop of sesame oil." She doesn't mind this, except when he says his mother tops and tails bean sprouts individually (which Liz has no reason to doubt is true), and then she tells him where to get off.

She used to hate cooking, especially in those huge messy kitchens in the places where her parents lived, where there always seemed to be fifteen clumsy people chopping up woody carrots into lumps to go with heaps of brown rice, and a cat licking its bottom on the table. This is different. She's learning something, and when she looks at the big jars of green plum wine she's made herself and stored beneath the trapdoor in the kitchen floor, she feels proud, like a housewife from a different age.

She is a housewife, really, because she doesn't have a real

job. Her scholarship ran out a long time ago, and though she still works on her thesis she no longer feels any sense of urgency about it. She started it and she would like to finish, but that moderate degree of satisfaction is all she expects of it. Sooner or later she'll probably have to teach, because that's what gaijin do, if they have no business sense, but she doesn't think she'd be very good at it, so she keeps putting it off. She does some private tutoring, and that gives her money of her own. In any case, she has complete control of Tomokazu's salary, in the Japanese way, and gives him an allowance for his daily expenses, which is getting to feel less and less odd. She is quite frugal, and good at saving. That comes naturally to her, since she has never had much money and never acquired any real idea of how to spend it. What her friends have always derided as a hopeless lack of imagination scores her quite a few points with Tomokazu's family, though recently his mother offered to take her to the sales and, once there, steered her in the direction of some respectable designer skirts. This has somehow led to her buying a leather handbag and having her hair trimmed. She doesn't mind. She might as well look the part. She might even get to be good at it, be a proper housewife, bossy and sensible, a materfamilias. She might have a baby.

People are already asking her about it, and she and Tomokazu are not doing anything to prevent it, but so far there is no baby. Tomokazu's cousin says, "Why not? Maybe Tomokazu doesn't know how to make a baby?" This is a Japanese idea of a joke.

Liz tries not to let it get to her. She tells herself it's only the other side of a frankness that she has learned something about, one way and another. Just before she was married, she went to visit some friends in a country town, people she knew, not intimately, from before she came to Japan, when the husband was studying at her university, and she used to help him with his English essays, and he helped her with her Japanese. They took her for a drive, to see something interesting, they said. She remembers they went on a highway, like any other highway, where small factories encroached upon scrappy farms, and there was a huge driving range, surrounded by walls of netting, and littered with masses of golfballs like snowdrifts. They turned off here, drove not far away from the highway, and parked outside a shrine. "Because you're getting married," said her friend's wife. Liz didn't get the idea until they went through the torii gate, and then she did. There were phalluses everywhere. Inside the simple shrine building there were dozens of them, all sizes, carved ones and pieces of wood that just happened to look like phalluses, and one really huge red lacquered one that stood taller than Liz herself, and had pride of place by the altar. The three of them respectfully clapped hands and said a prayer just as you would at an ordinary shrine—at least, Liz supposed her friends said a prayer, though she herself was too astonished to be capable of formulating one. In the garden, instead of ordinary garden stones, there were stone phalluses. A naturally-shaped one, as thick as three fence-posts, leaned horizontally over a pond, and dripped water, a languid fountain. A group of middle-aged farmers' wives on a bus trip were playing around it, splashing each other with handfuls of the water for luck, and laughing like schoolgirls. Liz tried to imagine her grandmother's branch of the Country Women's Association in their place, and failed. At the shop a young man in pure white kimono sold her a postcard with a picture of the big lacquered one being carried in a portable shrine on the shoulders of the crowd on festival day. It stuck out at both ends in a way that could only be called cute. "Now you will be happy," said her friend's wife with satisfaction, as they got back in the car. At least, Liz thought, I was right to buy the sex mook.

Recently, her mother-in-law has remarked that it might be a good idea to go to a shrine for getting pregnant. Liz is not against this. There's a shrine or a temple for everything, for every possible human worry, and from the beginning she's appreciated that, although the very existence of a shrine has sometimes drawn her attention to a worry she didn't even know she had.

Once, exploring, she and Tomakazu came across a temple where a lot of old ladies were praying. "What's this one for?" asked Liz.

"They want a good old-age time," said Tomokazu. "They're praying to be strong, praying their daughters-in-law won't have to take care of them, you know, change their diapers." Liz felt chilled. These old ladies would have all been daughters-in-law. They would know the kinds of things that could happen. But where does she herself fit into this terrible vision? She and her pretty, sturdy mother-in-law?

Generally, though, she finds it comforting, the way the Japanese religions deal with life, and the passing of time. She likes the way the New Year starts out, with everything fresh, and a name for everything: the first meal, the first love-making, her mother-in-law's first tea ceremony.

She enjoys throwing beans around the house in February

and shouting, "Devils out! Good fortune in!" The thought of the ancestors coming back from the dead at O-Bon is beautiful to her. Her mother-in-law puts miniature vegetables, spirit food, before the household shrine. There's dancing in the schoolyard round a drum tower, and fireworks all over the place, and at the end the paper lanterns floating on the pond, lighting the spirits back, slowly sinking one by one.

She no longer knows when Easter is, and ignores the kind of Christmas they have in the department stores as far as possible, but at the same time she now sees a point to all religions, which she never did before. Maybe it has to do with growing up, and having something to lose.

Tomokazu's attitude seems to be rather businesslike. He has described the sun deity Amaterasu Omikami to her as "the top-ranked goddess," and when she asked him about the relationship between the vast black-lacquered household shrine his mother keeps with such care, and the family tombs in the grounds of a faraway temple, he replied, "It's sort of a branch office."

And yet, once, after praying, he turned to her and said, "I never prayed till I met you."

At some shrines there are antique markets on Sunday mornings. Liz likes to go to these, although it's hard to make Tomokazu get up early enough. You have to be really early to get the good things. She buys old kimono. "What do you want them for?" asks Tomokazu, puzzled. She hasn't said yet, but she's thinking of cutting some of them up into little pieces to make a baby quilt. She has bought a book about patchwork. Probably her mother-in-law will think it's unhygienic and try to give her something new with sweet cartoon animals on it, but Liz has this vision of her baby lying in a shaft of sunlight under a quilt of many colours of old brocade, shot through here and there with gold thread, and that's what she's going to have. If.

Some gaijin she's met say they wouldn't want to have babies in Tokyo. It's too crowded, they say, the air is too dirty. All the places Liz lived as a child had endless trees and grass and fresh air, and she can't wait to have a baby in this city. She sees the little children rushing through the busy stations with their season tickets and tinkling lucky charms attached to their satchels and admires the way they dash, chattering, through the crowds, and hop on and off trains. Her child will be like that, a lively, competent city child, in a city where it's safe to be a child on the streets and in the subways. Her child will be the opposite of the child Liz. Her child will be cheerful and unafraid.

People say children here have a tough life because they have to study so hard. But Liz herself studied hard, and at least she'll see to it that her child does it for reasons that make sense. If you have to study to get places, well, there are worse things than that. A lot of kids in the back blocks of the world would be glad of the opportunity. Her child might even enjoy studying. If she inherits anything from Liz at all she might be good at it. If she likes, she can have one of those desks Liz has seen in the department stores, almost like a spaceship, with a built-in globe of the world that lights up, a calculator, an electric pencil sharpener and a cassette deck. Anything. But she will never have to study to escape being who she is.

Thinking about this child somehow fills Liz with confidence. Probably if she does get pregnant she'll find plenty to worry about, but the one thing she never doubts is that her child will be properly loved. And everything will be done right.

At the first shrine visit her mother-in-law will hold the baby in its brocade robe, probably the same one Tomokazu wore, and Tomokazu will do his thing with the tripod and the timer, and there will be a picture for the family album. Emperor and Empress dolls and all their retainers will sit in gorgeous rows every doll's festival day, with offerings set before them, pink and white cakes, and thimble-size cups of sweet sake. And when the child is three they'll put her in kimono with a red silk vest and take her to the Meiji Shrine, walking with all the other parents and children up that long path, the light falling through the dark branches of the cedars and catching the bright ornaments dangling from every little girl's shiny head. For Liz's child, for Tomokazu's child, all will be as it should be.

First, the baby has to be born.

Liz has decided to take action. Cathy has found, through a couple of gaijin she talks to in the changing room at the pool, a gynecologist who speaks some English and is supposed to be "very good." Liz hasn't been to a doctor of any kind for years, and the thought makes her nervous, but she hasn't told Tomokazu or her mother-in-law. Tomokazu would worry and want to consult his mother. His mother would certainly get on the phone to his aunt and to all their joint network, a truly formidable list, and come up with an introduction to "the most famous specialist in Tokyo," who would agree to see her as a particular favour to whichever of their friends had recommended him. Her mother-in-law would go with her to see him, and indeed, Liz would need her help with all the gynecological vocabulary. Then she'd be in the clutches of this doctor for the rest of her life, since she could never stop going to him, once everyone had gone to so much trouble to find him for her, and she'd never have any secrets, even the most intimate, from her mother-in-law ever again. So she gets on the train and goes way across town, and the farther the better.

The waiting room is like an oven. There are about fifty women in there, and three big heaters, as if they all need incubating. Liz takes off her jacket, but after a few minutes she's sweating. The other women look unbothered, even the pregnant ones. Most of the young women who are not obviously pregnant have older women with them. Liz wonders whether the ones who are alone are seeing about abortions. There are two gaijin women across the room, speaking French, but they don't look at Liz, and she begins to wish she'd asked Cathy to come with her. A toddler starts to scream, and the room reverberates with the sound. Liz tries to read the book she's brought, but the time goes very slowly. All around her the conversation is about the doctor. Sensei says this, sensei says that.

There's a stir in the lobby. A young woman, holding a very new baby, and an older one carrying bags and things, have come down the hall from the part of the building that seems to be a maternity clinic. (The whole place is called a hospital, though it doesn't resemble anything Liz would have thought of as one.) The sensei appears from the consulting room. She's a small, youngish woman in a white coat. Her hair is pulled back in a bun and she wears wire-rimmed glasses. Liz is impressed. The doctor looks exactly like a doctor ought to look. What a lot of bowing! It must be hard to bow that low while holding a baby, but the young woman manages it. Thank you, thank you, thank you, sensei! The sensei accepts the gratitude of mother and grandmother with smiles and smaller bows, pats the baby, and whisks back inside. Liz is thoughtful. It has never occurred to her before that a husband might not take a day off work to come and take his wife and new baby home, that it might be all what Cathy would call "women's stuff."

She has plenty of time to think about it, because nothing else happens for hours, except that she has to go into a tiny room by the receptionist's desk, pee into a bottle, and hand it through a window. Naturally, she wears the special toilet slippers out into the waiting room when she's finished, the most elementary gaffe of all, and has to turn back and fetch her regular slippers while everyone pretends not to notice, except the other gaijin, who smirk. Or perhaps not. It might be just fellow-feeling. She sits down again and opens her book, her face burning. Her hair is sticking to the back of her neck, and her blouse is damp and crumpled. Her whole self is damp and crumpled.

Women come and go. The waiting room begins to empty. The gaijin, one of whom is the patient and her friend the interpreter, see the doctor and leave, looking happy but no less collected than before. It dawns on Liz that she's being kept till near the end of the session, in case she should present difficulties that will take more time than the few minutes most people seem to get. She supposes this is a first-time gaijin privilege, but if she doesn't breathe some fresh air soon she thinks she might pass out.

Her name is called. She stumbles in and sits by the sensei's desk. There are still quite a few people in this smallish room, women lying on half-curtained examination couches, and nurses being busy. She blurts out her problem in English. Her voice sounds terribly loud.

The sensei beams. "I will help you make baby," she says.

Liz has to be examined, so she climbs up on the table, expecting the worst. Actually, the sensei is amazingly skillful. Her little hands probe so deftly and gently that it's all over before Liz knows it, and she doesn't even have time to think, as she always does at the dentist when metal things are stuck in her mouth: "What if there's an earthquake now?"

The nurse motions to Liz to get off the table, and in her relief she mistakes the direction and starts to slide off the end, realizing too late that there's an instrument tray attached there out of sight, and that she has put her foot in it. The nurse corrects her with an ill-concealed look of disgust. No doubt everything will have to be sterilized all over again. Humiliated, Liz scrambles back into her clothes and blunders through the curtain back to the desk, where the sensei is busily writing.

"I think you have a problem," announces the sensei.

"What problem?" asks Liz, alarmed.

"A problem," says the sensei firmly.

"But what is it?"

"Don't worry. I will help you."

Liz looks at the sensei, waiting for more, but that seems to be it. The sensei looks down at her notes.

"What can you do about it?" asks Liz desperately. The sensei doesn't reply. Liz is at a loss. Can it be that she doesn't speak much English after all?

But it would be too insulting to try it now in Japanese. "Please explain the treatment to me," says Liz, enunciating very clearly.

The sensei clears her throat and finally says, not looking at her, "Pills. Injections."

"What kind of pills?" The kind that give you sextuplets?

A long silence.

Then Liz gets it. She's not supposed to be asking these questions. Not yet, at least. It shows lack of faith. When the sensei offers to help you in such an important matter, you say thank you. Thank you, I put myself in your hands, sensei. That's the first thing you do. Then, when all goes well, as it might, God knows, you say thank you, thank you again.

The sensei has promised to help her and probably she could, whatever it is that needs to be done, and Liz has hurt her feelings. What now? Start in with the thanks, and promise to do whatever the sensei tells her to do? Be trusting, as a good patient should? Liz can't do it. Nor can she begin to explain why she needs to know everything at once. What would it all mean to her anyway? Does she want a baby or not? Who's the doctor here? The sensei is a busy woman who has spent all morning seeing a roomful of patients who have the right attitude, who really want babies, (except those who want abortions), and know a good doctor when they see one. Even gaijin. Liz has blown it.

She's tired, and hotter than ever, and she sits there looking sullen in just the way she'd thought she'd grown out of, until the doctor says, "I'll give you some medicine to begin with," adding, "it is Chinese herbal medicine, not dangerous." That's how offended she is. "And please take your temperature every day."

"Thank you," says Liz, and the sensei gives a very small sideways bow and turns back to her notes.

The pharmacist at the desk hands over a packet of pills with no name on them, a temperature chart, and a digital thermometer. The receptionist tells her rather coldly to take care of herself. Liz gets out of there.

"I'll bet she didn't want to test Tomokazu," says Cathy on the phone afterwards.

"No. It seems to be me."

"Oh, phooey!" says Cathy. "That only means they'd rather put you through everything they can think of first. What, disturb the danna-sama's equilibrium? Embarrass him? They'll pin it on you if they can."

"It's not a question of blame," says Liz rather stiffly.

"You know that. I know that," says Cathy. "Does everyone else know that?"

"Anyway," says Liz, "I don't think I want to go back there. I can't take pills with no name. Injections! Injections of what?"

"What indeed? I can just see you with six dear little babies. Tomoaki, Tomohiro, Tomoyuki . . ."

"Oh, stop!" cries Liz, laughing in spite of herself.

Tomokazu likes the digital thermometer. The display shows a little stick man who runs when the temperature is normal and lies down when it's feverish. They take each other's temperature several times, just for fun.

Then he says, "Seriously, I think you should talk to my mother."

"No," says Liz, and bursts into tears.

While he's comforting her she catches out of the corner of her eye something that's happening on TV, and sits up. It's some kind of ceremony, some folk religion survival in a little village by the sea. Women are burning dolls, traditional dolls, throwing them on a kind of pyre. "What's that?" she asks, sniffling.

He pays attention. "Ah, that's a ceremony," he says. "In a village."

"I can see that."

"Very ancient."

"What for?"

"Seems like . . . for women's problems," he says cautiously.

"Like mine?"

"Maybe. The dolls take the problems away in the fire."

"They're having a good time," says Liz. "Better than I had today. Maybe they know what they're doing. Yes, I think they're onto something!"

She snuggles down against him. He kisses her hands. "You feel okay?"

"Yes."

"That's good. Really, it's not so terrible. It might be all right. If not, it can't be helped, we can have a good life. I want to be with you, with or without baby, you know? Understand?"

"I don't want to go back to the doctor."

"I didn't ask you to do this," he says. "So now I say don't. Let's wait. We are young."

That's true, they are young. Still, for the next few weeks, everything she sees seems to reinforce the longings that sent her to the doctor. As she passes the playground on the corner one morning, she stops to watch: an old lady in grey kimono hanging by her arms on a climbing frame, encouraged by a small child, who is clapping; a young mother sitting idly on a swing with her baby on her knee; another chasing a toddler in a bunny suit who, as Liz stands there, falls down, and sits crying in the dirt, his ears flopping over. Liz feels something stab inside her, and hurries on.

Too soon she finds herself inside a hospital again. Tomokazu's aunt is ill. It has all happened very rapidly, or perhaps not as rapidly as all that, but Liz and Tomokazu have not been told till now. She has a cancer of some kind. Though nobody is saying so, Liz understands it can't be anything else. Her daughter has quit her job so as to spend all her time at the hospital, and Tomokazu's mother is now there constantly too, doing all the things that need to be done, that Liz is sure nurses are supposed to do. Only here all the nonmedical things seem to be the family's responsibility.

This hospital looks like a huge grey naval base. Inside, too, every wall is painted battleship grey. The ceilings are grey and the floors are shabby grey linoleum. Liz thinks she has never seen such a horrible colour. How could they do this to sick people? Under the neon light even Tomokazu looks sick.

The elevator doors open onto a long grey corridor. Tomokazu's uncle is waiting for them, smoking a cigarette, which he stubs out as he catches sight of them. He leads them to a bleak glass-walled waiting room and moves chairs together for them to sit on. He asks if they want coffee, and disregarding their protests, goes out to the coffee machine and comes back with plastic cups which he sets carefully before them.

"How's your work going?" he asks Tomokazu.

As Tomokazu begins to reply, a nurse runs out of the room opposite, another nurse hurriedly appears, and they both go back into the room. In the moment before the door closes, Liz has an impression of movement, fear and panic.

"She has these episodes, when she can't breathe," says Tomokazu's uncle. "She has not been well this afternoon. But I'm sure you can see her later." Liz understands. He has left his wife's side to wait for them, to sit with them, so they won't be left alone and uncertain outside the room, so they won't feel unwanted or intrusive. He is taking care of them.

The door remains closed for a long time. Liz can't bear to think of the struggle that is going on in there. Tomokazu's uncle continues to speak to them with gentle courtesy. Finally, the door opens again, and the nurses come out carrying bowls and tubes imperfectly concealed by white cloths.

Tomokazu's cousin Shizuko comes out after them, the young woman who made the silly joke about Liz's failure to conceive. Her face is very pale.

"She's better now," she says.

Liz has never seen anyone so sick. How little she has seen. She is not prepared. Tomokazu's aunt's face is of a colour that can only be the colour of death. Tears spring to Liz's eyes and she tries hard to control them. It is not her place to cry. She stands at the foot of the bed clutching the basket of flowers they've brought, till Tomokazu's mother takes it from her and puts it on the windowsill, turning it carefully so the sick woman sees the flowers from the best angle.

There's some small talk, about whether Tomokazu's company will send him abroad, about Shizuko's driving lessons. Tomokazu's aunt says, "Let's all go to a hot springs next year for a few days, when I'm well." She stops for breath between each word.

"I'll drive," says Shizuko pertly, bending to touch her mother's forehead with a folded damp towel.

"Good idea, Aunt," says Tomokazu. "Liz loves hot springs."

"Liz." Her eyes search for Liz, focus. "It's so good of you to come."

She moves her hand slightly, and her husband bends down

and gropes for a package in a bag by the bed. He passes it to Tomokazu, who gives it to Liz.

Liz takes the package from him uncomprehendingly, murmurs "Thank you," and bows awkwardly over the end of the bed. Tomokazu holds his aunt's hand for a moment, and then, with "Thank you," and "Take care," they are out of the room. His mother and cousin stay behind. His uncle walks with them to the elevator. "Thank you for coming," he repeats, "Thank you, until we meet again," and they all bow, as the doors close. Tomokazu reaches for Liz's hand. She imagines his uncle turning away and walking as fast as he can without running back to the room where his wife is dying.

At home, she opens the package. Inside is a silk cloth, the traditional kind you wrap things in. It has a pattern of blossoms against a background of clouds.

"It's beautiful," she says, gazing at it helplessly. She looks up at Tomokazu. "How did she do it? She's dying, how did she think of giving me a present, having it wrapped and brought from home—how did they remember, as if they don't all have enough to worry about? And the way your uncle treated us, as if we mattered."

He smiles, but he has no answer. Perhaps he doesn't get the question.

They both go to the funeral. Tomokazu's mother, whether from principle or foreknowledge, has recently insisted that Liz buy a formal black dress, in case of need, and given her a single row of pearls in a box from Mikimoto, so she has the right things. The pearls are for tears, said Tomokazu's mother. One must always wear pearls. Also black shoes, black stockings and black handbag. Liz has washed her hair and pulled it back from her face in the nearest thing she can manage to a French twist. Cathy once showed her this, but she has never tried it for herself before. When Tomokazu sees her, his eyes open, but he doesn't comment.

In the temple, the altar is heaped with yellow and white chrysanthemums, which seem to exude more light than the candles do in the dimness. A large, heavily airbrushed photo of Tomokazu's aunt, looking much younger but less pretty than Liz remembers her before her illness, is set in the middle. The priests are in fine brocade robes, but they sit on ordinary metal folding chairs. The ceremony is long. There is music, the piercing cry of ancient wind instruments Liz has never seen before, and chanting, which seems to be drawn from the air and to return to it in a single breath, without end.

Worry about the incense—to fuck up, now!—does not allow Liz to concentrate very well, but Tomokazu has coached her, and when the time comes she manages with only a slightly shaky hand.

Among the people who come, not to the funeral service itself but to pay their respects at the door of the temple while it's going on, Liz sees that snobby Englishwoman, Gwyneth Plummer. Out of the corner of her eye she sees that Gwyneth hesitates before the incense, but an elderly man behind her comes closer and shows her what to do. Gwyneth looks for a moment rather irritated, as if she actually knew all the time and was only reviewing her moves, and has now been deprived of credit for knowing, but her face, as she places her hands together and looks up at the altar, is really sad. Liz meets her eye and nods, and Tomokazu gives a pleased start when he sees her. After all, she didn't have to come, thinks Liz. Maybe we should ask her to dinner. I don't think I'll ever really like her, but I could try.

At the end of the service, something happens that Tomokazu has not mentioned to Liz. The open coffin is brought out, so that the family can say goodbye. When she realises what's happening, Liz feels a surge of alarm. She has never seen an open coffin before, and indeed it isn't the custom at home. She has never seen a dead person. She doesn't think she can, without having thought about it first. There is much more to come, probably worse, and she has prepared herself, she thinks, but she doesn't know if she can do this, too.

Tomokazu's uncle gets up heavily and bends over the coffin, and on his face is an expression of such tenderness that Liz turns her eyes away. She has sometimes seen just such an expression on Tomokazu's face, at just such an angle, looking down at her.

As Tomokazu moves forward with the others, she bends her head and stays a little behind him, and doesn't look. Nobody knows. Then the lid is put on the coffin, and a nail is placed in a hole in the edge of the lid, and each person has to tap lightly on the nail with a stone that is passed from hand to hand. Liz takes her turn.

Outside in the sunlight, the hearse, its roof glistening with gilt and mother-of-pearl, is waiting. Shizuko holds her mother's portrait from the altar, though Liz can't see it for the reflection off the glass. Her father, in his hands a black lacquered wooden tablet inscribed with his wife's posthumous Buddhist name, gives formal thanks to everyone in a low, hoarse voice. Now she is at peace in the next world after so much pain, he says.

Liz and Tomokazu stand side by side. Liz thinks how different everyone looks. Even Tomokazu's sister, over there with her mother, seems somehow like a real person, grown-up in black and pearls. Liz looks at Tomokazu in his black suit and thinks: We are really married. I am a married lady at a family funeral. How many more times will we do this through our lives together, until I am at his funeral or he is at mine?

Driving to the crematorium they pass Gwyneth Plummer standing alone at a bus stop. Liz would have liked to get out and say hello to her, even to Gwyneth, a foolish thought. Nothing will stop what is happening now. Through the tinted glass she sees Gwyneth's head turn and her eyes follow the black cars.

There is a very plain waiting room where they sit in strained silence until they are called into an inner room where a kind of tray is placed on a stretcher. On the tray there are some small, grey, shapeless pieces of bone. That is what they are. Liz's head feels light with the effort of not thinking. This is what she has decided to do, not think. In turn, they each pick up a piece of the bone with chopsticks that are very cold to the touch, and place it in a white ceramic urn. Liz is last. She does it slowly and carefully, and her hand does not shake. The soft bone makes a very small dry sound when she finally lets it drop in the urn. She has done it, something she never thought she could do. Then a man places the urn in a plain wooden box, and wraps the box in a white cloth. Liz thinks of Tomokazu's aunt in her white crepe underslip, laughing and holding out her arms as her sister helps her on with her kimono, but she must not think, and she twists her hands together. Beside her, Shizuko begins to sob. "Such a small box!" she cries. "Mother!" Liz, trembling with pity and relief, puts an arm around her and leads her out.

At Tomokazu's parents' house, when they finally return, his grandmother is waiting for them. She is holding a white saucer with salt in it, so that they can purify themselves before entering. Liz is glad. She would like very much not to bring death into the house. Even though she is standing down in the tiled entrance with her shoes on, and Grandmother is up on the step in slippers, the old lady is so little that Liz has to bend over to take a pinch of salt. She sprinkles it on her shoulders and enters the house.

"You look tired," says Grandmother.

"A little," says Liz, taken somewhat aback at being directly spoken to. This is a first.

The old lady has also prepared dinner, though she moves so slowly that it must have taken her most of the day. Tomokazu's mother eats hardly anything. She looks much older than Liz has seen her look before. After the meal, from force of habit she gets up and begins to clear away. Liz and Tomokazu's sister both protest, and Liz takes the tray from her. "We'll do it," she says. "Please go and get some rest."

"Thank you, Liz," says her mother-in-law. "You're very good."

Her father in-law says to Tomokazu, "You found a good wife by yourself, after all."

It gives her a strange feeling, being approved of.

As they're walking back home to their own place, she says, "I think I'll try to get my thesis finished soon."

"I've thought so," says Tomokazu.

"Even if we never have a baby. . . ."

"It's all right."

"Yes, really it is."

Are these the magic words?

❖ ❖ ❖

Liz sees a doctor nearer home, a woman her mother-in-law has highly recommended. "What's one more sensei," said Cathy, "in a lifetime? Get used to it." Liz is careful. She doesn't put a foot wrong on her first visit. But she'll never know what difference it makes, because this sensei turns out to be easy-going, even jolly, and willingly draws little diagrams for her, with kanji she can look up when she gets home. Relax, says the sensei. Wait.

The day she finds out for sure that she's pregnant, she's already arranged to meet Tomokazu in Shinjuku for dinner. As it happens, it's the anniversary of the day they first met in the library, and so it's meant to be a celebration anyhow. They drink a lot of toasts. Liz drinks orange juice, for the baby's sake, but she feels as high as it it were champagne.

"I think our baby will be a son," declares Tomokazu. A son! Somehow, this is a downer. In all her fantasies, she had a daughter. It was all clear in her mind. But there's no reason—it could just as well be a boy. And if that could be different, everything could be different.

All at once, sitting there opposite Tomokazu, his face flushed with beer and happiness, Liz is overwhelmed. It is as if she's been playing at the water's edge and a great wave has appeared out of nowhere and knocked her down, blinding her and filling her ears with roaring. She feels as frightened as she has ever been in her life.

What can she have been thinking of? What has she done?

Her baby will be a haafu. God, what problems it could have! It might never fit in anywhere. Or it might fit in too well! Yes, her mother-in-law will hold it on its first shrine visit, and probably the rest of its life. She herself might never have any say in anything. They always know so well what they want, and how to get it. Why should they listen to her? They manage everything so perfectly. How could she have ever thought to match them? Her baby will have all that they value some day. The beautiful vases! They'll want to teach it things. And what can she teach it, what does she know? She doesn't even know how to speak to a child in Japanese, they have special words and she doesn't know any of them. What's the baby word for car? There is one, and you have to be ready to scream it if you're going to stop your child from being run over! She has always been so tongue-tied with children, what on earth made her think she'd know what to do with one of her own? She will be a foreigner to it! Anyhow, don't they say good parenting is passed down from generation to generation? In that case, since neither of her own parents had the faintest idea, she's bound to be a total incompetent. There are so many things you have to do! She doesn't even know what half of them are. And mothers have to be out in society, you're not allowed to be shy, if you're a mother! They play volleyball at the kindergarten, and go to the PTA, all of which must be dreadful. And what about her thesis, so carelessly pushed into the background after all those years of study? She must have been crazy not to have finished, when she showed so much promise. She had a scholarship! She might never finish it now, and what if she does? What use will it be? She's done everything all wrong! Her mouth feels dry, and her heart beats terribly, as she pushes back her chair and runs out of the restaurant.

In the street, she looks wildly around. There is light everywhere, blazing neon, zipping up and down in bursts of colour that seem to explode behind her eyes. This is Kabukicho. She's been here dozens of times, and always had fun, and never minded its tackiness and noise. Now she doesn't know where to turn to escape. She's standing outside an amusement arcade, full of beeping, shrieking game machines, when Tomokazu comes rushing down the stairs from the restaurant, carrying her bag and jacket. Of course, he's had to stop to pay the bill.

"Are you all right?" he asks, taking her arm. "Do you feel sick?

She pulls away. "Yes, no, I'm okay, don't grab me!"

That's when she notices, right by them at the door of the arcade, ringed with flashing lights, a game table with holes all over it. Tentatively popping out from random holes, peering and retreating, are little round brown heads.

"Look!" she cries, "It's a mole game! Oh, I want to try it! Have you got a hundred yen?" She holds out her hand urgently.

He finds quite a few coins in his pocket. "Are you sure you want to play?" he asks doubtfully.

"Yes, yes!" And now she really does. She's seen it often, and it's very simple. What happens is, when you put in the money, the moles start jumping up and down quite fast, in and out of their holes, and you take a big padded hammer and try to hit them on the head with it. You have to hit them hard, and if you get one, it squeaks and falls back in its hole, and you score a point. Some of the moles are wearing miniature blue plastic crash helmets.

The first time she plays, all the moles are far too fast for her. She doesn't hit a single one. She puts in more money. The next time is better, and gradually she begins to get the hang of it. The moles squeak so pathetically, and they have such sweet faces, with big sad eyes, somehow that's why it's so much fun! She hits more and more moles each time, and when she hits them their squeaking makes her giggle. Then they come faster and faster and in more irregular patterns, but she manages to keep up, more or less. She bashes away at them, laughing till tears come to her eyes.

Tomokazu watches her, half-laughing, too, at first, but after a while he starts to look anxious, and says, "Liz, please stop now." He's embarrassed, and it's true, people passing by are slowing down to sneak glances at her. Even when she becomes aware of this, she doesn't stop, she can't, not till all the money is used up and she's so exhausted she has to let the last few moles go.

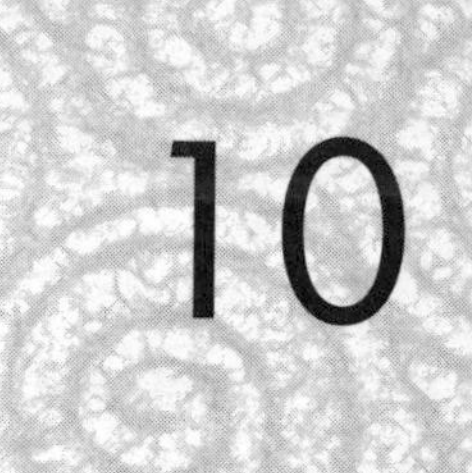

10

Waiting for Midnight

ELAINE PULLS HER woolly cap over her ears and stamps her feet. There's a brazier in the temple forecourt, and red sparks fly up every time someone feeds it with a few more sticks of kindling, but from her place on the queue she can't feel the effect.

The temple doors are open but the light of lanterns and candles doesn't spill out the way electric light would. The scene is framed by darkness. Priests are chanting the sutras. The impression they give, kneeling beneath the image of the Buddha, against a background of flowers and golden lotuses, is of stillness, except for the moving hand of the one who beats the rhythm on the wooden mokugyo and at intervals in the chant strikes the bowl-shaped gongs, one low and resonant, one a bright chime. Their deep voices fill the space around them and reach out into the dark.

People keep arriving. Their silhouettes appear in front of the temple steps, then join the ragged queue that begins in the shadow of the bell and winds through the garden. No-one's come from farther than a few blocks away, and everyone looks kind of rumpled, as if they've just got up from the floor in front of the television—leaving it still on, showing the crowds at famous shrines and temples all over the country or enka singers in brocade or spangles belting it out to an empty room—flung on down jackets and mufflers, hustled into sneakers, and hurried down the road, gasping in the icy air. Elaine counts. She's number twenty-three. Twenty-one and twenty-two are a little boy of nursery-school age and his mother. (The father, thinks Elaine, is probably still snoring off a few whiskies. It looks like he's going to miss the New Year.) There's a baby too, almost buried under pink fluffy stuff, in a stroller. Maybe the mother plans to carry her up the stone steps to the bell platform. The mother's eye, as she looks around to see who's here, meets Elaine's in a friendly way, but Elaine doesn't feel like starting up a conversation or cooing at the baby, so she lets it pass.

She keeps on counting, and figures there'll soon be a couple of hundred people here, including kids. The bell should be rung a hundred and eight times, for the earthly passions and desires, but because this is just a neighbourhood thing they really let everybody do it, keeping on till they get to the end of the queue. Nevertheless, she's made it here early tonight because this will, or so she's almost decided, be her last time.

Most years since she came to live nearby she's managed to be here. Not that she doesn't see this temple at other times. She always likes to walk through on her way to the station, if she doesn't need to do any errands in the other direction, past the kindergarten. It's nothing special as temples go, not famous for anything, in fact unknown to anyone who doesn't live right here, but it's really pretty if you catch it on the right day. A sunny spring morning, especially after rain, brings out the scent of the wood it's built of and the incense that permeates it. There are plum trees and cherry trees in the garden, and often when she's been on her way to some boring job or stressful encounter she's wanted just to stay here and sit by the silent bell, and has had to force herself to go on. Then she's told herself that some day she'd bring a book and spend the whole morning, but she's never done it, never had the time. Still, here she is now at least, once more stamping her feet against the cold just before midnight on the last day of the year, waiting for the bell.

The bell, lit by a single naked bulb on a wire run from the priest's house, seems even larger than it does in daylight. It's huge, almost as tall as a person, and it hangs from under the curved roof of a pillared stone platform that you reach by climbing up the steps at the side. When it's your turn, when the resonance from the last ringing has died away, you duck under the rail. You put your hands together and bow to the bell, then you take hold of the rope and swing the horizontal log that is the striker tentatively a couple of times, then you draw it back and strike, not so hard as to make a great rough clang, which the priest disapproves of, but hard enough, and on just the right place, the medallion that's part of the pattern moulded into the bronze, so that the sound can be heard through the night air in the neighbourhood around, and so that it will reverberate, ringing and ringing while you take a step back, and bow your head again, and the next person eagerly comes up. Elaine feels a sense of anticipation, something she hasn't felt in a long time. She can't think of anything she loves more than hitting the bell full on, and hearing that wonderful sound.

You only get one chance, and she's seen people fumble it completely and make some poor little thud, but she's always done it right.

The baby starts to fuss. Typical, thinks Elaine. She doesn't approve of baby carriages, on principle. All the babies she ever hears crying are in them. They never cry on their mothers' backs, and it seems a shame that so many young women prefer to push their babies now, and think they're so smart and modern. However, what's it to her? She doesn't have a baby, and she won't be here much longer. The little boy takes the baby's hand. "It's all right," she hears him whisper. "We're going to ring the bell soon."

Elaine has just spent a few months back home seriously looking for jobs. Talking to people. Her timing's not bad, they say. Jobs are opening up, better jobs than she's been offered before. Her thesis is really almost finished, there's nothing more she can do to drag it out. So this is what's ahead: a decent, tenure-track job, one of several that seem possible. A couple of books. Tenure. A full professorship, maybe somewhere major. She's not being unrealistic. This is her future. It's the future she's worked towards for years, and now she has to force herself to take it up.

She came back on a cheap flight via Anchorage, Alaska. It was one of those horror flights that you think will never end, diverted to Washington, D.C. after takeoff from New York, then delayed four hours in Chicago because of blizzard conditions, and again in Seattle. Coming into Anchorage, the first time she's done this in winter, she looked down at the sea. It was frozen. At first she couldn't believe it. No-one had ever told her about this. She stared hard at the expanse of water. It looked like the sea should, with waves, white-capped, on the point of breaking, but there was no movement. The waves curled towards the shore, and on the beaches they made patterns, as if about to withdraw, but the patterns never changed. Elaine tried to remember something about the temperature at which salt water freezes, from high-school physics, and drew a blank. She found herself reaching for the earphones, plugging her ears with plastic and platinum to take her mind off the dreadful silence of those unbroken waves, but her eyes kept turning downwards in fascination.

When they landed at Anchorage, she was almost crazy for want of a book. Because of all the delays, she'd finished everything she had to read, including the magazines in English and Japanese supplied on the plane, and the airline magazine right down to the diagram of the emergency exits. At the terminal, while the plane was refueling, and the Japanese returning home for New Year's roamed the duty-free counters obsessively buying boxes of chocolate-coated macadamia nuts and bottles of Chivas Regal to fill the time, she searched for a bookstall. It didn't take long. There was no bookstall. There were a few racks of fundamentalist pamphlets. Otherwise, nothing. She spent the next hour and a half slumped in a plastic seat gazing out at the buzz of little private planes coming and going, appearing out of the snow-filled clouds and receding into them, and fell into a melancholy that has lasted, that this time even the furious activity of Tokyo at year's end has failed to shift. Perhaps it's because she's made the decision to follow the logic of her life, not its natural inclination, that she now feels herself to be somehow suspended on the crest of a frozen wave. Everything has come to a standstill.

She's told everyone that she's going back home next year. After all the time she's been thinking aloud about it, now some of them seem to think she means it.

Larry's got a job at a women's college in Kyushu in any case. He'll be going in the spring. "You have to keep moving on," he said when he told her. "So you never get old. That's my theory." Elaine is skeptical. She herself has a feeling that she's moving right on into middle age, although that could be because she's going home and Larry's not. Anyway, she didn't say this to Larry, but she's noticed the grey hairs among the blond, and the wrinkles round his mock-innocent eyes. She hopes, as he must, too, if he's given it a thought, which he probably has not, that their friendship will survive, in one form or another. That it was not just for this time.

Liz, her baby at her breast—the fat, placid baby, Tomonori, to whom she determinedly speaks only in Japanese, but there you are, that's very Liz—said, "Well, I've thought for a long time that you should be getting on with your life. Tomokazu thinks so, too. We were talking about you only the other day. After all, there's nothing really to keep you here—I mean, you know, nothing like this."

"What a pity you're not supposed to punch a nursing mother on the nose," said Cathy, when Elaine told her. And then she started to cry. Elaine, strangely calm, patted her shoulder until she said, "It's okay. I'll stop. I'll save it. Because I don't believe you'll really go. I don't believe you can."

A few flakes of snow fall gently down on Elaine's sleeve. Ordinary snow, not as beautiful as that first snow. She'd arrived in October, and found a place to live, and met her Professor, and established herself at the library, all that. By winter, she was ready to see Kyoto. She travelled down on the overnight bus, and somebody's grandfather dozed on her shoulder all the way, so she couldn't sleep at all. The next morning, leaving her backpack in a locker at the bus station, she made her way to her first temple, Nanzenji. She was very tired, not only from the trip but because for months she'd been in a state of shock and excitement, just starting out, every day changing her mind about the country, deciding it was a bland, barren industrial society where tradition and spirituality were dead, then, contrarily, deciding it was bound in impenetrable customs that ought to be swept away forthwith, and so on. As if it were up to her to decide. At Nanzenji, this dark winter's afternoon, she'd walked up an aisle of tall black cedars and was just emerging from under the great gate when snow began to fall. It was a kind of snow she'd never seen before, huge dry snowflakes like blossoms falling out of the sky, and when she put out her hand to catch them she could see the pattern in each one, the intricate, lacy pattern she'd thought you needed a microscope to see, and it stayed and stayed. She found out later that it was called "peony snow." As she stood there, she heard the sound of a gong, and a line of monks in grey robes and conical hats came into her field of vision, walking through the slowly falling snow, everything silent except for the gong and the shuffle of their feet. And she was lost. She thought then that she would never leave.

"Watch me do it," she said to Cathy.

"I'm watching," said Cathy.

Now the mother of the children is watching her, too. She's dying to talk. "Is this your first time?" she asks Elaine.

"No," says Elaine.

"So you live around here?"

"Yes. Over by the kindergarten."

"I go to the kindergarten," says the little boy, swinging on the side of the stroller. "I made a snowflake out of paper."

"Don't swing," says his mother. "Your Japanese is very good."

Elaine, who has said only half a dozen words, doesn't bother to deny it. "I suppose you've been in Japan a long time?"

"A long time," says Elaine. The words seem too spare, but the woman is satisfied. She smiles at Elaine and bends to tuck the baby's ear under its pink quilted hood.

"Do you like this sound?" asks the child. "I like the way it goes on."

Elaine says, "I do, too," but then she doesn't know what else to say, and is relieved when he hops a little way down the path, the better to see where the sound comes from. Waiting here on the queue, looking into the lighted space where the monks sit, she can make out the rounded shape of the mokugyo, the wooden fish, strangely carved so that it looks not like a fish but like a curled-up octopus, or a high-domed turtle, or an ornate skull. It shines with a dark patina, and the sound made by the slight, rapid movement of the skin-padded stick in the monk's hand is soft, but at the same time not soft at all.

"Be careful, don't hop near the fire," calls the child's mother.

This fire in the brazier makes her think of a New Year's Day years ago, when she was alone in Tokyo. Her gaijin friends, (Cathy, Liz, Larry, that nice big Australian woman who was around then, the one who should have married a sumo wrestler, Janet—one of those people who come and go, to whom you tell your story, spill out your doubts and fears, and who then carry all you've told them back to the place they've come from, where they do with it nothing at all, only sometimes they might wonder whatever happened to you), all those people must have gone home for Christmas, or to Hokkaido skiing or to Bangkok or somewhere, and the Japanese she knew back to their hometowns. Maybe she'd just broken up with a boy, she doesn't quite remember.

She'd decided to do something that sounded cheerful, not just to go to the shrine on the first day of the year—what year was this?—but to walk a route that goes to seven shrines and temples, each one dedicated to a different one of the seven lucky gods: Daikoku, Hotei, Bishamon, Jurojin, Ebisu, Fukurokuju, Benten. (Her party piece, tested whenever they were drunk and silly enough. Cathy knew Santa's reindeer, Larry knew the seven dwarfs. Elaine always won hands down with the Shichifukujin.) At the first shrine, crowded and bright with festive kimono in the pale winter afternoon sun, she bought a little boat and a miniature figure of the first god, and at each one another figure, so that finally she had a boat full of gods, with Benten-sama, the female deity, holding her lute and standing in the bow. She planned to set it up on a corner of her old desk, the only possible space in the six-mat room she lived in then. It was a great thing to do, trailing from place to place with all the other people carrying their boats. There were families, and quiet people doing it alone. At some of the stops there was hot sweet sake, always a good thing.

Probably that was why it took longer to get through than she'd thought it would, looking at the sketchy map, and why, when it was getting really dark, she somehow lost track of the other stragglers, and completely missed her way. There she was, in the middle of nowhere. And the streets looked differ-